A Bounty of Darkness

Markus Matthews

A Bounty of Darkness
Copyright © 2022 by Markus Matthews

All rights reserved. No part of this publication may be reproduced, distributed, or transmitted in any form or by any means, including photocopying, recording, or other electronic or mechanical methods, without the prior written permission of the author, except in the case of brief quotations embodied in critical reviews and certain other non-commercial uses permitted by copyright law.

Tellwell Talent
www.tellwell.ca

ISBN
978-0-2288-7877-3 (Hardcover)
978-0-2288-7876-6 (Paperback)
978-0-2288-7878-0 (eBook)

Books by Markus Matthews

The Bounty Series
A Bounty with Strings
A Bounty of Evil
A Personal Bounty
Bounty Calls
The Sin City Bounty
A Bounty of Fury
A Bounty of Darkness

This book is dedicated to the teachers in
my life that didn't just mail it in.

Chapter 1

Saturday, October 8

My excitement grew as I watched the little girl through the binoculars.

Before I ended up legally barred from being within 500 feet of schools, a monitoring bracelet around my ankle, and law enforcement checking Ministry of Transport records to see if I owned a sketchy late-model van with blacked-out windows, I should probably have clarified that statement.

At the beginning of the week, my team and I took on a new case: a rogue Werewolf with a $50,000 bounty on his head. He was wanted for assaulting his pregnant girlfriend so badly that she and her unborn child were both fighting for their lives in intensive care. As someone whose fondest wish was to start a family, I found this crime particularly heinous. This was one of those cases where the bounty was secondary; getting this monster off the street was its own reward.

Tracking down him down had been remarkably easy and had taken us less than a day. I never understood why people put so much personal information on online. Via his social media feeds, we found he had a sister. The sister had a small house in Hamilton's North End. Blue was able to spy on the house from the shadows and found him hiding out in a back bedroom. The problem was the sister had two small kids which would make a takedown tricky.

We decided to monitor the house and wait for an opportunity where the kids weren't home. Unfortunately, it had been five days and we hadn't gotten a good chance. Worse yet, the full moon was tomorrow night. Normally most Weres on the night of a full moon would either lock themselves up or go out with their pack to a remote location to keep regular people safe. Our target wasn't currently a member of a pack, and while she was spying Blue hadn't seen anything in the house capable of restraining him. That meant we needed to take him down before the full moon.

This brought us to our current situation. The little girl I was watching was my teammate, Stella. Stella might look like an eleven-year-old girl, but she was actually over one hundred years old. Today though, she was trying to look like a high school junior. She'd ditched her signature white *Little House on the Prairie* dress, shiny black dress shoes, and long-braided pigtails for a much more modern-looking outfit. Her dark hair was straightened and tied back in a simple ponytail which made her look like she was Liv's younger sister. She was wearing a light jacket with a T-shirt under it, black yoga pants, and a pair of Nike sneakers.

    Stella usually wore the same dress all the time due to her ability to turn into a monstrously powerful Hyde. That transformation would destroy any outfit she wore and when she turned back to her normal human form, she'd be back in that same dated dress. I never understood how that dress survived and magically reappeared each time and had finally just accepted that was how it worked.

    I was excited as I watched Stella from my perch on the roof of a nearby apartment building because it looked like our plan was working.

    Stella was on the porch with her clipboard talking to the Werewolf's sister. We needed the sister and her kids out of the house. To accomplish this, we'd purchased one adult and two children's tickets to the movies for tonight's 7:10 p.m. show of the latest Pixar movie. Stella whipped up a fake survey about children's juice preferences and was currently going through the motions of asking questions.

    Blue, our shadow traveling alien was currently standing on the sidewalk in front of the house in her holographic old man disguise. Stella and Blue were the logical choices for this little ruse. Stella, with her youthful looks and, more importantly, her very human scent and heart rate, made her one of the only members of our team that could get that close to the house without tipping off the rogue Werewolf. Blue's slow heart rate and alien scent would have been picked up by the rogue if she had been on the porch with Stella.

    A young girl and her eighty-something-year-old grandfather would also help ease the rogue's suspicions. Law enforcement or bounty hunters wouldn't use a minor or the elderly in such a dangerous situation.

    I pumped my fist as Stella handed over the envelope with the tickets and the sister's face lit up with a huge smile.

I watched my two teammates travel down the block and disappear from sight. Their work done, I knew Blue and Stella would use the shadows to travel back home.

I secured my binoculars and called on my Air powers to lift me into the sky and headed for home.

It was a sunny and mild fall day and flying over the Hamilton escarpment with all the multi-hued trees just added to my good mood. The colorful mix of red, orange, and yellow leaves was a spectacular sight. My day got even better as I heard the distinctive sound of four Merlin engines growling away in the distance but getting louder with each passing second. I scanned the air and spotted the World War II-era Lancaster coming towards me.

The Lancaster, or Vera as she was affectionately known, was a common sight over Hamilton as she operated out of the Canadian Warplane Heritage Museum. There were only two Lancasters in flying condition left in the world. As the other Lancaster was operated by the Royal Air Force (RAF) for the Battle of Britain Memorial Flight, Vera was the only Lancaster in the world that a civilian could buy a ride in. As someone who built model WWII planes and loved aircraft from that era, I was always in awe every time I saw her. Perhaps aside from a steel mill, Vera would be the quintessential icon to represent Hamilton.

I gave a friendly wave to the pilots and got a slight wing waggle from them in response as we passed by each other.

A few minutes later, I circled over the house that was our team's base, making sure that nothing was out of place. My paranoia was probably misplaced on a bright day like today but seeing what was left of our original house meant I had my reasons.

During our last case against the Master, our house had been blown up by a missile from one of more than a dozen robots that had been sent to attack us. That hadn't been the only time that we'd been attacked at home since I'd expanded from bounty hunting solo to adding my new teammates. We'd also been attacked by dark elves back in our early days.

After the case with the Master finished, we'd purchased the house beside our old one to live in while the original was rebuilt. The foundations and the frame to the first story were in place but it would be months until it was finished.

We probably could have had the house built quicker, but I'd taken the opportunity to add some modifications. This new house would have much more steel in it than a standard house; it also had a vault in the basement to protect Liv, our vampire companion, during her daytime slumber. The windows were going to be bulletproof, and we would have solid steel security doors. In short, I was building more of a fortress than a house.

In the meantime, I had Walter, a wizard acquaintance of mine, move the wards that surrounded the old house to our new one to add more protection to our current abode.

I touched down on the front step and let myself in. I wasn't shocked to see that Stella was already back in her usual outfit.

She greeted me as I came through the door. "Good news. Blue's confirmed that the sister is going to use the movie passes. The brother was suspicious but after finding out that she got them from a 'young high school girl,' he seemed to let it go."

I smiled and began taking off my armor. It looked like our plan worked and we were all set for our takedown this evening.

***

While Stella had been instrumental in getting the sister and the kids out of the house, we were going to be without her services for the actual takedown. She'd had a scientific conference in Philadelphia that she'd wanted to attend this evening and had it on her calendar for months. That meant we didn't have use of her powerful Hyde form for tonight's strike.

Not having Stella's wit and strength was a concern but any one of us should be enough to subdue a rogue Werewolf and take him into custody. According to Blue, the house was a cramped one-story job with a basement, which made me feel better about not having Stella around. As Stella's Hyde form stood close to seven feet tall and weighed over 600 pounds, tight spaces weren't her ideal operating environment.

Blue pulled me from my musings. "The sister and the kids have just left."

I nodded and smiled as I heard Liv emerge from the basement as the sun had just set.

Blue had used the shadows earlier to visit our secret lab to use the Food-O-Tron to get Olivia a couple of pints of blood. The Food-O-Tron was a magical device that had been created by Stella's late stepfather. It had the ability to replicate any food that was programmed into it, which fortunately included human blood. It also saved us a small fortunate in keeping Bree and the rest of us well fed.

Once Liv downed her liquid breakfast, we were ready to go.

I lowered the faceplate to my armor and looked over my teammates. Liv was at the head of the line just in front of the shadows beside Blue in our living room. Liv played idly with the power-blocking cuffs in her hand, looking almost bored. Bree, in her standing hybrid Werepanther form, was next in line. I put my armored hand lightly on Bree's dark-furred shoulder to let her know I was behind her and ready to go.

The last member of our team was nowhere to be seen. Alteea, our pixie companion, had elected to pass on this mission. Pixies feared Weres and Alteea wanted nothing to do with this one. Her normal role with the team was to fly high and record everything on her magically resized miniature iPhone. Those recordings helped us file bounty claims and generally made things easier when dealing with law enforcement. The enclosed environment would have made her role more difficult, so the loss of her presence wasn't a huge deal.

Blue wasn't going in either, as she was going to hang back and monitor everything from the shadows. We'd decided on this course for two reasons. The first was the cramped conditions of the house. Liv, Bree, and I would be confined enough that adding a fourth didn't make much sense. The second reason was Blue could monitor everything from the shadows and, on the off chance that the rogue escaped, would be able to track him via the shadows wherever he went.

We'd just completed a comms check when Blue asked, "Ready?"

Liv nodded, Bree growled, and I said, "Ready."

Blue turned to the shadows, made a gesture with her hands, and opened a portal. "Go!"

Liv disappeared into the shadows quicker than I could blink. Bree surged forward and I was right on her heels. I followed Bree as she vanished into the shadows.

I came out in a small three-piece bathroom that, even in the darkness, I could tell had seen better days. The linoleum was cracked and worn, and the grout was grimy and blackened. As I wasn't hosting a home improvement show, I decided to ignore the décor and get on with the mission.

I stepped out of the bathroom and heard a scuffle coming from the room on my left. I entered the bedroom to find Liv on the floor, frantically looking around for something while Bree and the Were exchanged blows on the bed. It dawned on me that I couldn't see the power-blocking cuffs and realized that's what Liv was searching for. If we slapped those on the Were, he'd be unable to use his strength against us and they'd stop him from being able to access his powers.

"Hey!" exclaimed Liv as Bree was thrown off the bed and crashed down on top of her.

The rogue Werewolf began trembling as he began to change from his human form into his wolf one. I didn't hesitate and sent a powerful bolt of lightning at him. He cried out in shock as the electricity flowed through him before going limp in his still-human form on the bed.

I cursed under my breath as I worried that I'd overdone the power on the lightning and wondered if I killed him.

Before I could check if he was alive, something big and heavy hit my armored form from behind and I too ended up on the floor. I swore as the pain hit me, and I tasted blood from accidentally biting my tongue. Even through the armor, I felt something strong clamp down on my leg and begin pulling me out of the room along the worn hardwood floor.

I turned my head and saw a huge black and brown dog with its massive jaws locked on my lower right leg. By its size, I'd briefly worried it was a Werewolf before realizing it was just a dog. It growled as it pulled me along the floor. I was about to call another blast of lightning but checked that impulse at the last moment. The dog had no aura around it, which meant it was just a normal dog. Well, normal but huge, as it had to weigh more than a hundred pounds, but I still didn't want to fry the poor animal with electricity.

"BREE!" I yelled as I continued my slow journey down the hall.

I was halfway down the hall by the time Bree's dark form landed beside me. She lowered her head towards the dog and let out a growl that shook the windows. The dog lowered its ears, released my leg, and its claws scrambled for traction on the hardwood as it tried to scamper off. It took off with its tail between its legs.

A few moments later there was a crash from the front of the house, followed by a soft whimpering from the deeper in the house.

Bree held out a paw and helped me to my feet.

"Found them!" said Liv from the bedroom.

Bree and I returned to the room as Liv was putting the cuffs on the rogue.

"Is he still breathing?" I asked with concern. Liv nodded as she secured the second power-blocking cuff into place. "Great, grab him and let's get out of here."

Liv hefted our target and tossed him over her shoulder like he barely weighed anything. Considering the rogue was probably close to 200 pounds, it was an impressive feat.

Bree led the way back to the bathroom and Liv and I followed her. We disappeared into the shadows and in moments we were gone.

***

Three hours later, we were back at the house, sitting around the kitchen table having a late snack. We dropped the rogue off at the central police station downtown and it took much longer to process him than I expected. Hamilton police had had a busy couple of days as crime and odd incidents had picked up dramatically. I attributed this to the approaching full moon. The full moon was always the busiest day of the month for law enforcement.

It took close to two and half hours for them to take the rogue into custody, do up a report, and give us our bounty claim number.

Stella was back from her conference and seemed excited about what she'd learned. Blue on the other hand wasn't as pleasant and said, "Tonight's operation was poorly executed and we need to discuss how to do things better in the future. What do you three have to say for yourselves?"

Liv grinned and hit a button on her phone. I groaned as "Who Let the Dogs Out" began blasting from a wireless speaker in the living room. Liv and Bree began dancing around in their chairs and pointing at me and laughing.

I shook my head and rubbed my temples. There were times I hated my teammates.

I was about to tell them to turn off the music, but Blue beat me to it. She glared at Liv and Bree wordlessly. Liv sheepishly turned off the noise but snickered.

"Since Liv brought it up, let's start with the dog," I said. "Why didn't you inform us about the dog before we went in?"

Blue shrugged and said, "I hardly thought family pets would be a concern."

"Family pet?! That was fucking Cujo!"

"Arf! Arf!" added Liv, referring to the song again with a giggle.

I ignored Liv and turned to Blue, "In the future, please add the presence of any animals in the house to your report."

Blue nodded. "I suppose you have a point. I will endeavor to make sure the intelligence I provide is more thorough." Blue shifted her attention from me to Liv and Bree. "I fail to see why both of you are so jovial, as you both performed poorly tonight."

Blue spent the next thirty minutes tearing us a new one. I had to admit we deserved it, as that hadn't been our finest work. Between Liv losing the cuffs, Bree getting tossed off the bed, and me being tackled by a dog, Blue had a lot to criticize.

At least, in the end, we'd taken him down without endangering the sister or the kids, taken the rogue off the streets before the full moon, and gotten the bounty. Other than our pride, nothing had been seriously injured.

For now, I'd take that as a win.

Chapter 2

Sunday, October 9

Around one that morning, I was just getting ready for bed when my phone rang. I spotted Rob's name and number on the display and answered it. Rob Quinn was my best friend and a Hamilton police officer. I hoped the call was a personal one, but that hope died the moment I said hello.

"*Hurricane, there is no easy way to say this, so I'll just come out with it. Curveball's dead.*"

I almost laughed, as this had to be a sick joke. I'd just seen Charlie last Sunday when the members of my foundation met for our weekly training session. She was supposed to be coming by tomorrow night for the next one. Sparks dripped from my hands as shock and anger kicked in, and I hastily tampered down my powers to avoid frying my phone. Questions began rapidly forming in my mind.

Rob's concerned voice brought me back to the here and now. "*Zack?*"

"Sorry, I'm here. What happened?"

"*We don't know. I'm at Andropov's Pizzeria on James Street North. Units only arrived on the scene twenty minutes ago and I got here five minutes ago. EIRT are en route. There are three bodies. I called you as soon as I found out that Curveball was one of them.*"

"*I'll be there shortly,*" I said as I started putting my armor back on.

"*It is an active crime scene; you won't be allowed in.*"

"*We'll see about that,*" and with that, I hung up.

My hands shook as I fumbled with my armor and my eyes began welling up. I desperately wanted to believe that this was some sort of horrible mistake. My anger grew as I struggled to get my left gauntlet on. I just wanted to lash out at something. An image of Charlie's young face popped into my head and the tears began flowing. I was turning into an emotional wreck, jumping between anger and grief, but neither of those things would get me answers. I forced myself to take a deep breath and centered myself.

I nodded in satisfaction as I finally secured my gauntlet.

One step at a time, I thought as I began putting together a plan.

I needed more than just myself on this. "STELLA, BLUE, GET UP!" I yelled in the direction of the room they shared beside mine. The rest of the team with their enhanced hearing would be alerted too.

I heard movement almost instantaneously on the other side of the wall and finished putting on the last of my armor. I tucked my phone into one of the compartments on the armor, gave a quick look round to make sure I had all that I needed, and exited my room.

My entire team was outside my room and waiting for me. "Rob just called. Charlie's been killed—" I paused as Bree and Stella gasped and then continued. "They are at a place called Andropov's Pizzeria on James Street North. Blue, find it, and get eyes on it. Please open a portal to it ASAP."

Stella asked, "What happened?"

"I don't know. The police have only been on the scene a short time. Charlie wasn't the only casualty; there were two others."

"I'm so sorry, Zack," said Liv as she stepped in to hug me.

I shook my head and moved back out of her reach. Liv gave me a wounded look at my rejection. "I appreciate the gesture but I'm barely holding it together . . . I need to focus on finding out what happened."

Liv nodded in understanding, but before she could say anything else, Blue said, "I have found it and can open a portal nearby."

I'd planned on doing this part on my own but changed my mind. "Liv, Bree, Alteea, you guys are with me. Blue, keep an eye on everything from the shadows. I suspect we won't be allowed into the crime scene, so I want you to find out what you can. Stella, get on the computer and see what you can find out from Twitter and other sources. See if there have been any other attacks in nearby areas tonight."

"Do you want me to change?" asked Bree.

"No," I said. "Whoever did this is gone. I want you to have your nose and ears open and let me know what you find out. Alteea, glamor up, and when we go through, hit the crime scene."

"Yes, Master."

Blue made a gesture with her hands and gave us a nod that the portal was open. Alteea was the first through and I followed her.

I came out into a darkened alley and was hit by the scent of rotting food from the dumpster beside me. Thankfully, the stench wasn't that bad due to the cooler weather this time of year. I spotted Alteea's rainbow aura making a beeline down the alley towards the two police officers and the yellow police tape they were putting up at the back door of the restaurant.

Liv popped out of the shadows with Bree just behind her. Bree caught my attention when she shuddered and then stumbled slightly before catching herself.

"Fuck!" exclaimed Bree as she trembled again.

"You okay?" I asked, confused at her behavior.

"No. Don't you feel it?"

I shook my head. Bree looked at me like I was crazy and turned to Liv, "Do you feel it?"

"Feel what?" asked Liv who was just as puzzled as I was.

Bree rubbed her arms like she was cold and shivered. "Something feels wrong. It's like darkness and death are all around us. My beast is pacing in my head and it's afraid."

Her words put me on high alert. Bree was not one to be dramatic about things, and fear wasn't an emotion that her beast often had. What the heck could scare a Werepanther? I called on my powers and looked around anxiously. "Is there anything nearby that we should be concerned about?"

Bree frowned. "No. I'm not picking up any scents, but that dumpster isn't helping. I also don't hear anything other than some mice and rats nearby."

"Liv, you see or hear anything?"

"Nope. The closest things to us are the cops at the end of the alley. It's just us here."

"Okay, stay alert and follow me."

I began walking towards the two cops. Bree and Liv were right behind me. Whether it was Bree's dire warning or something else, the shadows in the alley seemed to have a sinister element to them and my stomach knotted up as we walked.

"Zack," said Bree, "the feeling is getting stronger."

The hairs on the back of my neck went up and something almost primitive deep inside of me warned me to leave. Bree's earlier words about wrongness, darkness, and death now resonated with me. "Liv, you feel anything?"

"Nope. Nothing. I do smell blood, though. Human, and lots of it."

We got closer and one of the cops jumped in surprise as he noticed us. His partner immediately reached for his weapon but didn't draw.

"This crime scene is a restricted area. Go back the way you came," said the first cop. He relaxed slightly and his partner's hand dropped away from his weapon as I stepped into the light. "Hurricane, as much as I want to, I can't let you in."

"Can you get Rob Quinn and whoever's in charge?"

He nodded and he keyed the radio on his vest, turned away, and made the call.

Less than a minute later, I spotted Rob ducking under the police tape at the opening of the alley on the other side of the restaurant. He hustled towards us, stopping just in front of me.

"I'm sorry about Charlie but I told you wouldn't be allowed on scene."

"Rob, she was my friend and a member of my foundation. I'm pretty sure that after her mom, I'm her next emergency contact . . ."

He shook his head. "If I let you in, I'll lose my badge. Please don't make me make that choice."

I was about to tell him to screw his badge but took a deep breath. Rob loved being a cop and if I cost him his job, I knew that would put a serious strain on our friendship. I also knew that if I did ask, Rob would have picked me over his job. I owed him too much to force that decision. "You said EIRT was being called in; I'm assuming, then, this is an Enhanced-related crime?"

"Rumor has it that the victims' wounds are consistent with a vampire attack. Looks like it was actually multiple vampires involved."

Vampires and Weres were the most common Enhanced Individuals out there. It wasn't a huge surprise that vampires might be responsible for this attack.

A vampire would have been a bad match for Charlie, and two or more meant she'd been seriously outclassed. Liv, in our training sessions, had an eleven-and-one record against Charlie. Charlie struggled to cope with Liv's inhuman speed.

But murders were usually committed by rogue vampires. When a vampire went rogue, they were almost unthinking in their quest for blood, little better than wild animals. They were almost always solo. If multiple vampires had been involved in this crime, it wasn't just a rogue attack. Something else was going on.

The other thing was that vampires didn't give off this feeling of dread that was around us. It wasn't just me and Bree who felt it either. The cops were overly nervous and alert too, so they sensed whatever we were feeling. We were missing something here.

A guy in a suit came out from the restaurant. The plain, badly fitted suit he was wearing just screamed detective. Cops didn't tend to waste their money on expensive tailored suits. He spotted us and headed over.

He introduced himself as Detective Frank Little. "Hurricane, sorry for your loss. I understand that you knew the deceased?"

In the light, Detective Little looked familiar, but I was having trouble remembering where I knew him from. He was in his mid-thirties, about six-foot-tall, brown hair, and was in pretty good shape, though had a couple of extra pounds on him. "Charlie was a friend and a member of my foundation. Sorry—do I know you?"

The detective smiled. "We met more than ten years ago. You saved me and my partner from a ghoul attack when I was a rookie. I didn't have the mustache back then, my hair was shorter, and I was probably twenty pounds lighter."

That night came rushing back to me and it clicked as I remembered him. He and his partner had been responding to a disturbance at a cemetery in West Hamilton and interrupted a ghoul feeding on a corpse it had dug up. It had been sheer luck that I'd been flying over and spotted the ghoul's bloodred, brown, and black aura.

Ghouls were undead, like zombies but smarter, faster, and more vicious. Unlike zombies, ghouls preferred carrion, corpses especially. Generally, they avoided live humans, but if cornered or provoked, they'd attack. They also weren't that common; I'd only encountered them twice in my life, so it was easy to remember which incident the detective referred to. Thankfully, frying them with lightning was an effective way of dealing with them, and I'd hit that one before it even knew I was there. The incident was over almost as soon as it started. Unfortunately, I hadn't gotten there fast enough to prevent his partner from getting hurt.

"I remember. Did your partner recover?"

He nodded. "Yeah, they brought in a healer and priest that night. He was back on duty not even a week later."

I nodded at that. "Glad to hear that he didn't suffer any complications or issues from the attack. Now, I don't mean to be rude, but how about access to the crime scene?"

The detective shook his head. "I owe you, Hurricane, but even if I could allow you on the scene, I wouldn't. Having a civilian on the scene would cause all sorts of issues. My partner is senior, and it's his call. Unlike me, he isn't a fan of yours. Murdock is a good friend of his . . ."

I cursed at this. SWAT Sergeant Murdock and I had a history and none of it was good. If this guy was a buddy of his, there was no way I was getting into that crime scene. At least I had a couple of aces up my sleeve, as Alteea was already in there and Blue was spying on it from the shadows. Between the two of them, we'd get a pretty good picture of what happened. It still sucked, though, as I wanted to be there, and Bree's and Liv's enhanced senses would also have been an asset to have in there too.

Detective Little spoke, pulling me from my thoughts, "We're waiting for EIRT to arrive and most likely we'll lose control of the scene anyways. We also have a call into the English Vampire Court to get a representative here in case any of the victims are reborn. Weren't you and your team acting as the Court's representatives during the last rogue vampire attack?" He finished with a wink.

My neck twinged as I remembered that attack. We'd been pursuing a bounty on a vampire that had attacked and killed two people in Hamilton and caught him in the act that night. Unfortunately, there had been a second one and he'd gotten the drop on me and torn a large chunk of my neck out with his fangs. I'd only survived due to the quick action of my teammates, and it was one of the main reasons I bought the armor I was currently wearing; I wanted to prevent something like that from happening again.

I mentally smiled. My new detective friend had just given us our way in.

Chapter 3

Sunday, October 9

Fifteen minutes later the detective was back inside the crime scene, and I called Stella and asked her to contact the English Vampire Court and to have them make us their representatives in this matter.

I knew that they'd only be too happy to pass the matter off to us. If we didn't take it, they'd have to contact one of their local members here and that individual would have to drop everything and deal with it. It was a responsibility that no vampire really wanted.

The English Vampire Court's representative had two jobs in cases like this: the first was to remain with the victims on the slight chance they would be reborn as vampires. In this particular case, the odds of one of the three victims inside becoming vampires were exceptionally thin. The attacking vampire would have had to share blood with them, and even then, it was unlikely. It did happen, though. Liv was walking, talking, undead proof that it did.

The second part of the job was to work with law enforcement to bring the vampire to justice. Vampire courts and human authorities had had this arrangement since just after World War II when Enhanceds came out into the light, so to speak.

As representatives, we'd be full partners with law enforcement and have access to all the case files and any other information pertaining to this case.

Stella's voice came over the comms in my helmet, *"I just spoke to Sarah. She will make the calls to make us the Court's official representatives in this matter. You should have access to the crime scene shortly."*

"Good work, Stella."

I'd barely ended the call when I spotted a black SUV with flashing lights in its grille pull up in front of the alley's entrance. A heavily armed team of EIRT agents got out. I smiled when I spotted the unmistakable blond, muscled form of Bobby Knight.

At least something was going right on this shitty night.

Bobby had been a Hamilton Police SWAT Sergeant before leaving to join EIRT, probably close to ten years ago now. He'd been excellent in that role and was just as good as an EIRT agent. Murdock had been Bobby's SWAT replacement. Murdock wasn't half the cop Bobby had been—one of the reasons I had such problems with him.

I quickly glanced over the six-person EIRT team. I spotted a multi-colored aura on one of the members that marked him as a mage. The rest of the team was human. I let out a sigh of relief at that. EIRT teams usually had one or two Enhanced Individuals as part of the team. My fear had been that one would be a vampire, Were, or something else with extraordinary senses that would be able to detect Alteea. A mage, though, would be oblivious to her presence.

Her being detected once we were the English Vampire Court's representatives from a legal perspective would have been okay but awkward. It would be obvious that I sent her in ahead of time, which would have made things uncomfortable. I also liked to keep her presence hidden as much as possible. Alteea saved our asses a couple of times, mainly because people weren't aware she was around.

Bobby and his team came down the alley and Bobby spotted us. "Rob! Hurricane! Nice to see you both. I wish the circumstances were better."

Rob gave Bobby a typical bro hug and I tipped my head towards him. The pleasant expression on his face disappeared as he turned to me and said, "I heard that you knew one of the victims? My condolences, by the way."

"Thank you." I then explained how I knew Charlie. Bobby's frown deepened. "If you were a cop and you were this close to the victim, you wouldn't be allowed within a hundred feet of this crime scene. I don't like this, but as you are the English Vampire Court's representatives, I have no choice but to allow you on the scene. I'll warn you that if you step outside procedures or let your emotions get the better of you, I'll have you escorted off the premises, understood?"

My temper flared for a moment, but I kept it under control. I knew it wasn't personal. Bobby wasn't questioning my team's abilities. He was just concerned about three powerful and emotional Enhanced Individuals being on his crime scene and messing it up. As my friend, he probably hated giving me that lecture. "Understood."

Bobby nodded. "I'd also appreciate if it was just you and one other team member. It will be only me and Mac," Bobby pointed at the mage beside him, "going in there. The fewer people in, the less chance of contaminating the crime scene."

I was about to protest this, as I wanted both Liv and Bree in there, when Bree cut me off, "Zack, you and Liv go." I turned to Bree and lifted an eyebrow at her. "The dark vibes around this whole place are getting to me. And what's worse is they're getting to my beast too. The full moon is tonight so she's already hard to control; this is just making it worse. I also don't want to see Char—"

Bree closed her eyes, locked her jaw, and clenched her fists. Her body started to shudder like she was about to change for a brief moment but then went still.

I realized that she was barely holding it together. I opened a channel on the comms. *"Blue, please open a portal where we came through."*

"Roger that."

Bree's eyes opened and a forlorn expression appeared on her face. "Zack, I'm—"

I held up my hand and cut her off. "Nothing to apologize for. Liv and I can handle this. You head home and help Stella and Blue."

Bree stayed motionless for a moment, as though she was conflicted. After a few seconds, she slowly nodded, turned, and headed back down the alley towards where we arrived.

I watched her go to make sure that she got through the portal okay. I deeply respected her decision. It is never easy to admit weakness. She did the right thing; rather than risk losing control of her beast, she removed herself from the situation. I was also feeling the weight of the dark, oppressive vibe around me and a large part of me just wanted to leave too. Bree sensed that darkness before I did, so she obviously was getting a stronger dose of it. Considering the added burden of her beast's reaction, it was impressive that she'd managed to stay here as long as she had.

I heard Bobby directing his team behind me. He sent one officer back to the SUV to get protective gear and ordered the other three agents to liaise with Hamilton police around the perimeter and canvas the neighborhood for possible witnesses.

Once I spotted Bree disappear back into the shadows, I turned back to Bobby and the rest.

Detective Little came out of the back door of the restaurant behind another older detective in a suit. The lead detective was tall and thin and had his gray hair cut almost military short, probably to help hide the male-pattern baldness that hit a large area at the front of his former hairline.

He shot Liv and me an unpleasant look and then promptly ignored us and turned his full attention to Bobby and the mage. Detective Little gave us a short nod as he passed by.

Once the introductions were out of the way, the older detective got down to business. "Three victims inside all show signs of a vampire attack. The couple at the front of the kitchen were restrained in chairs and physically assaulted before being drained."

I frowned at that. Why would vampires tie their victims to a chair and assault them before feeding on them? It made no sense. It also ruled out rogue vampires in the grip of bloodlust; they would have just fed. The vampires who committed this act were under control and of sound mind. The restraints and assault almost made it seem like the vampires were interrogating the couple.

"The couple were the owners, Vanya and Mila Andropov. The male deceased is sixty-one, and the female is fifty-nine. We are looking into family members to contact. The third victim is the hero known as Curveball, Charlene Peters, seventeen. It looks like she interrupted the attack and was killed by the vampires in retaliation. She is at the back of the kitchen."

My gut tightened up and my knees went weak at hearing Curveball's name, and I struggled to keep it together. I refused to give in to my emotions. I owed Charlie more than that. I forced myself to focus on the facts and not fall apart.

Bobby asked, "How were they discovered?"

"Two officers on foot patrol. The back door here had been propped open and one of the officers spotted blood on the floor and they took a closer look. Once they spotted the first victim, they entered to provide medical assistance and called it in. Once they determined that all three victims were beyond medical help, they exited the building and secured the scene."

"Forensics and the coroner en route?"

The detective nodded, "Both should be here shortly."

"Good. We'll take over the scene now but please remain on-site, as we might have more questions for you and your partner."

The detective stiffened at that but just nodded unhappily in response.

Bobby turned to me and said, "Ready?"

I nodded and the older detective balked, "Hold on, why are you taking two civilians in?"

Bobby shifted his attention back to the detective and said, "They have been appointed official representatives of the English Vampire Court in this matter."

The older detective shook his head in disgust, fished a pack of smokes from his jacket, and stomped off down the alley with his partner on his heels.

Bobby lifted the crime scene tape and Liv and I ducked underneath it. We followed Bobby and the mage to the door.

There was an EIRT agent at the back door of the restaurant wearing boot covers and latex gloves. He had a box in front of him that contained more. He handed a pair to Bobby, the mage, and Liv. Noticing my armored hands, he just handed me boot covers. I awkwardly put them on over my armored feet. To my surprise, the agent had two evidence bags for me as well when I stood back up. He put one over my left gauntlet and then snapped an elastic band over my wrist to hold it in place and did the same with my right hand.

The bags on my hands made me feel like a kid with oversized mittens. I was tempted to kick up a fuss, but I knew Bobby was already unhappy with me being on his crime scene and didn't want to push him, so I stayed quiet. The awkward hand covers really didn't matter, as we weren't supposed to touch anything anyways. The bags wouldn't interfere with my powers, though if I shot out lightning, I'd be spending time afterward scraping melted and burnt plastic off my armor.

We entered through the steel side door. Bobby and the mage blocked a good area of my view, but I spotted the blood on the floor. Charlie's pale hand and the dark sleeve of her sports jersey stuck out from behind the ice machine that was just ahead. I dropped my gaze to the plain reddish-brown tiles that seemed to be common in restaurant kitchens. Many of the restaurants I'd briefly worked in trying to support myself during my hero days used the same tile.

A rainbow aura shot by me, and I assumed that Alteea was now sitting on Liv's shoulder.

Bobby and the mage stopped in front of the area where Charlie was and I said, "Can we start with the owners first?"

I wanted to see them first while my mind was reasonably clear. I knew seeing Charlie would cloud my judgment.

"Sure," said Bobby softly and he and mage began moving again.

The blood on the floor brought up another concern. I looked over my shoulder to Liv and asked, "You going to be okay in here?"

"Yeah, I had a few pints while Bree and I were watching TV before this. I'm good."

The Food-O-Tron at our secret lab was able to replicate human blood. Blue, before going to bed, would usually take Liv and Bree to the lab so they could grab blood and food for the night.

I pointedly looked away from where I knew Charlie was and followed Bobby and the mage deeper into the kitchen. It was more open here. There was a food prep area with stainless steel tables to the right and the ovens, deep fryers, and cooking area were to the left. Between the prep station and the kitchen proper were two chairs and the victims.

I stopped dead as I got a look at their faces and suppressed a gasp. I'd seen more dead bodies in my time than I'd like to admit but these two were different. Most corpses looked more or less peaceful. These two, though, had their heads back and their mouths wide open like they were in the middle of screaming. Their faces were locked in identical looks pure fear and terror.

I'd also seen vampire victims before and none of them had expressions remotely like what I was seeing.

By the gaping wounds on their necks, I had no doubt that both had died from a vampire attack, though. Both victims also had bruises and deep cuts on their faces and arms. Someone had used both as punching bags before they died.

Bobby and the mage walked slowly around the two victims, examining them.

I sensed Liv beside me and said, "Do you smell anything odd?"

I was usually nose blind, and before gaining vampire and Were companions, didn't see much value in scent. After being around them and seeing how much they could detect via scent, I highly valued their abilities.

"Blood dominates everything, and I'm getting things you would expect, like tomatoes and herbs, but I'm also picking up something odd."

I turned to look at Liv. She had her eyes closed and was sniffing the air intently.

"There is a faint musty smell of decay lurking under everything, but it is fading, and I can't describe it any better than that. Sorry, Bree is the better bloodhound of the two of us."

We spent the next ten minutes carefully avoiding the blood splatter on the ground as we walked around the bodies and examined the area. There was what looked like the outline of the tip of a male dress shoe in a small pool of blood beside the male victim. There was also a partial heel print of another dress shoe in some flour that was on the floor a few feet away from the bodies. But either of those might have been from the officers that were first on scene and not connected to the attackers. I used my visor to take pictures of the shoe prints and everything else.

Liv spotted a baseball lying near one of the fryers in the kitchen and I almost broke down at the sight of it. I had no doubt that was one of Charlie's. It made me feel a little better when I reasoned that if the ball was here, Charlie at least went down swinging. Not that it did her much good in the end.

Bobby and the mage had already moved on to examining Charlie, and I knew Liv and I had gotten all we could from examining the other two bodies. Now I was just stalling.

My stomach knotted up. I really didn't want to do this. I wanted to remember Charlie as the vibrant tomboy with marvelous blue eyes that always had a twinkle of mischief in them. I knew, though, that if I saw Charlie's corpse that image would dominate my memories of her.

"Zack?" said Liv. "Let me deal with Charlie. I'll take pictures and have Stella and Blue go over them. You don't need to do this."

My body warmed at her words. Without saying anything, Liv knew exactly what I'd been struggling with. A part of me was tempted to take Liv up on her offer, but I'd never forgive myself for not doing it. Charlie had given her all here tonight and I owed her nothing less.

I shook my head and wandered over to where Charlie lay. Bobby and the mage were standing between Charlie and me, blocking my view.

As I got closer, they both stepped back, and I stopped in my tracks. Charlie was lying on her back with her feet away from me, extending into a short hallway. I cursed when I saw that Charlie's mouth was also wide open in an unending scream, the same look of terror the older couple had mirrored on her face. Her neck was a bloody mess that was torn open on both sides as if the two vampires each fed on her simultaneously. Her right hand was bloody and bruised. Her bat lay a foot or so from her outstretched right hand. The end of the bat had a dark stain on it that I realized was blood. I wondered if was hers or her attackers. There were also bloodstains on the floor, the walls, and the restaurant equipment around her.

I spotted something small and dark down the hallway by her feet. I realized that it was her catcher's mask and neck guard, her helmet was resting against the wall. One of the straps on the helmet was frayed as if it had been ripped apart.

I focused on that ripped strap and remembered the night when Charlie came to training with her new gear. She used money from my foundation to replace her old worn equipment. She'd had an extra bounce in her step and her eyes shined with pride as she showed it off to us. My eyes began welling up again.

I took a deep breath and centered myself. I wasn't going to fall apart now. I channeled Blue. Blue was exceptionally good at looking at a scene and surmising what happened. I needed to do that here.

Charlie had made her stand here at the opening to the short hallway. On her left was the ice machine and on her right was a large standing commercial fridge. I turned and looked behind me and could clearly see the victims and the two chairs they were in. That meant Charlie would have had the vampires in her sights in front of her and they only had a narrow entry to reach her. Blue would have been proud of her tactical choice.

She would have harassed them with the baseballs to get their attention and pull them away from the victims. I was willing to bet that the blood on the end of the bat was from one of the vampires. She tagged one with it but probably didn't have time to take the second before it got her. Once it closed, Charlie would have fought, which was backed up by her bloodied and bruised hands and the bloodstains all over the place, but her strength wouldn't be able to match her attacker's and she'd be overwhelmed. The second vampire would have probably rejoined the fight at that point too, which just made a bad situation even worse.

But how did Charlie end up lying on her back? If she'd been facing them, she would have either fallen forwards onto her front or fallen back deeper into the hallway. I figured that during the struggle she might have got turned around. Or maybe she did fall face forward and the vampires flipped her over, either to search her or continue feeding.

Bobby interrupted my thoughts by walking by me, heading toward the front of the restaurant, and I shifted out of his way.

I got back to my mental exercise of recreating Charlie's last stand. I thought again about the vampires searching her. Where was Charlie's phone? Did they take it?

I excitedly opened a channel to Blue, *"Blue, Charlie's phone doesn't seem to be at the scene. Can you see if Stella can trace it?"*

"No need. We have the phone here. It was under the ice machine in the shadows, so I acquired it. The battery was dead, so we are recharging it now."

I mentally shook my head at Blue. She'd removed evidence from a crime scene, which wouldn't be well received if anyone found out. We'd have had full access to it as the English Vampire Court's representatives, so there was no need to take it.

On the other hand, if she hadn't stolen it, it might have been hours or even days before that happened.

Bobby was still out in the front of the restaurant and the mage seemed to be occupied casting some sort of spell, so I risked saying, *"Don't power it on at the house. Use the lab."* Being in our underground lab with no cell connection would ensure that the phone couldn't be traced.

Oddly enough, while I couldn't see Blue, I instantly pictured her tail making sharp motions in disapproval as she said, *"As Olivia is fond of saying, 'relax, not my first cow convention.'"*

The irony of her getting an expression wrong that was meant to reassure was funny, but I wasn't in a laughing mood. Bobby reentered the kitchen and I ended my call with Blue.

As Bobby approached, he said, "Robbery wasn't a motive, or at least not for cash anyways. There is cash under the counter in plain sight and the cash register is intact."

I nodded. I'd have been surprised if this had been a robbery, so his news wasn't a shock.

The back door to the restaurant opened and three people wearing protective gear, cameras, and large bags walked in. I assumed the forensics team had arrived.

I was about to give the place a last look around and then get out of their way when a call came through on my visor. I cringed as I saw the name show up on the caller ID. I *so* didn't want to take this call. I took a deep breath and answered it.

"Mr. Stevens, Diane Peters here, Charlie's mom. Charlie's late and isn't answering her phone or texts; I'm worried something's happened to her . . ."

I didn't want to give her the news over a phone and scrambled to come up with what to say, "That's not like Charlie; let me make some calls and I'll get back to you."

She thanked me and ended the call.

Liv blurred up beside me. "Go, I got this."

I puzzled for a second at Liv's comment and then realized that she'd heard the entire conversation with Charlie's mom. "You sure? You'll need to stay here until just before dawn."

"Not my first rodeo. I'll call Blue to get a lift home. I'll be fine. Go."

I was tempted to tell her that the term was now 'cow convention,' but I knew that would just get me a blank look in response and just nodded.

We moved aside for the forensic techs and then I closed the distance between me and Bobby. "I just got a call from Curveball's mom. I'm leaving and going to break the news in person to her. Liv will stay here in case any of the victims have a new surprise lease on life."

Bobby gave me a look of profound sympathy. I was willing to bet he'd had to break this type of news to a victim's loved ones before. "I'll send you a copy of my report once it is complete. I'll also make sure that a copy of the forensics and coroner's reports are sent your way as well. It was good seeing you again, Hurricane; hopefully, the next time we meet it will be under better circumstances. Sorry again about your loss."

"Thanks, Bobby," and with that, I turned and left. The moment I got out of the restaurant, I used my powers to lift myself into the sky and headed for Charlie's house.

Chapter 4

Sunday, October 9

It was close to 4 a.m. when I got back to the house. To my surprise, everyone was still up. Bree came up to me and hugged me. "Sorry I chickened out back there."

I shook my head. "You did the right thing. Liv and I had it covered. It's all good."

"How is Charlie's mom doing?"

"About how you'd expect. Charlie's grandmother lives there too; I didn't know that. The two of them are taking care of each other now. The grandmother is a tough old girl. She just had one request: find who did this to her grandchild and make them pay. And that's exactly what we're going to do."

Bree nodded and returned to the table. Both Charlie's mother and grandmother had been devastated by the news. They'd also been incredibly gracious to me. A part of me wished they'd yelled at me and blamed me for all of this. I knew Charlie would have been out on patrol whether she'd been a part of my foundation or not. For Charlie, being a hero had been her calling. Despite all that, I still felt responsible. If I hadn't sponsored her, maybe she'd have been forced to get a part-time job and might not have been out there tonight.

I couldn't change the past, but I was going to fulfill her grandma's request no matter what it took. "Any news?"

Stella nodded. "The pizzeria had cameras, but they only covered the front of the restaurant. Blue spied on the cops and techs as they were looking over the recorded video from the cameras, but they came up with no possible suspects. It looks like the suspects must have come in the back door. The English Vampire Court also sent a list of all vampires they are aware of that live in the province."

I cursed mentally about the first part of Stella's statement, as a picture of the suspects would have been nice, but the vampire list would be useful. That was assuming that the vampires responsible were local and not just passing through. It seemed more likely to me that nomadic vampires were the culprits. Local vampires were either members of the English Vampire Court or were free vampires that abided by the Court's rules. Nomadic vampires weren't members of any court and tended to feel that the modern no-killing-while-feeding restrictions were undignified.

Stella's voice pulled me from my thoughts. "I saved our best lead for last. Curveball recorded the entire thing on her phone."

My pulse picked up at that. "She got video of the whole thing? How?"

Stella's face fell. "She recorded video, but it is really just audio. The video is just shots of the underside of the ice machine. She hit record and tossed it under the ice machine before confronting the assailants. We've listened to it a few times. There were three perpetrators."

Three vampires meant Charlie had been well and truly screwed the moment she stepped into that kitchen. There was no way she could have taken that many down. My anger grew but I forced it down. "Okay, let's hear it."

Stella went pale and shook her head. "Zack, I'll warn you that listening isn't easy. Let us transcribe it and you can read it instead."

"I appreciate what you are trying to do but play the video."

Stella nodded slowly. "We have it hooked up in the living room on the TV. The speakers are better than the phone's."

Stella got up from the table, but Bree and Blue remained seated. I lifted a questioning eyebrow at them.

Bree shook her head. "I've listened to it three times already." She shuddered and added, "That's enough for me."

I nodded in understanding and worried that maybe I should take Stella's advice and wait for a transcript. But I needed to hear the recording for myself just in case I caught something the others had missed. Stella, Blue, and Bree were very capable and the chances that I'd pick up something they missed were remote, but I owed it to Charlie to do everything possible to bring her killers to justice.

I glanced at Blue and as soon as I saw the entranced look on her face, I knew why she wasn't joining us. She had a book tilted on the table and was staring deep into the shadows. I assumed she was spying on the investigation, looking for more clues.

I followed Stella to the living room. On the large screen was a paused video with Curveball's masked face in the shot.

"Take a seat," said Stella, pointing at the couch while she picked up the phone.

"I'll stand."

"Sit. Trust me, Zack."

I was going to argue but took a deep breath and sat down on the couch. Stella gave me a nod of approval and hit play.

An image of Curveball's blacked-out catcher's mask bounced around the screen and her 'bat-voice' came from the speakers. A forlorn smile came to me as I heard it. Curveball preferred to be mistaken for a male when out on patrol, so she'd purposely deepened her voice when in costume. I always thought she went too far with the voice and sounded like Batman. Originally, I'd found the faux voice slightly annoying, but over time it had become endearing.

"I heard a scream of distress and am investigating where it came from."

A smile of pride reached my lips at the formal tone of her words. She was using our training by recording everything in case the footage had to be used in court at a later date.

The camera went still as she stopped running. The buildings in the background rotated and I realized she was turning in a slow circle. A sound of an impact, followed by a grunt of pain, was barely audible over Curveball's breathing.

"The noise came from that restaurant over there," said Curveball in her faux voice over the speakers.

The image bounced around, and I could hear shoes on the pavement as she ran. She flipped the camera around, and I recognized the back door to the restaurant as it moved around in the shot. The door was propped open and the hallway with the ice machine loomed beyond it.

When she reached the doorway, she stopped.

Two hard smacks and another cry of pain came from the kitchen, followed by a desperate accented male voice, *"Please stop. We know nothing about this headpiece you keep asking about."*

So the vampires had been interrogating the couple. They were searching for a 'headpiece,' whatever the heck that was. For some reason, an image of King Tut's ceremonial funeral mask popped into my head. I doubted they were searching for that, but maybe some sort of ornate crown or mask was this mystery headpiece they were looking for.

The camera moved again as Curveball entered the kitchen. A part of me mentally screamed at Charlie to turn back but I knew that wish was futile as this was a recording and not live.

A gravelly, almost reptilian, voice that chilled me to my core replied, *"If you don't know, then you are of no use to me . . ."*

With those words, the image on the screen flashed around as Curveball placed the phone on the ground. She used her foot to push the phone under the ice machine, and the image went dark.

A woman screamed and then Curveball's bat-voice filled the air, *"Yo, Skeletor! Why don't you and your two fanged friends pick on someone not tied to a chair?"*

I puzzled over the Skeletor comment. What did the skull-headed villain from *He-Man* have to do with vampires? I wondered if the guy was wearing a skull mask to hide his identity or to intimidate his victims.

The chilling voice I'd heard earlier pulled me from my speculations. *"Deal with the child."*

"Yes, Master," came the response from identical monotone voices. The replies had to have been from the other vampires, but the flat dull tones were odd. Vampires were a lot of things but dull wasn't one of them. Most vampires had strong, robust voices and usually liked to hear themselves talk; these ones sounded like they were in a trance.

The distinctive sound of a hardball making contact with flesh filled the speakers.

"Oh my! Curveball gets a double to center field. The crowd goes wild."

I smiled at Curveball's verbal taunt.

The ring of an aluminum bat hitting something hard filled the air. I assumed Curveball tagged one of the vampires with it. I remembered the bloodstain on the end of the bat.

"STRIKE ONE!" said Curveball in an upbeat voice that almost made me laugh.

I would have if the stakes weren't so high and if I hadn't known the results of this encounter.

A surprised, *'Shit!'* in Curveball's regular voice was followed by the sounds of hits being exchanged.

"*Get off me!*" said Curveball with a hint of panic in her voice as the sounds of the scuffle continued.

My gut knotted up. I knew things were going badly for her now.

A grunt was followed by a rattling sound that puzzled me. The object sounded like something plastic. The image of the discarded mask behind Curveball's body came flashing back to me and I knew it was her helmet, mask, and neck protector hitting the tiled floor.

A surprised yelp of pain echoed in the room.

"*No!*" cried Charlie as a snarl and wet sounds filled the air.

I clenched my fists when I realized the vampires were feeding on her. The stomach-turning sounds continued for what seemed like forever, but in reality, it was probably only thirty seconds.

A sigh of pleasure filled the air and then the impact of plastic and the dull thump of something heavy hitting the floor followed. I clearly pictured Charlie falling to her knees, the plastic knee guards impacting the floor, and then her lifeless body falling face-first into the tile.

I wiped the free-flowing tears away from my face.

Damn it, Charlie! Why didn't you call us? I thought to myself.

I shook my head because I knew why she hadn't called; there hadn't been enough time. Even if she'd hit dial and tossed the phone, it would have taken us time to figure out what was happening, track her phone, and then get there. We wouldn't have arrived in time.

Slow, sharp footsteps were the only sounds I could hear now. The steps got louder as they approached.

"*Turn her over,*" said the cold, hissing voice.

My eyes widened as a soft feminine groan came over the speakers; Charlie was still alive.

A low, almost whisper-soft, chanting started. I just made out what sounded like words but couldn't catch any of them. They weren't English.

Stella hit pause. "Blue picked out a couple of words of Russian—night, darkness, and gift—when she listened to it. The rest of the words she said weren't Russian, English, or French, and she didn't know what language they were. I think this was some sort of ritual or spell."

I almost dismissed that idea outright; vampires couldn't do magic. Something about the process of becoming a vampire blocked all other Enhanced abilities. So, if a mage, elemental, or Super became a vampire, their powers disappeared.

Two of the perpetrators were vampires but what if the leader of the group wasn't? Vampires, though, didn't call anyone but higher-ranked vampires 'Master.' The vampires had sounded like they were in a trance, though, so they might be enspelled. That was a disturbing thought. Vampires had high mental resistance to compulsion. Heck, most of the time they were the ones mentally dominating their victims. If they were enthralled, that meant whoever this mysterious third member was, he was exceptionally powerful.

I also kicked around the three words and the fact that they were in Russian. The couple's names and surname were also Russian, and I doubted that was a coincidence. This crime was turning out to be more than just some random vampire killings. What all of it meant I didn't have the faintest clue, but we needed to get to the bottom of this mystery if we wanted to catch them.

Stella lifted an eyebrow at me, as though she were asking if I was ready to resume watching. I nodded and Stella hit play.

I jumped as a scream of absolute terror and pain that shook me to my core suddenly flooded the room. I dug my nails into my palms as I sat there helplessly listening to Charlie's last moments on Earth. The scream ended almost as quickly as it started, and everything went quiet.

"Ah, a strong soul. I shall enjoy breaking this one," said the hissing voice.

Sounds of them moving around and something else filled the room. I strained to hear the soft rhythmic tones and then realized it was someone praying.

The leader said, *"Feed, but don't kill them."*

Two quick rushes of air were followed by cries, pleading, then sharp gasps of pain; the vampires had blurred off to feed.

The footsteps of the leader rapped across the floor and faded as he moved back deeper into the kitchen.

For the next thirty seconds, there were barely any sounds coming through the speakers and I wondered if this was where the phone had run out of power.

The gravelly voice broke the silence. *"Enough. It is time."*

I cringed as another female scream of terror filled the air shortly after that. Ten seconds later, another scream, this one deeper sounding, echoed around the room. Those screams chilled me to the bone, as I'd never heard anything like them before tonight. I knew these screams would haunt me to my dying days.

"*Fetch the horseless carriage,*" said the leader.

I frowned at that statement. The term 'horseless carriage' hadn't been used in more than a century, which meant the leader was at least a hundred years old, and I suspected a great deal older. Magic users like mages had very long lifespans, so it was more than possible.

A whoosh of air followed, and I assumed one of the vampires blurred by and out of the restaurant. The staccato taps of the leader's shoes on the tile grew louder as he approached. I couldn't hear the other vampire that I assumed was still with him, but that wasn't a surprise. Living with Liv, I was all too aware of how quiet vampires could be when they walked.

The sound of the footsteps changed as the leader left the tiled floor and I assumed stepped out onto the pavement. The steps gradually faded off into the night and were gone.

Stella smothered a yawn and hit pause. "The recording goes on for another twenty minutes and then ends. Other than a bit of faint traffic noise, there is nothing there."

I mentally sympathized with Stella over her yawn as I suppressed one of my own. "I know it's late and thank you for staying up. As vampires are our main suspects in this case, we'll probably be working a lot of late nights going forward. We'll stay up until dawn when Liv gets home and then sleep during the day. You okay with that?"

"I assumed as much."

We joined Bree and Blue at the kitchen table.

Blue broke her trance-like state of staring off into the shadows just as we sat down.

"It is fascinating observing the forensic technicians performing their duties. They are very efficient and methodical. Their efficiency has been impacted due to Olivia's assistance and I would not be surprised to find the head technician executing searches of vampire banishment rituals," said Blue with a pointy-toothed smile.

Olivia hanging around the restaurant until dawn wasn't the most exciting way for her to spend an evening. The most dangerous vampire of all is a bored vampire, so I felt a great deal of sympathy for the forensic techs. I bought Blue and Bree up to speed with the plan to stay up until dawn and sleep during the day due to the nocturnal aspects of the case. Bree just shrugged as she was usually up until dawn anyways hanging out with Liv at night, so this was nothing new for her.

"I concur," said Blue with an approving nod.

"As we have a few hours until Blue needs to retrieve Olivia, let's go over what we know and develop a plan for going after the things responsible for these murders . . ."

Chapter 5

Sunday, October 9

I was annoyed and pleasantly surprised as my alarm blared beside me, waking me out of a deep sleep. The annoyance was due to being forced to get up when all I really wanted to do was roll over and grab another couple of hours of sleep. On the other hand, I was surprised to have slept at all. I'd expected to have trouble getting to sleep. I figured my mind would have been going over the case and Charlie's death but staying up till dawn had exhausted me and I was out almost the same time as my head hit the pillow.

I liked my sleep and usually needed more than five hours of it to function, but I wanted to get started tracking down Charlie's killers as soon as possible.

I stumbled downstairs like a zombie but instead of moaning for brains, my chant was for coffee.

Stella and Blue were already up and seated at the kitchen table with laptops open and papers around them hard at work. I knew they were working on less sleep than I was and yet they both looked disgustingly alert and refreshed. Other than grunting at them, I ignored them and continued on my quest for life-giving caffeine.

A few minutes later, with the nectar of the gods in hand and doing its magic in getting my sluggish brain to fire, I joined them at the table.

Not much had changed from this morning, as Blue and Stella had only started their research twenty minutes before my arrival after they'd had breakfast, or maybe, as it was gone noon, that would be considered lunch. Stella was looking for supernatural incidents involving Russians. Blue was researching headpieces with a Russian connection to them.

We'd decided last night that the Russian used in the leader's spellcasting and the fact that the murdered couple were of Russian descent was too much of a coincidence to ignore. Limiting the searches to Russian-based supernatural incidents and headpieces with a Russian connection narrowed down the possibilities. We were probably still in needle-in-a-haystack territory but at least this made it a smaller haystack.

Once the sun went down tonight, both Blue and Stella would go over the list of vampires that the English Vampire Court had provided and start ruling out suspects.

After a quick breakfast and another coffee, I got up to go upstairs to my office.

"Remember to work quietly," said Stella, not looking up from her laptop.

I frowned for a moment in confusion then remembered tonight was the full moon and Bree was still sleeping. I'd wondered why Stella and Blue were working at the kitchen table and not up in the office.

Bree was usually very good about controlling her temper and her beast, but the day of the full moon was the one exception. During full moons, Bree was a walking, snarling ball of rage that took very little to detonate. Our usual plan was to let her sleep until mid-afternoon and then get some food in her. The moment she was fed, Blue would portal her out to the pack meeting compound in Barrie. She and the rest of the Weres would travel from there to a remote location and spend the night in their furred forms howling at the moon and chasing deer. Tomorrow morning we'd get back the happy Bree we all knew and loved.

That also meant we were without the use of Bree's services this evening, but that couldn't be helped.

I crept up the stairs like my life depended on it and slipped into my office without making a sound. I plugged in the headphones to the PC and turned it on. I held my breath as the fans whirled up and the computer beeped and clicked as it booted. I gently exhaled in relief, as I heard no movement or noise from the far end of the upstairs.

I wanted to figure out more about this mysterious skull-masked leader of the group. We were convinced that two of the three culprits were vampires, but we were leaning towards the leader being something else. The spellcasting we heard added weight to that theory. His heavy footsteps also suggested he wasn't a vampire. Usually, vampires made little noise when they walked. Lastly, the pall of dread and despair that had blanketed everything like a shroud last night wasn't something vampires usually produced.

The last clue, though, was tricky. Vampires, as they aged, developed unique powers. Master vampires could create powerful illusions, mind control large numbers of people, manipulate emotions, detect truth or lies, change into mist, and many other wonderful and scary things. These talents varied greatly from one older vampire to the next. It was possible that the gloomy aura over everything was one such power, but I was leaning towards it being something else.

I opened a browser and started doing Google kung fu on skull masks and individuals and organizations that used skull masks.

Two hours later, I closed the browser in frustration. There was plenty of information online about skull masks. Historically they were used by the Aztecs and tribes in New Guinea. In the present day, there were protesters all over the world that had been seen in skull masks. Some gangs and cartels used them as their signatures. There was an assassin out of India that wore a skull mask as his calling card. There was speculation that the assassin was Enhanced due to his lightning-fast reflexes and some of the amazing physical feats he'd pulled off during jobs. The problem was none of these were even remotely pertinent to our case.

I decided to try a different approach and go more old school, and I glanced at the barely quarter-full bookshelf that contained my reference library on Enhanced Individuals. Every time I set eyes on that shelf, I was filled with sadness and loss. My old reference library had been destroyed when our house was blown up by the Master's robots months ago.

I'd initially attempted to modernize my efforts to replace it. Enhanced Net was an online reference service that had scanned numerous Enhanced reference books. They'd struck agreements with the Mages' Council, some Vampire Courts, and universities around the world for access to their archives and had scanned in some truly wonderful and rare books. They had a vast repository that was growing daily as they added more and more volumes to it.

I'd been excited about it at first and paid for a subscription to their service, which wasn't cheap. However, the site almost had too much information, and I struggled to use their search tools to find things I was looking for.

About a month ago, I decided to start rebuilding my own library, but it was currently a pale shadow of its former glory. I had gotten in the benchmarks, like the twenty volumes of *Lawson's Guide to Mythical Creatures* and all three volumes of Correia's *Essential Guide to Monster*

Hunting, but I was missing so much—more than half of my original library that I'd inherited from my mother when she passed. Many of those books were out of print and circulation and would be hard, if not impossible, to replace.

I'd ordered two copies of everything and had another budding collection back at the lab where Stella had graciously allowed me some shelf space in her library there. A couple of the rarer books that I'd only managed to acquire one copy of, I kept at the lab, as it was more secure than here. I'd probably change that around once our house next door had been rebuilt, as I had a large fireproof cabinet in the plans for my new office, but for now, this made more sense.

I was tempted to have Blue transport me to the lab, so I'd have access to those extra volumes but decided to make do with what I had here for now. I used the index for *Lawson's Guide to Mythical Creatures* to look up magic users and magic-using creatures, which turned out to be a very long list. I then used the index to look up beings that left an aura of fear, death, or despair in their wake. That also turned out to be a sizable list.

I froze in my work as the sounds of things being thrown around echoed down the hall and realized our moon monster had awakened. I rapidly went over all the things I'd done in the last few minutes, trying to figure out if I'd made enough noise to wake Bree, but thankfully came up empty.

Her door creaked ominously as she opened it. I went still and held my breath, not daring to move. Her heavy footsteps approached the doorway to my office but then she stomped by without even glancing in my direction.

I waited until her steps reached the main level and then exhaled in relief. My coffee cup was empty but to get more meant heading downstairs and possibly getting in the path of Hurricane Bree. I did a quick risk/reward evaluation in my head and decided that I could do without coffee until Bree left for Barrie and her pack meeting.

An hour later, Bree had been gone for twenty minutes, I had a fresh coffee, and I had finished cross-referencing my two lists. I was left with three unlikely candidates. The first one was an ancient immortal witch of legend that lived in the Black Forest in Germany, which I quickly eliminated. I somehow doubted she'd traveled over here to grab a slice of pizza and murder the older couple that ran the pizzeria. Also, the hissing voice I'd heard on Charlie's recording was masculine.

A demon was the next creature on the list capable of casting magic and leaving behind an aura of despair. A demon would also be powerful enough to enslave a couple of vampires to work for it. However, I highly doubted one would wear a mask. Demons were vain and arrogant and one of the last creatures I expected to hide their identity. Demons, though, did come in all shapes and sizes, so I guess one might have had a skull for a head. Full demons also had the ability to teleport, however, so why would one use a vehicle? While the bodies had been cut, gnawed on, and beaten, the carnage that a demon usually inflicted was so much worse. Demons also ate the hearts of the victim as, it was theorized, that's where the human soul was contained. None of the victims had had their chests ripped open.

The last being on the list was the best fit. A lich certainly could do magic and left an aura of death and despair in its wake. A lich was also the top of the undead class of creatures, sharing the top spot with master vampires. A master vampire versus a lich would be one heck of a fight, and one I'd love to see as long as it was filmed remotely on another planet. I wouldn't like to be even remotely close to where that fight took place.

Liches were also able to control the undead. Ghouls, zombies, wights, and other lesser undead would instantly fall under a lich's sway. Vampires might too, but only if they were young enough and mentally weak. The skull mask wasn't needed either, as liches were basically animated skeletons.

A lich was almost a perfect fit for the profile of these murders. The issue was that liches were exceedingly rare. If I was a betting man and had the choice between a lich being in Hamilton or a unicorn grazing in downtown Gore Park, my money would be on the unicorn every time.

Liches were necromancers that had reached the pinnacle of their craft and managed to cheat death itself. Reapers and entity of Death itself weren't pushovers, and to beat them, you'd need some serious mojo, which most necromancers never achieved. Most necromancers never came close to becoming liches, as they usually killed themselves by messing around with the powerful death and blood magics. Necromancers were also one of the few Enhanceds under an automatic death sentence; law enforcement and bounty hunters would shoot first and ask questions later. That stance tended to keep their numbers quite low. Due to these reasons, there were probably less than a handful of liches that had existed in all of human history.

As unlikely as a lich was as our suspect, I'd keep an open mind. There had only been two reported incidents of full demons on Canadian soil and yet, yours truly had taken on one of those, so anything was possible.

I sighed and reached for the volume of *Lawson's Guide to Mythical Creatures* that contained information on liches.

***

At dinner that night, I brought up my lich theory to the team. I still wasn't convinced that it was a lich but on the remote chance that it was, I wanted everyone prepared for the possibility.

Stella picked up on my reluctance and said, "I'm confused. Everything you listed points to a lich as our main suspect but I'm getting the feeling you're not convinced."

I swallowed a mouthful of potato and said, "There have been less than ten liches in all of recorded history; they are incredibly rare. I guess I'm having trouble believing that one would be lurking around Hamilton of all places. Also, if there was a lich in the area, there should be signs. Their very presence causes odd events to occur in any area they inhabit. We haven't heard of anything strange, or stranger than usual, happening around Hamilton."

Blue got a faraway look in her purple eyes, as if considering something, and then said, "The local authorities were busier than usual when we dropped off our last bounty."

I'd written that off at the time to the approaching full moon but maybe there was more to it than that.

Liv put down her pint mug of blood and said, "The last few days I felt restless, almost like something out there is calling to me."

"And you're just mentioning this now?" I asked.

Liv shrugged. "I didn't think it was a big deal. I figured I was just bored because Bree and I hadn't gone deer hunting or clubbing in a bit."

I let it go and wondered if those two things were signs that a lich was in the area. Both seemed a bit tentative and weak, but I wouldn't write them off just yet.

"If it is a lich, what are its powers and capabilities?" asked Stella.

"In short, they're super-powerful magic users that can control hordes of undead."

"That doesn't sound so tough," said Liv.

I shook my head. "We haven't had to deal with a lot of mages and such, but a strong magic user is one of the most dangerous things out there. They have spells that can level blocks of a city effortlessly. A lich uses the normal elemental spells like fireballs and lightning but also uses much darker magics. Death and blood magic are nasty. Add in that he can surround himself with an army of undead that we'd have to contend with to get to him and we are looking at an ugly fight."

"Oh," said Liv with a more somber expression, which suddenly change to a grin. "If these things are so dangerous, what type of bounty do they have on them?"

"Odin only knows. I don't recall a lich being taken down since the bounty program was established. If I had to guess, it would probably be in the millions, like the bounty for the demon was."

Liv fist pumped the air. "Yes! Mama has new shoes in her future."

I noticed Blue had sat up a little straighter and her tail was making happy circles behind her. I rolled my eyes at them. I was going to point out that huge bounties like this weren't handed out because they were easy, but just went back to eating my food knowing that it would be a wasted effort. There were times my team was a bit too mercenary.

***

Stella, Blue, and I had retired to the office upstairs after dinner to continue doing research. That session was disturbed just after ten when my phone rang. Dave Collins's name was on the display. Dave was a cop and friend of Rob's.

"Hurricane, I'm outside at East Hamilton Cemetery and we have a zombie issue. SWAT and EIRT have been called but both are delayed. For undead, these things are pretty lively and I'm not sure the gates will hold until they get here."

"Hold tight, Dave. We'll be there in less than five."

"Thanks," Dave paused and I heard a loud screech of metal in the background, and then he added, *"The gates are holding but the quicker you can get here the better."*

The moment I ended the call, Liv appeared at the doorway to the office with an excited grin. "Did someone say 'zombies'?" I nodded and she added, "Sweet, I need to change."

Vampire hearing was frightening at times, and this was one of those times. Liv had managed to eavesdrop on my call from downstairs while she'd been watching TV. "Be quick. The moment I get my armor on, we're outta here. Meet in the living room."

"'K, bye," said Liv as she blurred down the stairs.

Blue and Stella were already out of their chairs, and I quickly explained the side of the call they'd missed.

Once I was done, Blue went to her room to get her gear and Stella followed me to mine. Stella never carried anything into battle, so she was usually at a loose end while she waited for the rest of us to get ready. Blue had suggested that when speed was of the essence that Stella assist me with my armor, as out of all of us, I was usually the one that took the most time to get ready. Stella's assistance helped shave time off my prep process.

Just as I was attaching the last piece of my armor, Stella dashed over to my closet and pulled out one of my generic white T-shirts, and tossed it to me. For a brief second, I was confused, but then smiled and stuffed it into a storage compartment on my armor.

Stella and I joined Blue, Liv, and Alteea in the living room not even three minutes after I'd ended the call from Dave.

I stopped dead in my tracks as I spotted Liv. She had changed into what looked like an old plain white sports bra that had seen better days, a pair of worn and ripped cutoff jean shorts, a pair of shiny red Wellington boots, and had her silver-edged Katana strapped in a sheath over her on her back. "Yo, Paddington Warrior-Princess, what's the deal with the outfit?"

Liv frowned. "Do you know how hard it is to clean zombie guts off clothes? These—" she gestured to the bra and shorts, "—are getting burned when we are done. I'll rinse off the boots."

I nodded as I couldn't argue her reasoning.

Blue made a quick gesture with her hands and said, "The portal is open. We'll come out close to where law enforcement has set up their perimeter."

"Great. I'll go first and the rest of you follow. We'll assess the situation on scene. Alteea, stay high and film everything."

I didn't wait for anyone's reply and stepped forward into the shadows.

Chapter 6

Sunday, October 9

I came out of the shadows to a cool, crisp autumn night. The full moon ominously ghosted in and out of the thick grey clouds overhead, creating scenery that would fit in with a horror movie. I was standing in the shadows of the cemetery's high bricked walls and could hear the moans of the undead coming from the other side.

To my left was a ring of police cruisers that were parked in a large semicircle in front of the main gates. Their red and blue lights flashed and lit the night up like a disco. Hamilton police officers were nervously crouched behind their cars, pointing shotguns and pistols towards the gate. They tightened their grips on their weapons at the shriek of metal that pierced the air as the gates bowed out from the weight of the zombies pushing aggressively against them.

I spotted Dave's tall lanky form huddled among the officers and made a beeline over to him. There were more cruisers parked at either end of the street, blocking off traffic and pedestrians to the area.

A murmur went up from the officers as I approached. I assumed they were warning each other of my team's presence. I approved; it is always nice to avoid friendly fire incidents.

"Hurricane, thanks for getting here quickly," said Dave. "ETA on SWAT is unknown as they are tied up with a hostage situation in Ancaster. The closest EIRT team is an hour away."

Ancaster was a suburb on Hamilton's west side. As we were close to Stoney Creek on Hamilton's far-east side, even if they finished up now, it would take them probably close to thirty minutes to get here. That meant we were on our own for the time being.

I glanced at the zombies behind the straining gates and my concern grew. Normally zombies shuffled slowly, but these ones were quite vigorous in their efforts. "You have to love full moons . . ."

Dave gave a weary nod at that.

My team joined us, and Liv was almost bouncing with excitement. The girl did love a good zombie ass-kicking. Blue's tail made wide happy circles behind her as she gazed over the horde of undead and I realized that Liv wasn't the only one looking forward to this.

"Huddle up, team." Once they got closer, I said, "Here is what we are going to do..."

A minute later, I was standing about ten feet in front of the black iron gates with Stella just behind me. Blue and Liv were each against the wall on either of the gates. I scanned the skies and spotted Alteea's aura off to my right and a good twenty-five feet up in the air.

"Ready?" I asked.

Blue and Liv nodded.

I called on my Air powers and raised my hands towards the gate. I let the power build for a few seconds and then released a powerful blast of air. The mass of zombies managed to hold their ground briefly and then by ones and twos were tossed back deeper in the cemetery. A flood of them suddenly tumbled back from the almost hurricane-force winds I was sending at them. Five zombies were stubbornly gripping the iron gates and were blown horizontal to the ground. I narrowed my arc and picked each one off until they'd all been thrown back into the grounds.

I dropped my hands and yelled, "Clear!"

Liv executed a leap that took her straight over the ten-foot-high wall and disappeared inside the cemetery. Blue leaped up and caught the lip of the wall, deftly pulled herself up and over, and joined Liv. A bright light appeared in the darkness just inside the wall as Blue ignited her Keetiyatomi blade.

I used my Air power to lift myself and Stella into the air and flew over the gates. Liv and Blue had already engaged the outer edges of the zombie horde, which were getting back to their feet.

Once we were over the main bunch of zombies, hovering in mid-air, I asked, "Ready?"

Below us, zombies were clawing at the air and looking up like someone had rung a dinner bell. Stella's youthful face grinned and she flashed me two thumbs up.

A moment later, I cut the air beneath Stella and watched as she plummeted down. You'd think watching what looked like a young girl falling towards a hungry horde of zombies might have gotten a concerned reaction from me, but you'd be dead wrong.

Stella instantly transformed into her monstrous Hyde form and her large misshapen feet drove at least three zombies back into the earth from whence they came. Stella grunted as she landed and snatched a couple of zombies off their feet and crushed their skulls in her hands like they were made out of papier-mâché. The two now-headless zombies collapsed and went still. More zombies surged forward to take their places.

I left Stella to it. She was the least of my concerns, as zombies had no chance of biting or clawing through her impervious Hyde skin. She was the perfect zombie-killing machine.

I circled in the air to check on Liv and Blue. Liv had a big beaming smile on her face as she lopped off heads, limbs, and whatever else got near her whirling blade. She was completely surrounded by the undead but didn't care. One jumped on her back, and she just reached behind herself with her free hand, yanked it off, tossed it away, and continued fighting.

Blue's fighting style was more cautious than Liv's. Blue would dart forward, behead a zombie or two with an efficient swipe of her flaming blade and then dance back before she was engulfed by the horde. She'd then pivot, take out another zombie, and retreat again. Every movement that Blue made was calculated and graceful and demonstrated her years of discipline with a blade.

The three of them were aptly suited for this work. Blue's alien DNA made her immune to the zombie virus, ditto for Liv due to her vampire nature, and Stella's skin was too tough for zombies to bite through. Even if a zombie did manage to somehow bite Stella, if she changed back to her human form, the infection would be gone due to something that happened during the transformation process. I was envious of that ability, as Stella never got colds either. Satisfied my team had things well in hand, I turned my attention to more pressing matters.

I slowly circled around while I hovered in the air above the horde. You know your life is pretty odd when a mass of bloodthirsty, or maybe that should be brain-thirsty, undead isn't your primary concern. I strained my eyes against the night, searching for an aura anywhere out in the cemetery grounds. Zombies don't raise themselves from the grave. Something or someone had disturbed their deathly slumber and anything that did that wasn't something I wanted to take lightly.

I completed a full rotation and came up emptyhanded. I wasn't sure if I was relieved or disappointed. On the one hand, it was nice not having to deal with something capable of raising the dead. On the other hand, it meant that whoever had done this was still lurking out there and could stage a repeat performance on another night.

I pushed some air behind me and began doing a slow, careful lap of the cemetery grounds. I flew over row after row of disturbed graves but saw nothing more than that. I was searching for an altar, a sacrifice, or signs of a magic ritual. Most things that could raise the dead needed those to assist in the process.

I spotted a lone zombie trying to push against the brick wall near the west corner of the grounds. I shook my head. Whether it was people or zombies, there was always that one special idiot that stood out.

I landed on the wall above him and sat down, "Hey, Waldo, whatcha doing?"

Waldo continued pushing against the brick wall but looked up at me with milky white eyes and growled at me before turning his attention back to the wall.

"Yeah, the weather is unseasonably mild for this time of year. You think the Leafs have a shot at the Stanley Cup this year?"

Waldo grunted again and then let out an angry growl.

"You're probably right—they need better defense if they are going to make a run at it."

As fun as my one-sided conversation was, I needed to deal with my friend. My powers weren't ideal for beheading zombies, so I called on my Air powers and used them to lift Waldo a foot or so off the ground to send him in the direction of my team, who were well equipped to dispose of him. I then carefully turned him around so he was pointed in the direction of the other zombies. I floated him about ten feet away, as there were a few tombstones between him and his friends, and then lowered him to the ground.

Waldo began walking away but after a few steps, stopped and turned back around.

"Buddy, your friends are the other way. There is a nice lady zombie in a shiny green dress that wants to meet you," I said as I used my powers to lift and turn him around.

Once again, Waldo took a couple of steps but then turned back in my direction.

I sighed.

So much for the easy way, I thought, shaking my head.

I called on my Electrical powers and let them build for a moment. Just before Waldo reached the wall again, I released a massive blast of lightning at him. The bright blue lightning lit up the night, and a few seconds later, so did Waldo as he ignited.

Fire was another way of taking care of a zombie. Old dried-up corpses went up like cordwood. The problem was using lightning to create fire takes a fair amount of juice. I probably drained about twenty percent of my power doing that, so it was not something that I wanted to do on a regular basis.

Waldo's flaming remains dropped to the ground and went still. I briefly worried about it setting the grass on fire, but we'd had plenty of rain recently so it should be okay.

Waldo's behavior was odd, and I wondered if something had caused him to head in this direction. I stood up on the wall and looked around. To the left was the main road that led to the entrance of the cemetery. About fifty feet down the road there were a couple of police cruisers blocking off access. To my right were houses that backed onto the cemetery. I scanned their yards looking for auras but didn't see anything.

I used my powers to fly over the first row of houses and take a closer look at each of them. I didn't spot anything out of the ordinary. I shrugged and figured Waldo was just messed up or something and headed back to the cemetery to continue my lap around the perimeter.

I completed my lap of the grounds and found nothing of interest, which wasn't a good sign. The lack of altar or sacrifice narrowed down the list of things capable of raising the dead considerably. Off the top of my head, four came to mind: a master vampire, a full demon, and an exceptionally powerful necromancer or a lich. I cursed to myself at the last one.

The discussion I'd had earlier with my team about an odd phenomenon occurring when a lich was in the area came rushing back. The dead rising from their graves for no good reason certainly fit. Add that to the restless urges that Liv had been experiencing and the busy couple of days Hamilton police were having and it looked more and more like we might have a lich problem.

If it was a lich, then this was a major issue. I kicked around calling Acting Director Cooper at GRC13 and getting their help and resources to deal with it. I dismissed that idea almost as quickly as I'd thought of it, as we didn't have any solid proof we were dealing with a lich. They were so rare that if I did bring up my concerns and laid out my weak evidence, he'd probably laugh me out of his office or order a psychiatric evaluation for me.

I realized that for now, the best thing to do was keep my lich theory under my hat and cross the bridge of GRC13 assistance if and when we had more proof.

I turned in the air and headed back towards my team.

The mass of zombies had been thinned out considerably. Maybe twenty percent were still standing.

I shook my head and smiled as I spotted a now topless Liv still swinging away and hacking down zombies.

I spotted Stella pounding another zombie into paste and I watched in awe as Blue beheaded three with a single sweeping stroke of her magic sword.

It dawned on me that we were looking at a pretty good payday here. Zombies were $500 a head and there had to be close to 300 of them. The only downside was the paperwork was going to suck, as we had to file a claim per zombie. That was a lot of pictures and forms.

Twenty minutes later, Blue and Liv raced to cut down the last remaining zombie. Blue got the honor by barely a hair and gave Liv a pointy-toothed grin.

I landed beside them and fished the T-shirt out of its compartment. "You think you might ever get through a zombie encounter fully clothed?"

Liv shrugged. "Not my fault zombies are all grabby and shit," she paused as she caught the T-shirt I tossed to her, and added, "Besides, I might lose clothes, but they lose limbs and heads; I think I get the better end of the deal."

The beaming smile on her face made me wonder if there was some transference going on here. It wouldn't surprise me if Liv pictured the zombies as every guy who'd made an unwanted physical advance on her in her life. That would explain why she seemed so overjoyed about hacking them to pieces. Beats paying for therapy, and even better, she got paid for it too.

Liv frowned as she looked at her sword and then drove the point into the grass a few inches, freeing up her hands. She slipped on the

T-shirt and said, "Thanks." I nodded and she asked, "Anyone seen Mr. Slicey's holder?"

Blue shook her head and I just shrugged.

Liv extracted the sword from the ground and blurred off—I assumed to go find the missing sheath.

Stella's crisp English accent filled the air as she joined me and Blue. "Do you have my phone? We'll need pictures for the bounty claims."

Blue pulled out Stella's and her own phone from a pouch and handed one of them to Stella.

"You start on this side, and I'll cover the other," said Stella as she brought up the camera app on her phone. Blue nodded and the two of them started taking pictures.

"Found it!" yelled Liv from thirty feet away as she retrieved her sheath from a pile of zombie remains.

"Great," I yelled back, "do a lap and make sure that all the zombies are down."

Liv blurred off.

As my team had the scene in hand, I took to the air to let Hamilton's finest know the threat was over for now.

Chapter 7

Monday, October 10

The next day, I awoke with a smile just after noon as a clap of thunder boomed above the house. My powers were humming with all that wonderful static electricity in the air.

Last night, we hadn't gotten home until the wee hours in the morning. It had taken Stella and Blue more than an hour to photograph all the zombies. Just after they'd finished, an EIRT team showed up. It was another two hours of answering their questions and for them to give us the bounty claim numbers.

Once we'd gotten home, we spent almost until dawn filling out and submitting the claim forms. The final number was 302 zombies, which made a nice payout, and even Liv didn't gripe too much about all the paperwork.

After a quick shower, lots of coffee, and a bite to eat, I joined Stella and Blue in our home office. I instantly noticed the new pictures on the wall but wasn't sure what I was looking at.

"The autopsy report came in," said Stella as she got up and joined me.

The bare chests of all three victims were laid out in multiple pictures. All three had five small, round, and deep bruises in the left-center of their chests.

"The medical examiner believes those bruises are from the fingers and thumb of one of the assailants," said Stella.

As soon as she said that the images made more sense. Four of the bruises were grouped together with the last bruise offset from the rest.

Stella added, "The bruises on all three victims were directly over their hearts." She then pointed at the three pictures below. Each one contained what looked like a blackened shriveled raisin. "Those are the victims' hearts."

I staggered slightly at that. I'm no biology major or medical professional but I knew what a healthy human heart looked like, and these dried out and decrepit things weren't even remotely close. They looked like something that had been left out in the desert sun for months. What the heck could do that to a human heart, and more importantly, why?

My stomach knotted up as a possible answer came to me. It was speculated that the heart was where the soul was kept, that was why demons ate their victims' hearts. Liches harvested souls to fuel their death magics. If this had been done to them while they were still alive, it was no wonder the victims had screamed the way they did.

My eyes welled up as I thought about Charlie's final moments. It hit me that if the autopsy had been completed, the medical examiner would release the body and there would be a service held for Charlie soon. I pushed those thoughts aside for now and told Stella my theory about the shriveled hearts.

"Between the zombies last night and this, it is looking more and more likely that a lich is our prime suspect," said Stella.

I nodded. A lich was bad news, but at least if we were right, we knew what we were dealing with. We still had to find it first, though. "Any leads from your search of Russian supernatural incidents, Russian headpieces, or the vampire list the English Court provided?"

"Nothing on supernatural incidents. As far as Russian headpieces, there were a few articles on the Czar's crown that explained it contained magic to protect the wearer from mental assaults. The problem is the crown was lost during the Russian Revolution and hasn't been seen since that time. Most experts believe that it was melted down for its gold and jewels," said Stella.

I pondered the crown and asked, "Did the articles mention the crown had any other powers?"

"No. Why?"

"Mages have great mental discipline and are usually quite resistant to mental attacks. As liches have mage-like abilities, they would also be very mentally disciplined. A crown that provides mental defense doesn't seem like the most useful item for a lich. I'd be willing to bet he's not looking for the crown."

Stella seemed a bit crestfallen but then perked up. "Blue might have a lead for us regarding the two vampires."

Blue nodded. "The list for vampires in our immediate area is very short. Besides Olivia, there is an older vampire who lives near McMaster with his human servant. I was able to spy on them and they do not seem to be under any sort of trance or guise. Two younger male vampires live together in old Ancaster. They weren't home last night when I spied on their home from the shadows. Even more curious is they are not home now. There is a cold cellar in the basement with a heavy-duty steel door, but the door is open, and the cellar is empty."

My excitement grew at that. We knew the vampires who'd been with the lich were male from their voices, so two missing male vampires seemed like a good lead. Their absence from home during the night wasn't a big surprise, but it was odd they wouldn't have returned during the day. Most vampires had secure resting areas they retreated to during the day and very few took the risk of sleeping outside those areas. "How long have they been vampires?"

Blue opened a document on her laptop and after a bit said, "Seventeen and fifteen years respectively."

That wasn't super young, but it was young enough for them to probably be susceptible to a lich's powers. "Do they work?"

Blue checked the document again. "Yes, one is a computer programmer, and the other does computer security."

That made it unlikely they were away for work. A lot of computer programmers did contract work from home. The computer security expert could be focused on remote network intrusion and website security, which would mean most of the work could be done at home as well.

We needed to take a closer look at these two. Normally, I liked to do things legally. As the English Vampire Court's representatives, we could probably go through law enforcement to get a warrant but that would take time. "Blue, what type of security systems do they have on the house and is there anyone living there besides them?"

Blue smiled, as she knew where I was going with that question. "They have a security alarm, but it is just sensors on the doors and windows and external camera, no motion sensors inside the house. They are the only occupants of the dwelling."

I nodded and was about to have Blue open us a portal when another thought occurred to me. "Any pets?"

Stella giggled at that and Blue just shook her head.

"Great, let's hit the living room and pay the house a visit."

***

The three of us came out of the shadows into an unfinished basement. I spotted the open steel door to the cold cellar off to my left. In front of me was a bare wood staircase that led to the upstairs. To my right were two rooms that were drywalled in but unpainted. The one room had a steel utility door and I assumed it was probably the furnace room. The other didn't have a door and I could see a basic white laundry sink and shiny red washer beside it, as well as the edge of what was probably the matching dryer beyond it.

I turned around and there were boxes stacked up in the corner labeled in black marker as towels, cutlery, books, and computer parts. In the opposite corner was a ping-pong table that had one side folded up and a paddle resting on the lower part.

It all seemed very normal and didn't strike me as the lair for a pair of murderous vampires.

Blue wandered over and swung open the heavy door to the cold cellar. Stella and I joined her, and we peeked inside the door. There were two cots and a small bar fridge inside. Blue went in and opened the fridge. There were a few bags of blood inside the fridge and nothing else.

The main level was a stark contrast to the unfinished basement. The place was immaculate and tastefully decorated in a sleek modern style. There were neutral colors on the walls, dark hardwood throughout, cream leather furnishings in the living room, and the thinnest large screen TV I'd ever seen. I'd been expecting more of a frat house vibe for two young male vampires.

"What are we looking for?" asked Stella.

"Signs of how long they have been away. The police were busy for the two days before the full moon, so we can assume the lich has been in town since Thursday or Friday. If these two have been missing since around that time, we can probably assume they are the two vampires with the lich. If they have been missing longer than that, this might be unrelated to our case."

Stella tugged her braid. "Blue mentioned that they have computer-related careers; their computers then should give us the best idea of when they were last here."

"I observed computers upstairs in the two home offices they have up there," said Blue.

"Can you run me home for a moment? I need to pick up my USB boot drive," said Stella.

Blue nodded but I asked, "What is the boot drive for?"

"As one of them does computer security, the computers are probably password protected and encrypted. If I boot off the USB drive, I can bypass that security. I won't be able to access any data due to the encryption, but I can look at date stamps on the files."

I was pretty sure I understood what Stella was doing. The system files were updated every time the computer booted from them. As Stella was booting from a third-party device, the files on the hard drives wouldn't be touched. She could look at the date stamps to find the most recent ones and that would tell us when they were last here. I assumed this was due to both of them having computer-related careers. Most computer geeks lived and breathed on their computers.

She and Blue disappeared into a darkened powder room, leaving me on my own. Their absence made me very aware of how illegal our current activity was. It would be my luck that a cleaning or blood delivery service stopped by and found me here. My black armor with its distinctive gold *H.H.* logo on the chest meant I would be instantly recognizable. I mentally urged Stella and Blue to return quickly so we could get out of here sooner than later.

I headed to the kitchen. A kitchen was another good place to check when someone had last been home. However, as these were vampires who didn't eat regular food, I didn't have high hopes on the kitchen providing the answers I was looking for.

The kitchen amused me as it had a top-of-the-line range, fridge, dishwasher, and all the small appliances a chef would give his favorite apron for. The six-burner gas stove was spotless, and I wondered if it had ever been used. I opened the fridge and other than a box of baking soda, a half-empty bottle of Chardonnay, and six bags of blood, it was empty. Adjacent to the fridge was a well-stocked standing wine fridge that probably held over a hundred bottles of wine in it. I assumed the wine was kept on hand for entertaining human friends.

I found some open and discarded mail in the recycle bin in the cabinet under the sink. The most recent was dated was from the second of October, which was just over a week ago. Assuming a day or two in the mail, that probably meant they were here on the third or fourth.

I froze when I heard a noise upstairs but then heard Stella's voice and realized that she and Blue had returned.

I wandered around the main level. I found the alarm panel in the front hall which was armed. The alarm company would have records of when the alarm was set and that would give us a better indication of when they were last here. I made a note of the alarm provider. Stella might be able to hack their records, or we could use our law enforcement contacts to get the information.

I wondered if interviewing their neighbors would give us any answers. If our target had been human, I probably would have made the effort. As they were vampires and kept nocturnal hours, I doubted the neighbors would be much use in knowing when they were last home.

Stella came downstairs about fifteen minutes later. "There are two smartphones upstairs charging, so neither vampire took their phone with them."

I was taken aback by that. Most people, and that included vampires, lived and breathed by their phones and I assumed that the vampires wouldn't have willingly left theirs behind if they had a choice. This lent credence to them being enthralled by the lich. It also meant that we couldn't track them by their phones. That last thought had me wondering if the lich was more familiar with technology than I would have imagined. I quickly dismissed that idea, though, as someone who refers to a car as a "horseless carriage" didn't strike me as a technology guru. "Any luck with the computers?"

Stella nodded, "The last time either of the computers was on was 1:37 a.m. Friday."

That fit our timeline, and I was beginning to like these two for our vampire attackers. Now we just needed to find out where they were hiding.

Chapter 8

Monday, October 10

A few minutes later we were back at the house. The three of us made a brief pause at the kitchen to make a coffee and a couple of teas and then regrouped in the office upstairs.

I thought about our recent trip and realized that even though we'd been to the vampires' home, I still didn't have a clue about what they looked like. There had been no pictures of them in the basement or on the main level. There might have been pictures upstairs but I hadn't been up there to check.

I turned to Stella and asked, "In the file the English Court gave us, does it contain any pictures of the two vampires?"

Stella, in the middle of blowing on her tea to cool it down, paused, and then shook her head. "No, but I can get them." I cocked an eyebrow at her, and she explained, "As the official representatives of the English Vampire Court in this matter, they have given us full remote access to all files on Canadian personnel."

That was a perk I hadn't been aware of. "Great, find the pictures and send them to me."

While Stella was busying tracking down the pictures, I had research of my own that I needed to pursue. I'd been thinking more about this possible lich as our main suspect. As liches had been incredibly rare, it might mean that we had a very short suspect list. I opened a browser and began looking into each incident where a lich had been involved.

The first known sighting of a lich was around 1290 BC in Egypt during the reign of Pharaoh Seti I. The lich was believed to be an Egyptian priest who had been executed for using dark magic hundreds of years before. Seti and his warriors fought a large battle with the lich and his forces defeated it. There was some debate on whether the lich was banished or destroyed. The translation could have meant either.

Another lich appeared in Egypt around 1240 BC during Ramesses II's reign. Ramesses was the son and heir of Seti I. Similarly to his father, Ramesses and his forces defeated the lich and scattered its ashes to the winds. Scholars believe that this lich was the same one that Seti had faced fifty years earlier.

I agreed with the scholars—it seemed likely that Seti and Ramesses had fought the same lich. The fact that they'd scattered its ashes also meant I could eliminate this lich from my suspect list.

The next lich appeared in 332 BC in Gaza and was encountered by Alexander the Great on his campaign to capture Egypt. Alexander and his troops took Gaza by siege and encountered the lich while securing the city. An epic battle in the streets of Gaza occurred where they beat the lich in battle. A great pyre was erected outside the city where all remains of the lich and its undead forces were burned.

As this lich had also been in the region of Egypt, there was some debate on whether or not this one had been the same one that Seti I and Ramesses II had encountered. Here, most scholars believed it was two separate ones mainly due to the almost one thousand years between the encounters.

This was an interesting theory. but whether it had been one or two liches, one or both looked to have been eliminated.

The next appearance of a lich in history was in 218 BC during the second Punic War between Carthage and Rome. It was encountered by Hannibal in the foothills of the Pyrenees Mountains on his trek to invade Rome overland. The details on the battle were sparse, other than it seemed like elephants were really good at trampling over hordes of undead and the lich was defeated and destroyed.

I shook my head at the next lich sighting as it occurred in 790 AD in Toulouse by Charlemagne. While liches were few in number, they certainly did have a habit of coming up against some of the most influential people in history. The battle between the lich and Charlemagne took place over three nights. Charlemagne's forces won in the end but at a great cost in lives. The details on what happened to the lich at the end of the battle weren't clear, so it may have survived, which meant I had a possible suspect.

While liches were theoretically immortal, I doubted a 1,300-year-old lich from what would become France was lurking around Hamilton looking for a Russian headpiece.

The next lich to appear was in 1159 AD and once again in Toulouse. This time it was Henry II of England and Louis VII of France that encountered it. It took almost a week of battle and the combined powers of both kings to defeat the lich. At the end of the battle, Henry ordered everything within a hundred feet of where the lich fell to be burned. Once the large fire had burned out, Henry had the ground salted and then commissioned a group of priests to spend the next month blessing and consecrating the ground.

I had to hand it to Henry; he was a thorough type of guy.

Once again, most scholars believed that this lich was the same one Charlemagne had encountered hundreds of years earlier, due to both incidents happening in Toulouse and the fact that the details about what happened to the lich after Charlemagne's battle were sparse.

I sighed and scratched off the one suspect I had on my list.

The next lich sighting occurred on September 26, 1805, when Napoleon Bonaparte's troops disturbed a lich while marching through Austria on their way to what would become the Battle of Austerlitz. French infantry and cavalry engaged the lich and were routed, but it seemed the lich wasn't familiar with what cannons could do and was blown to pieces under a devastating hale of cannon shot. French troops burned the ground where the encounter took place and continued on their way.

I'd initially got excited about this connection to the Battle of Austerlitz, which was a fight between the French Empire and the Russian and Austrian Empires. The Russian connection was what had me excited. However, it looked like French troops had eliminated that lich from existence.

The final lich on record appeared in Tunisia in 1943. It attacked American soldiers, and General George S. Patton happened to be in the area. The report stated that Patton, noticing the combat with the lich, had his driver pull over his Jeep. He leaped out and, bold as brass, drew his Colt .45 sidearm and began taking potshots at the lich in the distance. The lich was so distracted by this it failed to notice the company of anti-tank guns positioning themselves on a nearby ridge. The anti-tank guns rained a barrage of high-explosive shells down on the lich. The area where the lich had been standing was leveled so badly that not a single piece of it could be found afterward.

I inwardly groaned at Napoleon's cannon and Patton's anti-tank gun solution because if Blue saw those, she'd think the anti-tank missile she had stashed away in her room at the lab would be the perfect solution for dealing with our current lich. The last thing I needed was to give the crazy alien an excuse to make large explosions.

I closed the browser in frustration. While the history of lich activities had been interesting, it hadn't provided a single clue about our lich. It also puzzled me that every lich had been defeated by some of the most well-known figures in history. If we did have one here in Hamilton, I doubted that anyone in this city or even the entire province of Ontario would go down as a pivotal person in history. So, what was this lich doing here?

Blue pulled me from my thoughts, reminding me that we wouldn't have use of her services tonight as she had a date with Dmitri.

Dmitri Petrov was a Werebear that led one of Canada's two elite GRC13 anti-monster squads. The two of them had been dating since they'd met when our teams worked together to take down a full-blown demon earlier this year.

It was a bit odd that they were going out on a date on a Monday night, but I remembered Dmitri's schedule was all over the place, so they had to get together whenever they could.

With the lich out there and wanting to bring Charlie's killers to justice, I seriously considered asking her to cancel the date. I went in another direction instead. "Thanks for the reminder. Can you keep your phone on in case something comes up where we need you?"

Blue nodded and went back to her own research.

My email chimed and I saw a new message from Stella. I opened it and it had full names and descriptions of the two missing vampires. There were two photos attached and I opened them to get my first look. I rolled my eyes as both were good-looking. One of them was the first vampire I'd ever seen with red hair. Only a small part of the population had ginger hair—hopefully that would make spotting him that much easier.

I thanked Stella and then called the number I had for Detective Little.

It rang five times and I expected it to go to voicemail when the detective answered it.

We chatted briefly and he mentioned that the day had been a madhouse and that the city seemed to be going nuts. I mentally sighed at that, as this might be another sign that the lich was still in the area. I didn't mention the lich and instead got to the reason for my call.

"I'm going to shoot you an email that contains pictures and description of two vampires that are of interest to this case."

I was pleased that Detective Little promised to add the pictures and descriptions to the daily briefing and would hand it over to media affairs to be released to TV and newspapers.

I made a call to Bobby Knight at EIRT and he too said he would get the pictures and descriptions out on his end.

We'd cast our net, now we just needed to get lucky.

***

The local evening news didn't mention anything about the vampires. I'd have been surprised if they'd had, as I'd only turned over the pictures and descriptions to the detective a couple of hours ago. I hoped that it would be on the morning news.

After dinner, it was just Stella and I left in the house. Blue was out on her date with Dmitri and Liv, Bree, and Alteea were out hunting deer in some woods just outside of the city. I tried to convince Liv and Bree to stay and do research, but Liv was adamant that she needed to get out of the house. She said the call she had been sensing had been getting stronger and that if she stayed in the house, she'd go crazy.

I was concerned that this calling was increasing in strength and wondered if that meant the lich was also getting stronger. I also wondered if Olivia was playing this up just to get out of doing research, which she wasn't a fan of.

Stella and I ended back up in the office doing research on Russian headpieces and not having much luck.

A couple of hours later, I was surprised to see Blue walk through the office door and even more surprised to see Dmitri right behind her. Blue had a smile on her face, a twinkle in her purple eyes, and her tail was flicking rapidly behind her, which meant she was excited about something.

"This office isn't the most exciting date destination," I said.

Blue waved her hand dismissively at my comment and said, "Dmitri, tell them the story you told me."

Dmitri rolled his eyes. "You are excited about nothing. The story is—what is word?—fable, told to Russian children to make them go to sleep or eat their vegetables." Blue gave him a hard stare, and he sighed.

"Fine. During dinner, Blue was talking about case and the lich. With Russian connection, I joked that it sounded like the Night Lord had returned.

"During the reign of Tsar Peter the Great, an army of the dead arose and swept across the plains, killing all in their path led by a powerful necromancer called the Night Lord. The Night Lord had a magic artifact called the Staff of Darkness that turned day into night, allowing the dead to walk the earth without pause. The staff had a magnificent ruby at its head that shone with a crimson red light in the night.

"Tsar Peter marshaled his forces of knights, foot soldiers, and priests, and rode out to stop the Night Lord. An epic battle occurred between the two groups and lasted for three days without pause. By the third day, the battle was going badly for the Tsar and his forces, for each person that fell rose to join the Night Lord's army.

"A small group of Knights Hospitaller, pious warriors committed to God, made a suicidal charge across the battlefield. One of their number managed to knock the Staff of Darkness from the Night Lord's hand. Another knight, who had been dismounted, picked up the staff and removed the headpiece from it. There was a large explosion. The darkness that had been blocking the sun disappeared and the sun rays lit the battlefield, destroying the army of the dead where they stood.

"Peter and a group of nobles rushed to the spot where the Night Lord had been. The area was blackened and flattened. All that remained were some battered bits of armor and the Staff of Darkness lay in the center in two pieces. There was no sign of the Night Lord or the knights that had defeated him.

"Peter picked up the staff and gave it and a pouch of gold to a young knight. He ordered the knight to ride west and not to stop until he reached the sea. He told the knight not to return and to keep the staff as far from Russia as possible.

"The headpiece to the staff he handed to a trusted noble and made him vow to protect it until the end of time."

My interest went up massively when Dmitri referred to the headpiece. All this time we thought it was a crown, but it might be part of a staff.

Dmitri continued, "The ruby that sat in the headpiece was gone. Some say that it was destroyed in the blast when the staff was broken in two. Cynical people think that Peter pocketed the ruby for himself. Either way, no one has seen it since that day."

Stella was looking at me with a grin, and I had to admit pieces started falling into place for me too. Besides the headpiece, the other important detail was that the Night Lord was a powerful necromancer. The most powerful of necromancers became liches. Add in that this was all Russian-based and it really did fit.

"Thank you both for interrupting your date to tell us about the Night Lord."

"Bah!" said Dmitri. "Night Lord children's story. Like your King Arthur and his roundtable."

Blue suggested that they continue their date, and we said our goodbyes to them as they left.

"What do you think? Could this be more than a children's story?" I asked Stella.

Stella tugged on one of her braids and didn't answer right away. "I think it could be real. Before Enhanced Individuals were exposed to the world during World War II, anything mythical or magic was written off as children's tales or fables. That might be the case here."

"My Russian history isn't good, when did Peter the Great reign?"

Stella frowned. "Late seventeenth century and early eighteenth century, I believe."

That meant this had occurred around 1700. If the Night Lord did exist, it meant we have a four-hundred-year-old lich on our hands. What concerned me most was this Staff of Darkness and that the lich seemed to be trying to put it back together. An artifact that could turn day into night and block out the sun wasn't something to be taken lightly. This made it a major magical artifact like the Spear of Destiny or the Holy Grail.

Major magical artifacts weren't to be trifled with. They were the magic equivalent of a nuclear bomb.

If the lich was trying to assemble the staff, there were three pieces he needed to find: the ruby, the headpiece, and the shaft.

The ruby disappeared right after the staff was broken. I knew that necromancers sometimes used objects to hold their souls as a way to cheat death. The idea was that even if the necromancer was killed, if their soul was placed in an object, it couldn't be collected. So, assuming the ruby was the vessel and the source of the Night Lord's power, if this lich was the Night Lord, then he had the ruby.

We knew he was missing the headpiece, which was why he was looking for it here. According to Dmitri, the headpiece was given to a noble by Peter to be protected. So why was lich looking for it here in Hamilton of all places? I knew that a lot of Russian nobles fled the country in 1917 during the Russian Revolution. It wasn't inconceivable that an ancestor of that original noble might have fled to Canada with the headpiece in 1917.

The big question was, did the lich have just the ruby or did he also have the shaft of the staff as well? If he had both, then if he found the headpiece, he'd be able to reassemble the Staff of Darkness. If he restored the staff, I had no doubt that his power would grow considerably; we needed to stop that from happening at all costs.

I shared my thoughts with Stella, and she said, "I will start researching the shaft and see if there is any information on its whereabouts."

"Can you also see if there are any drawings or descriptions about the headpiece while you're at it?"

Stella just bobbed her head in acknowledgment as her hands danced across the keyboard.

With Stella looking into the two missing pieces of the Staff of Darkness, I was at a bit of a loose end. I could try and search too, but Stella was infinitely better than me at web research; she just seemed to have a knack for typing in the exact phrase that produced the best results.

I went over the case in my head, trying to think of other leads that I could go after, but nothing was jumping out at me.

Another part of me wondered if Olivia's restlessness was catching, as I had an overwhelming urge to get out of the house. Since Stella had things in hand here, I decided to do just that.

Chapter 9

Monday, October 10

After putting on my armor, I left the house and took to the sky with a smile; the Hamilton Hurricane was back on patrol. With the Hamilton Police being run ragged, and no Curveball patrolling the streets, I felt this was something that needed doing.

The evening temperatures were hovering just over the freezing mark but that didn't bother me. My armor was usually too warm anyways and with the hint of Ice Elemental I had in my blood, I really didn't feel the cold anyway. That was about all that Ice Elemental power was good for. Making so much as a snowball would pretty much drain my powers.

The sky and the view were nice and clear partially due to the cooler air, and the almost full moon shone brightly in the sky above me.

Nights like these used to be my favorites back in my old hero days.

Seeing the lights of the city and the cars in the distance as they traveled over the Skyway Bridge that connected Hamilton and Burlington was always a sight that took my breath away.

I flew towards the downtown core. If bad things were happening, the core always seemed to get a bigger share of the trouble than other areas of the city.

Tonight seemed to be no exception to that rule.

I'd barely begun my patrol when a flash of light from below caught my attention. The light had reflected off a knife that some guy was using to threaten a well-dressed elderly couple on the sidewalk below.

I shook my head at the would-be mugger. Holding up someone on a sidewalk on King Street was both bold and stupid. The main police station was only three blocks away and the chances of a cruiser driving by were high on a regular night. On this evening those chances were perhaps lower due to all of the unusual activity happening around the city, but the mugger wouldn't know that.

I circled around quickly in the air and dove towards the mugger. I was tempted to lash out with lightning to stun the perp, but the older couple were too close. I worried that one of them might have a pacemaker or they'd be hit by some of the lightning if I overshot.

I flew closer.

"I've been assaulted by tougher punks than you, son," said the old man.

"Edgar, just give him your wallet!" said the wife with urgency in her voice.

I stopped my descent less than a few feet behind the mugger.

"Listen to your—" said the mugger who was cut off by a *gack* noise as his whole body shook and trembled due to the electricity I'd just sent into his brain stem.

The knife and the stolen purse both dropped to the pavement.

A few moments later, the would-be mugger stopped shaking and went limp. I lowered my hand away from the area near the back of his neck and he collapsed down towards the pavement.

I frantically used my Air powers to catch him before he hit the sidewalk. It would be my luck he'd fall on his knife and stab himself or crack his skull open on the cement. Both would just create a lot of paperwork that I didn't want to fill out.

I floated him over to the side, away from the purse and the knife, and lowered him to the ground.

By the amount of juice I'd pumped into the mugger, I knew that he'd be out for a while. By the scabs on his arms and the way he'd been twitching even before I fried him, I suspected he was a junkie that was badly in need of a fix.

I picked up the knife and slipped it into one of the storage compartments on my armor. The knife was just a steak knife that had probably been stolen from one of the local restaurants in the area.

I grabbed the purse and handed it back to the older lady who was smiling widely.

"Thank you, Mr. Hurricane," she said as she took it back.

Her husband gave me a firm nod, which I took as his way of saying thanks.

"Just Hurricane, no mister. Do you folks mind waiting with me for the police to arrive so they can get your statements?"

They both agreed to wait.

I called dispatch from the communicator built into my visor. I was a bit surprised that it took almost ten rings before they answered. I told them what happened and where we were. Their response was they'd send an officer, but ETA was close to an hour. I sighed and ended the call.

I had better things to do than stand around for an hour and went a different route.

"It seems like the Hamilton Police are having a busy night. Rather than keeping you here, can I get your names and contact details, and an officer, or the crown, will follow up with you later if needed?"

They gave me their names, home address, and phone number, which were recorded on video by the camera in my visor and I told them they were free to go.

"Um, Mr. Hurricane, can I impose on you for a picture? Our granddaughter was a huge fan of yours when she was younger." She smiled warmly and added, "She wanted to grow up and be a superhero."

"Did she become a superhero?" I asked.

"Oh, gracious no, she is studying to be a nurse."

I smiled at that answer. "A noble choice. She will probably help more people as a nurse than any superhero could during their career." I paused and added, "I'd love to have my photo taken with you."

The old lady nodded at that and handed an older model iPhone she retrieved from her purse off to her husband.

She moved beside me, and we posed together while Edgar fiddled with the iPhone.

The flash went off and Edgar started to lower the phone, so I said, "You might want to take another in case I blinked."

Edgar laughed at my joke. I was wearing a facemask with a visor, so whether I blinked or not was irrelevant. He did raise the phone and take another picture, though.

We wrapped up our little photoshoot and they headed on their way. I used my powers to lift the unconscious mugger and myself into the air and flew to the Hamilton Central Police Station.

Less than a minute later, I was walking in the main entrance with the mugger floating beside me. I spotted the Sarge on the desk and he saw me at the same time. Sarge was a longtime veteran of the force, and we went back from my hero days.

"Bounty hunting getting too boring for you, Hurricane?"

"Nah, just heard you guys were a little busy recently and thought I'd lend a hand for old times' sake."

I floated the mugger over to an empty bench off to my right and lowered him onto it.

"What did Gary do this time?"

I popped open my visor and approached the counter. "He tried to mug an elderly couple with this," I said as I pulled out the steak knife and placed it on the counter.

Sarge shook his head and opened a drawer and pulled out an evidence bag. He scooped up the knife, using the bag to avoid touching it, and began labeling it.

"I have the whole thing on video, including the names and contact details for the victims. Is your email address still the same?"

He nodded as he picked up the phone and called someone to come up and take Gary to holding.

I used my visor to edit the video from the beginning to the end of the encounter and then emailed it to Sarge.

He hung up the phone and looked over at Gary. "Is he okay?"

"Should be, I just used enough juice to stun him."

Sarge frowned. "I'll get some cuffs on him then. Gary can be a handful when he is awake."

"Do you need me for anything else?"

Sarge shook his head. "Nope. Good seeing you again, Hurricane."

"You too, Sarge."

I left the building and got back in the air. Sirens drew my attention east and I spotted what looked like a serious house fire in progress and poured on the speed.

The fire department was on scene by the time I got there, and all household members and pets were accounted for so there was no need for me to fly into the blaze. I was relieved at that. Going into burning buildings to rescue people was probably my least favorite thing I used to do as a hero. There were too many things that could go wrong in that dangerous environment.

Since the fire department had things in hand, I took to the sky again and set a course back to the downtown core. I passed a car accident on my way, but police and ambulances were on the scene, and it looked like everyone was getting medical care. Now it was just cleanup, so I continued on without stopping.

Car accidents were another thing I wasn't a fan of. It was gruesome what a couple of tons of steel, plastic, and glass could do to a human body. Some of my worst reoccurring nightmares were of car accident victims I'd seen in my past.

An hour later, I was doing my fourth or fifth lap of the core when I spotted a teen about to tag a building with spray paint.

He must have jumped a good two feet in the air when I cleared my throat behind him. He dropped the can of paint and went white as a ghost when he turned and spotted me standing there.

"I-I-I wasn't going to do anything," he stammered.

"Sure, you weren't. That can of paint, then, doesn't belong to you?"

He shook his head, "It was there when I got here."

"Good, in that case, you won't mind if I take it."

His eyes widened like saucers as I used my Air power to lift the can from the ground to my hand.

He rolled his eyes at me when I said, "Remember, son, stay in school and eat your vegetables."

I didn't wait for his reply before launching myself back into the air. I caught him flipping me the bird out of the corner of my eye but chose to ignore that, mainly because I deserved that for the cheesy school and veggie line.

I dumped the paint in a garbage can on the rooftop promenade of Jackson Square Shopping Centre and continued my patrol.

Every time I flew over the pizza place where Charlie was killed, it was like a punch to the gut. On a couple of laps, I'd purposely flown a wider route to avoid it. It hit me that I really hadn't had time to grieve Charlie's loss due to how busy the last few days had been. Avoiding that grief was probably one of the reasons I was patrolling the city currently. I pushed those thoughts to the side and promised myself that once this case was over, I'd deal with my emotions.

As it approached midnight, I set a course for Hess Village, a small strip of land on the western edge of the downtown core. It contained a number of pubs that were popular with McMaster University students and younger people in the city. Lots of alcohol and testosterone in a small area meant that something untoward was usually happening there at this time of night.

As I approached, I spotted a small crowd that had gathered in the street out front of one of the bars. There were two men in their late teens or early twenties throwing fists at each other in the center of the crowd.

Breaking up a bar fight wasn't something I usually did, but one of the guys near the middle had a purple, brown, and silver aura around him, which meant Werewolf. He and four of the people around him were wearing Mohawk College jackets. The other fighter wore a burgundy Mac jacket and so did the three guys behind him cheering him on. My fear was that if this escalated, and their buddies got involved, a Werewolf being in that group would make things get ugly fast.

The crowd went quiet as I landed right beside the two combatants. The fighter in the Mohawk jacket, at seeing me, backed up and raised his palms in a 'hey I want no trouble' gesture. The Mac student threw a wild haymaker that slammed into the chest plate of my armor. I winced as I heard his bones crack on impact.

He cursed and cradled his injured hand. By the guy's bloodshot eyes and the way he was swaying as he stood there, it was obvious he was hammered.

I looked over at his three buddies and asked, "Any one of you three sober?" The tallest one of the group nodded. "Good, take your buddy to hospital and get that hand checked out, okay?"

The three of them led him away.

"Alright, folks, nothing to see here, move along," I said to the crowd, which was already beginning to disperse.

The one I'd identified as a Werewolf gave me a defiant stare for a few seconds but allowed his buddies to pull him away and they headed off down the street.

A couple of girls in Mohawk College jackets asked for selfies with me and I took a minute to let them take a few pics. They thanked me and I launched myself back in the air.

I gave the core one last lap and then headed for home.

Chapter 10

Tuesday, October 11

It was past one in the morning by the time I made it home. As I was circling over the house, checking to make sure nothing odd was going on, Bree's new Toyota 4-Runner pulled up in the driveway. Her old one and Liv's Audi TT RS had been written off when our house was destroyed by the Master's robots.

Liv's new vehicle hadn't come in yet, as she had special ordered something. She was being very coy about what she had ordered and would only say that it was a surprise. A part of me was happy that Liv didn't have a new vehicle yet. The streets of Hamilton were much safer without her tearing around at insane speeds.

I landed as the girls were getting out of the truck. They were laughing and carrying on, so I had to assume that their hunt had been successful. The blood smeared across Liv's chin and neck was also a dead giveaway that things had gone their way.

We entered the house together, and the moment we were inside, Alteea dropped her glamor and appeared before our eyes. It seemed that Liv wasn't the only sloppy eater.

Liv giggled. "Look at you, little one. You're a mess."

Alteea shot Liv an indignant look, implying that vampires with blood all over them shouldn't be throwing stones.

Liv seemed to get the message. "Oh, yeah. I guess we both are a mess. Shower time!"

I smiled as Alteea did a loop in the air before flying up the stairs with Liv right behind her. Olivia was already peeling off her top as she headed up the stairs, giving me a lovely view of her bare back before she disappeared from sight.

Bree yawned and pulled my attention to her. Bree had her 'mmm, deer' expression that I'd grown used to seeing on her face after one of these hunts. Her eyelids were a touch heavier than usual, and there was a slight flush to her cheeks and a contented smile on her face.

"I'm assuming a catnap is in your future?" Bree grinned at my cat reference and nodded. "Have a quick one but once Liv is done with her shower, I want a quick team meeting in the office upstairs."

She waved an acknowledgment and disappeared towards the living room.

I joined Stella and Blue in the office. I'd barely sat down when Stella said, "Do you want the good news or the bad news?"

"I could use some good news for a change."

"The good news is that I found where the shaft of the Staff of Darkness was."

I keyed into the phrasing of that statement and asked, *"Was?"*

Stella's excited expression fell, "That's the bad news. Until about six months ago, the shaft was at the British Museum. It was stolen in a heist. The odd thing was that the museum didn't realize it was missing until a week after it had been stolen. The shaft wasn't on display but was in storage. The description listed it as *a six-foot-long wooden pole with a tapered end, intricately carved with Latin and Russian that referenced the night, darkness, souls, and other occult references. Origin unknown.* The pole had been part of the museum's collection since its founding in 1753. There is a picture of the shaft that I'll email you."

I cursed at her news, as I had no doubt that the lich or one of its minions pulled off the heist, which meant he had two of the three pieces of the Staff of Darkness. "Why did it take a week to find out it was missing?"

"The night of the heist, alarms were tripped off all over the building and all their cameras went on the fritz. Police were called. The museum's security staff and police swept the building multiple times but didn't find anyone or notice anything was missing or disturbed. The following day the curator had the museum employees do a full inventory. Due to the size of its collection and the fact that the staff had been in storage and not on display, it wasn't until a week later that they realized it was gone."

I'd been to the British Museum a few months back on a day trip with Stella and Blue. I'd been staggered at the amount of amazing historic items they had on display and the sheer size of the place. I'd tried mentally working out how much the items in some of the rooms were worth and was humbled by my rough estimates. Museum personnel must have been puzzled that with all the wealth in items they had, the only thing taken was an odd pole that they had storage. It also showed how focused the lich was that he ignored all of those other valuable items and just took the shaft.

Stella pulled me from the thoughts. "I have also found a description of the headpiece and some sketches of it. The descriptions vary but most describe it as brass, seven inches in height. The top of the headpiece was circular, with a small indent where the ruby was mounted, and just under that was an infinity symbol carved into the brass. The tapered base of the headpiece is four inches long and hollow."

The headpiece description didn't sound that special but at least the infinity symbol was unique enough that we'd know if we found it or not. We now knew exactly what we were looking for. "Good work. Print out some pictures of the sketches and we'll put them out to law enforcement and around town and see what comes up."

Stella nodded. "I have also been doing some research into the Russian community in Hamilton. Thankfully, it is a smaller group compared to others but large enough that we have our work cut out for us. There is a Russian Community Center in Westdale, which might be a good place to start our search. They might have a list of businesses owned by people of Russian descent in Hamilton."

I nodded at that. It was nice having smart teammates. Stella had done wonders in the few hours I'd been gone. The bottom line was, though, we needed to find that headpiece before the lich or things would get ugly fast.

***

An hour later, Liv, Bree, and Alteea were up to speed with everything we'd learned.

Stella and Blue were about to turn in for the night, as they wanted to visit that community center when it opened at 10:00 a.m. the next day. I wanted to join them on that trip, but that plan went out the window moments later when my phone rang.

I checked the display and saw Detective Little's name on it. As it was after two in the morning, I had a feeling this wouldn't be good news.

"Hurricane, there has been another vampire attack. One victim, the owner of Budimir's Dry Cleaning on Main near Kenilworth. We are on scene, and EIRT is en route."

"We'll be there shortly," I said and ended the call.

I brought Blue and Stella up to speed on the call and Blue was already searching the shadows to find the location.

Dry cleaning places were usually small, so I needed to limit who I was bringing. Liv was the first choice in case the victim was reborn as a vampire. It was tempting to bring Bree again to see if she could sense that presence that she had at the pizza place, but I suspected that EIRT would limit us to two people on scene.

In the end, I ruled out Bree, as I would be able to sense the feeling of despair at the dry cleaners once I was close to it. I figured that if I didn't sense anything, I could always have Blue send Bree down to double check for it.

Blue announced she had the location and was able to open a portal nearby.

"Liv, you and Alteea are with me. We'll meet in the living room in three minutes."

I'd taken off my armor when I got home, so I retired to my room with Stella, who helped me get armored up again.

Blue, Liv, and Alteea were waiting for me when I arrived downstairs. Blue opened the portal the moment she saw me.

"Portal open. When you come out on the outside, make a left. I will observe the crime scene from the shadows," said Blue.

I nodded and stepped through with Liv right behind me.

We came out in the shadows of a building on Kenilworth. To our left was Main Street and police cruisers had blocked off the intersection. There were also officers on foot at the intersection redirecting the light pedestrian traffic at this time in the morning. I assumed most were local residents trying to find out what all the fuss was about.

The officer at the corner waved us through when we approached and pointed at a small strip plaza on the other side of Main Street. I spotted the sign for the dry cleaners at the far end of the building. Beside it was a pawn shop, and a Chinese restaurant anchored the near end of the strip plaza.

The moment we crossed the street and stepped onto the sidewalk in front of the Chinese place, it hit me. A primal voice inside me told me to turn around and flee; there was nothing but death here. I stopped in my tracks and Liv walked halfway to the dry cleaners before noticing I wasn't still beside her.

She turned and scrunched her face at me in confusion.

I took a deep breath and started walking to her. The feeling of dread became more intense with each step.

If things are this bad at a place a lich visited, what would being in its presence be like? I thought with a shudder.

We reached the yellow police tape and one of the officers on duty out front opened the glass door to the dry cleaners and announced us.

Detective Little came out and had protective boot covers and latex gloves on. As he exited, Alteea's rainbow aura darted past him and disappeared inside the building.

"You made it here quick."

"The advantages of having a shadow traveler."

He held up his hands, showing off the gloves, and said, "Let me get you some gear from the car."

His partner came out while he'd been talking and the moment Detective Little finished, he said, "Not happening, Frank; I'm not letting civilians on to my crime scene."

Too late, I thought, as he had a pixie in there already and I had no doubt that Blue had gone over most of the place visually from the shadows.

Detective Little shook his head, "Max, you have no choice. They are official representatives of the English Vampire Court."

"I don't care. They aren't cops, they aren't Feds, so they aren't getting in here."

Detective Little was about to argue some more, but I cut him off, "Detective Little, if you'll allow me?"

He nodded and stepped back so he wasn't between me and his partner.

"Are you packing silver or wooden bullets?"

The older detective frowned. "No, what does that have to do with anything?"

"If the victim is reborn as a vampire, he is going to be very hungry and in the grip of bloodlust. If you don't want us in there, then he is your responsibility. I hope your marksmanship scores are high. Though without silver or wooden bullets, all you are going to do is piss it off. I'd save the last round for yourself."

There were times wearing an armored mask was advantageous, and this was one of those times. The look of deep concern on the detective's face and the fact that he quickly glanced over his shoulder, as if to reassure himself that a vampire wasn't lurking behind him, brought a smile to my face.

"Go get them some gear," he said to his partner.

Detective Little headed off past the row of cruisers parked in front of the building to an unmarked car on the end.

A few minutes later, I had boot covers on my feet and evidence bags strapped around my hands, and Liv was geared up, except with latex gloves instead of bags like I had, and we entered the shop.

"Human blood and lots of it," said Liv the moment we entered.

The smell of bleach and cleaning agents overpowered any other scents in the air for me, so I couldn't smell it.

She sniffed the air and added, "That musty scent from the pizza place is here too."

We'd discussed that musty scent earlier and Liv figured that it must be the lich. Vampires generally didn't have strong scents to them, or at least none of the ones Liv had met had.

The vampire attack, Russian link, and the feeling of dread and despair around us were enough for me to assume this was the lich and the two vampires again; the musty scent was just another thing that confirmed that for me.

I spotted a security camera as we walked past the front counter and hoped that it worked so we'd have video of the lich and the vampires. Video might give us the evidence I needed to confirm we had a lich on our hands.

We walked past the racks of cellophane-wrapped clothes waiting for pickup and went deeper into the store.

Near the back of the place, where all the machinery was located, was a man in his late fifties or early sixties tied to a cheap wooden and metal chair, like the kind schools used. He looked to be in good shape, like he exercised regularly. That might have been from working here, as I'd imagine that working in the heat the machines produced and hauling and ironing load after load of clothes was taxing work.

His head was tilted back, and his mouth was open in a silent scream of terror that matched the first three victims, leaving me little doubt that these had been the same attackers. The dual neck wounds from the two vampires were also a strong indicator.

The man had lots of deep bruising and shallow cuts on his face. He'd been worked over hard before his death.

We slowly walked around the body, being careful to avoid the blood spatter and drops on the floor.

When we got behind him, I lifted my eyebrows in surprise. The two metal rods that supported the wooden backrest had each been bent inwards a good inch or so where his arms were. His arms had been tied behind his back. I knew the chair was low budget, but it would still take a lot of strength to bend in the bars like that. Oddly enough, that drove home to me how much the man had suffered before they killed him.

"Who found the victim?" I asked.

Detective Little opened a notepad and said, "The victim's wife. The business closes at nine and he was usually home by ten. When he didn't arrive home, she wasn't concerned, as he occasionally stops at a local bar and has a drink after work. She went to bed but woke up just after 1:00 a.m., and noticing that her husband hadn't arrived home, grew concerned. She called the local bar he usually went to, and they said he hadn't been in. She went out looking for him. When she drove by here and saw the lights on, she stopped to check if he was here. The front door wasn't locked, which was odd, and she headed inside and found him. At that point, she called police."

"Where is she now?"

"She was extremely distraught, and after giving her statement, it grew worse. Paramedics sedated her and she is currently resting at the hospital."

I nodded and then made a silent prayer for her to have a swift recovery. I couldn't imagine what it would be like to find a loved one murdered and hoped she'd be okay. I clenched my fists and had to tamp down on my powers as my anger burst to the surface. The longer we took to track this monster down, the more victims there would be, leaving more loved ones with holes in their hearts.

I took a deep breath and forced myself to calm down. Getting angry wouldn't solve this case. I'd save that rage for when we met the lich.

I spotted the small hallway at the back of the place. It had three doors. On the right was a bathroom, and at the end was a back door to the outside. To the left was a closed unmarked door, which I assumed was a small office.

I pointed at the office and said, "Has anyone been in there?"

Detective Little shook his head. "It is just an office. I opened it to check that it was empty and then closed the door, why?"

"There was a security camera above the front cash . . ."

Detective Little nodded and headed towards the door and I followed him. He opened the door and turned on a light. It was a small office that consisted of a desk, a chair, and a file cabinet. There was an older-looking PC on the deck that was on but had a screen saver running.

Detective Little hit the space bar on the computer keyboard and I swore under my breath as a password prompt came up.

"Looks like we'll have to wait for the crime scene techs. They'll be here shortly."

I nodded but I was tempted to get Blue and Stella down here. I had no doubt that Stella would have access to this PC in minutes. I weighed the pros and cons and decided to wait for the techs. The hour or two delay wouldn't make much difference. Blue could also spy over their shoulders when they were watching the video, so we'd know what was on it the same time they did.

We'd just exited the office when an officer announced that EIRT had arrived.

A few minutes later, Bobby Knight and the mage from the other night arrived. They did their own walk around the body, and I just stood back and watched.

I was happy to see it was Bobby again, but my gut churned as I came to a decision. I was convinced we were dealing with a lich that was trying to reassemble a magic artifact of immense power. That made the stakes too high for my team to do this on its own. For me to lay out my case for it being a lich, however, I'd need to reveal that we'd taken Charlie's phone from the crime scene. I knew Bobby would be pissed at us for doing that.

No sooner had Bobby and the mage finished their inspection when the forensic team arrived, adding more people to an already cramped space.

"Bobby, can I talk to you outside?"

He nodded as he stepped back to let the techs by.

"Liv, stay here and watch the victim in case he is reborn."

She waved me off. I was pleased when I heard Detective Little asking one of the techs to examine the PC in the office.

Bobby, the mage, and I exited the dry cleaners and stripped off the protective gear we'd worn inside, dropping it in a small box that had been placed near the door for that purpose.

We walked about half a block from the place to a quiet area and I started laying out my case for the perpetrator being a lich.

The moment I mentioned the lich, the mage laughed and said, "Impossible. There has never been a lich spotted in North America in all of history."

"Yeah, and there had been only one full demon on Canadian soil before the one my team and GRC13 put down this year too . . ."

The mage gave a slight nod in acknowledgment of my point but said, "Since Enhanceds have been outed to the world, necromancers have been hunted relentlessly. I truly doubt that any necromancer would be able to gather the power to become a lich in the last eighty years."

"I believe this lich is 400 years old."

The mage was about to interrupt but Bobby cut him off, "Max, how about we let Hurricane lay out his case. We can debate it once he is done. While a lich seems impossible, Hurricane and his team have done the impossible a number of times. They've taken down a full demon, the Master, and the Rose this year alone."

I took a deep breath and started on everything we'd found and why we believed it was a lich. I mentally cringed at Bobby's body language when I brought up the phone, but he didn't say anything and let me finish.

To my surprise, the mage, as I'd laid things out, had gotten a more and more thoughtful look on his face, and once I'd finished said, "I can't deny that I sensed an unnerving presence at both crime scenes and there are very few Enhanceds that I can recall that have the ability to do something like that. I'll check with the Mage's Council and the archives about this Night Lord and the Staff of Darkness. If you're right, and I'm not saying you are, then this case is going to be everyone's top priority."

Bobby, though gritted teeth, said, "Hurricane, I should have you arrested for tampering with evidence, but I won't if I get that phone in my hands in the next five minutes."

I nodded and called Blue to bring the phone and had Stella send Bobby a copy of the video.

Blue appeared in less than a minute, handed Bobby the phone and the pin code, and then left.

Bobby said, "I hope for all our sakes, you are wrong about this, Hurricane."

Chapter 11

Tuesday, October 11

The blare of an alarm pulled me from a deep slumber, and I groaned as I sat up. By the time we'd wrapped up at the dry cleaners and had our after-action discussion about the crime scene, it was close to six this morning and getting up at nine was the last thing I wanted to do. I missed the days of my late teens and early twenties when I routinely was able to get by on little to no sleep.

After my discussion with Bobby and the mage, the rest of the night was uneventful. The victim hadn't been reborn as a vampire and the coroner had taken possession of the body at dawn.

The security camera had been a bust. The footage went haywire at 8:17 p.m. and showed nothing but static for ten minutes before a picture returned. The camera only recorded video so there was no audio. It had probably been set up that way to save hard drive space. The picture once again turned to static at 9:28 p.m. and stayed like that for ten minutes before returning to normal. So, we had no footage of the lich or the vampires. The only thing it established was their arrival and departure time.

After a couple much need coffees and a quick shower, I joined Blue and Stella for their visit to the Russian Community Center in Westdale.

We came out of the shadows beside the building to a nice sunny fall day. The temperature was warm for this time of year, and I was glad I'd left my armor at home. Blue was in her holographic old man disguise.

As we walked around to the front of the building, I admired the grounds. The grass was well cared for and the landscaping pristine. The building was older but in good shape. It looked like someone had given it a new coat of paint recently. The metal-framed glass doors at the front had a very institutional look to them. I was pretty sure my old high school had the same doors.

The lobby, too, had the same type of light green marble-like floor that my old high school had. Both were probably built in the fifties by the same builder. I suspected that this place started life as a public community center run by the city. It was probably bought out by the Russian community during a time when the city was hurting for cash.

There were signs on the wall in English and Russian listing the rules for the pool, sauna, and the main hall.

An older lady who looked to be in her seventies watched the three of us like hawks from the front reception area. I grinned, as she seemed to be giving Blue in her old man disguise a closer look than she did Stella or me. I recognized that look, as I probably had the same expression when I was checking Olivia out.

I was tempted to tease Blue about it, but I doubted she'd understand the humor of the situation.

We approached the counter and I asked to speak to the director or manager. I wasn't really sure what the title was for someone who ran a community center.

The lady shrugged and picked up a phone. She said something briefly in Russian and hung up.

"Someone will be with you shortly," she said and then pointed at some chairs off to the side.

I thanked her and the three of us took a seat and waited.

A few minutes later, a woman in her late twenties appeared at reception. She exchanged words with the receptionist and the older lady pointed at us.

We stood up as she approached and she said, "The director is off today. My name is Natalie and I'm his assistant, maybe I can help you."

I introduced the three of us and handed her my hero ID. I smiled to myself at how she perked up when I mentioned I was the Hamilton Hurricane. "We are working with law enforcement to investigate the tragic murders of Vanya and Mila Andropov and Budimir Volkov."

She frowned and said, "We were saddened to hear about their deaths. Mila attended our needlepoint classes on Wednesday nights. She will be missed. Though I don't understand what this has to do with us."

"Nothing directly," I said. "We have reason to believe, though, that the perpetrators are targeting businesses of people of Russian ancestry. We were hoping that you might have a list of your members' businesses so we can interview them and keep them safe."

Natalie nodded. "We have a business group that meets Monday nights. I have a list in my office that I will get for you. Give me two minutes."

It took Natalie closer to ten minutes before she returned and gave us the list. "The list I had printed out was an older one, so I had to get the latest one."

"Thank you. This should be very helpful." I pulled a couple copies of the drawings of the headpiece out and handed them to her along with a small stack of our business cards, "We believe this is what the perpetrators are looking for. Can you ask around if anyone has seen this artifact? Anyone who knows where this is or has it in their possession is in grave danger."

Natalie studied the image for a few seconds and shook her head, "I've never seen this before, but I will ask around and post these up around the facility."

"Thank you for your help."

She nodded and wandered off. I took a look at the list and whistled, as there had to be close to a hundred businesses, if not more. Stella held out her hand and I gave her the list.

A deep laugh from the front desk caught my attention. I turned and spotted Natalie showing the picture of the headpiece to the older receptionist. The receptionist said something loudly in Russian and then laughed again.

I looked over at Blue and raised an eyebrow.

Blue translated, "Staff of Darkness? Might as well be chasing Lenin's ghost..."

The old woman's cackling laugh echoed behind us as we left the building.

***

We ended up back in our home office after our trip to the Russian Community Center.

"I'd like to plot these addresses out on a map to put together a plan of attack," said Stella. "Both attacks were downtown, so starting with businesses there makes more sense than the ones up on the mountain."

I yawned and nodded in agreement with her logic.

"Even with my shadow abilities, it will require time to converse with all the merchants on this list," said Blue.

I suppressed another yawn and said, "I need more coffee."

As I got up, Stella said, "Zack, go get some sleep. The attacks have happened at night, and running yourself ragged now, isn't going to help anyone."

I was about to argue but realized that Stella had a point. Working on three hours of sleep wasn't going to help anyone. It wasn't even noon, and I was already wiped; what would I be like tonight? I'd planned on going out on patrol this evening, which meant I needed to get some sleep. "I'm going to grab some shut-eye. Wake me if anything happens."

Stella nodded and I left them to it. I cursed myself for my weakness, but burning myself out with lack of sleep wasn't going to help anyone.

I crawled out of bed at close to five that evening and was annoyed that I'd slept so long. On the upside, I felt normal again and the foggy haze that had plagued my thoughts that morning was gone. I checked the office to see if Stella and Blue were there, but it was empty. There was a brand-new large paper road map on the office wall.

I moved to take a closer look and spotted that the map was dotted with pins with round red plastic heads. I assumed each pin must represent a business on the list we got and felt overwhelmed at the task ahead. I did some quick math, figuring that each visit would probably take fifteen to twenty minutes to find and talk to the owner, which meant three to four visits per hour. It would take us three to five days to reach them all.

The good news was that was much faster than it would take the lich to visit them.

The problem was even if we visited all the businesses, it didn't mean that any of them would know about or have the headpiece. It could be that one of their spouses or relatives had it and they might not even be aware that they did. This thing could have been tucked away in a box in an attic and forgotten about. It might not even be a business owner that had it. What about all the people of Russian descent that worked for someone as employees? That number had to be much higher than business owners.

I tried to be optimistic and assumed the lich must have some reason for targeting business owners. Assuming one of the owners had it and we found it, what then? Having the headpiece in our possession meant he wouldn't be able to assemble the staff and attain his full power, which was a plus, but it wouldn't stop the attacks unless we found some way to let him know that we had it.

We needed to have other irons in the fire to find the lich. A lich was a powerful magic user, and an aberration of nature, surely there must be a way to track that. Our hunt for the full demon popped into my head. During that case we used a tracking spell that pointed to great evil and that allowed us to find him, I wondered if we could do the same here.

My thoughts were interrupted as I heard Stella and Blue coming up the stairs. They entered the office and Stella said, "Feeling better?"

I nodded. "Yeah, thanks. I just had an idea about finding the lich. I'm going to call Walter and have him make us another one of those magic devices that points towards evil."

Blue frowned and said, "Why not use the one he made us before?"

"It was destroyed in the fire when our old house was blown up."

Blue smiled and shook her head. "No. It is in my domicile at the lab. I will retrieve it now."

My excitement grew as she left the room.

Stella said, "Blue and I visited fourteen of the businesses on the list but had no luck. We stopped when her holographic disguise needed to recharge."

Stella pulled out a small box filled with green pins. She looked at the map and began replacing red pins with green to mark the ones they'd visited.

I noticed that all the businesses she was updating sat between the pizzeria and dry cleaners, which I thought was a clever plan on Stella's part.

Blue returned with the magic device and handed it to me. I shook my head at the simplicity of the design as it was just a metal arrow on a string. It certainly wasn't something that looked like it cost the ten grand I'd paid for it. Simplicity aside, the important thing was that it had worked.

I grabbed the end of the string and let the arrow drop. The arrow just slowly spun around on the string but didn't react. If it had detected a source of great evil within a hundred kilometers, the arrow would have started lifting in that direction. How hard it pulled was determined by how close the evil was.

"This doesn't make any sense. There is no way a lich isn't a source of great evil. The arrow should be going nuts right now," I said.

"Maybe the lich is not living within a hundred-kilometer radius of us," said Blue.

I shook my head. "It has to be hiding somewhere nearby. Why else has the city gone so crazy? We also had those zombies rise up the other night."

Stella tugged her braid and after a moment said, "Remember how the demon, once it knew we were tracking it, used spells on its hideouts to prevent us from finding it?" I nodded and Stella added, "The lich is a powerful magic user, so it probably has spells to stop us from tracking it too."

I cursed to myself, as that made sense. The lich would have to know that the murders would attract attention and would have taken precautions to stop authorities from tracking them. I handed the arrow back to Blue but had another idea.

"I need to call Walter."

I pulled out my phone and headed downstairs to make the call.

"*Your house already rebuilt?*" was the first thing Walter asked when he answered.

"No. Why?"

"*I'd assumed that you were calling me to move the wards back.*"

"The wards aren't the reason for my call. I have a project for you. Remember that evil-tracking device you built?"

"*Yeah.*"

"Could you build something similar that detects powerful magic?"

The line went quiet and just as I started to worry that the call had been disconnected, Walter said, "*Theoretically, it's possible, but why are you searching for powerful magic?*"

I took a deep breath and said, "I think there might be a lich in Hamilton."

"*I'm sorry; this line must be bad as I swore I just heard you say there's a lich in Hamilton.*"

"I did."

"*Dude, you know the chances of a lich being anywhere on the planet at this moment, never mind in freaking Hamilton?*"

I spent the next five minutes going over everything that happened in the last few days and when I finished, Walter said, "*That all sounds* bad but it has to be something other than lich. Whatever it is, I can build the device, but it will take me a few days, and it will have a much shorter range and cost more than the evil-tracking device."

"How much of a shorter range and how much more money?" I asked, dreading the answer to both questions.

"One-kilometer max and twenty thousand."

"Why so short?"

"Do you know how much magic is in the world? Ley lines, wards, magic users, fae, natural magic, just to name a few. The point is any longer than a kilometer in range and the device will pick up too many things and get confused."

While a kilometer range wasn't ideal, it was workable. It just meant it would take longer to track the lich. The price, too, wasn't that outrageous. "Alright, I can work with both, make the device."

"Hey, Zack, since you're such a good customer, I'll throw in a free case of unicorn repellent with your order," said Walter as he burst out laughing.

I knew he was making fun of me about my lich theory with that last comment. *"Walter, you should have been a comedian. Call me when it's done."*

I didn't wait for his reply as he was still laughing when I ended the call.

I thought more about the magic-detecting device. The short range was annoying, but we could divide the city up into two-kilometer grids and with Blue's shadow traveling abilities could probably complete the search fairly quickly. My biggest fear was that the lich could somehow mask or ward his power, in which case, the device would be useless. On the other hand, if it worked, this could be the best twenty thousand dollars I'd ever spent.

Chapter 12

Tuesday, October 11

That night we waited until Olivia rose to have dinner and turned it into a working one. The Russian business list, getting the vampires' pictures out to the police and media, and having Walter build the magic-detecting device was a good start, but the clock was ticking. The longer it took for us to track the lich down, the more bodies would pile up.

Stella was currently bringing all of us up to speed on the case. "The autopsy report for the victim at the dry cleaners came in. As we are eating, I won't go into details other than to mention that the same five circular bruises were found over the heart of the victim. The other anomalies from the pizzeria victims were found on this victim too."

I didn't have much doubt that the lich and vampires were the culprits for both scenes, but it was good to have more confirmation.

Stella continued, "Today the local media ran coverage on the vampires' descriptions. *Hamilton This Morning* covered it during their show and the *Hamilton Post* included pictures and descriptions in today's edition. According to Detective Little, Hamilton police also got briefings at the start of their shifts to be on the lookout for the vampires as persons of interest to the case."

Stella explained how Blue had canvassed local Russian businesses to bring Liv, Bree, and Alteea up to speed and I tuned out. I was hopeful that either a member of the public or an officer on patrol might spot the vampires.

Once Stella's briefing was done, I said, "I'm pleased with all the things we are doing to track the lich and the vampires down but want to spend the rest of this dinner brainstorming ideas on other ways to find them. Any thoughts?"

The silence I received in response to my question was deafening, but at least all my teammates had serious thoughtful expressions, which gave me hope.

After a good minute, Bree broke the silence first. "Are you still planning on going patrolling tonight?" I nodded and Bree added, "Take me with you?"

"Not that I don't enjoy your company, but why?"

"At the pizzeria, I felt the darkness and despair before we were even close to the restaurant. I was thinking that if the lich leaves that type of shroud over somewhere he's been, being in or near his presence must be even worse. My thought was if you flew me low over the city, I might be able to sense him."

I'd been kicking around doing something like that myself, but Bree seemed to be much more sensitive to it than I was. The downside to bringing her along was that it would be more taxing on my powers to fly both of us rather than just me. The upside was I probably wouldn't have to skim buildings at rooftop level to pick up a trace of the lich. The more I thought about it the more I liked the idea and agreed.

"You mentioned that as the lich's presence is an aberration to nature incidents like the zombies the other night can result from it. The increased crime rate in the city is another symptom of its presence. Can we assume that there is a limit to the range of the effects of its presence?" asked Blue.

I frowned, as I wasn't sure what she was getting at. "Do you mean like if the lich was in Hamilton, it couldn't cause issues in Toronto because it is too far away?" Blue nodded. "I think that is a valid assumption. Why do you ask?"

"My thought was that if the lich is residing in a fixed location, then maybe mapping out all the incidents might give us a rough idea of where the center of the disturbance is and possibly reveal his location."

I smiled at that, as Blue might have something there. The biggest issue was trying to figure out which crimes were due to the lich's influence and which ones would have happened anyways. Hopefully, the density of the crimes would help sort those two things out. "Your idea has merit. You can get a list of the crimes that happened in the last few days off the community crime map online. Or call Detective Little, as he should be able to get that list pretty quickly too."

Stella said, "I have different colored pins we can use to mark the map upstairs."

Stella and Blue got into a side discussion about the logistics and then Liv said, "You said that liches can control the lesser undead. I've felt restless since it arrived but can't pin the cause down to a certain direction. It feels like it's all around me. Would lesser undead like zombies be drawn to the lich?"

I realized what Liv was getting at. When we went after the demon, we bought an imp to track it, as demons can sense other demons. Liv wanted to do the same thing here. Get a zombie and see if it would lead us to the lich. However, a zombie would get distracted by any living thing it came across because it would want to feed. If we had a huge number of zombies, I suspected that a large group of them would start to cluster near the lich, but somehow I doubted creating and releasing thousands of zombies in Hamilton was the ideal solution we wanted to pursue.

I told Liv my concerns and thanked her for her idea.

The rest of dinner had all of us throwing out ideas, but none ended up being practical. I was still happy, though, that we came up with two new ways to possibly find the lich.

***

Bree and I began our patrol just after 10:00 p.m. At Bree's suggestion, we started over the dry cleaners and flew slowly towards the pizzeria.

Ten minutes later, we'd just passed Ferguson, when Bree said, "Zack, stop."

I pushed out some air in front of us to bring us to a halt and hovered in the air. Bree shuddered and said, "Back up a bit, slowly."

I turned us around and gently sent a small flow of air behind us to push us forward. King was a one-way street here, so we were now going against the flow of traffic beneath us. Thankfully, flying meant we weren't subject to traffic laws.

I hadn't sensed anything, but Bree obviously had by her demeanor. I was about to ask what she was experiencing when that familiar feeling of dread and fear hit me. My adrenaline kicked in as I realized that the lich might be near.

Bree pointed at the sign for a payday loan place and said, "It feels like it's coming from there."

I nodded and stopped us in the air. I called Stella's cell from my visor. *"Bree and I have found something; we are on King Street in front of a place called EZ Payday Loans—"*

Stella cut me off and said, *"Blue and I were there today. It was one of the Russian-owned businesses on our list. The owner, Boris, seemed like a shady individual. I got the feeling he was running more than just payday loans out of that place. Hold on."*

The line went quiet for a while, and I was just about to hang up and call Stella back when she came back on the line. *"Blue is spying on the place. Looks like Boris has become the lich's latest victim. Blue says that he matches the other victims. He's been tied to a chair, beaten, and has the same dual neck wounds as the others. Do you want us to use the shadows to get in there?"*

I mentally cursed to myself at both having another victim and not getting a shot at the lich. I kicked around Stella's question and asked, "Any chance Boris is alive?"

"Hold on," said Stella. I heard her asking Blue my question but didn't hear Blue's answer. *"Blue says no chance."*

"Don't enter the place then. Bree and I will check it out and see if we can get in. I'll call you back."

I ended the call and landed on the sidewalk with Bree in front of the payday loan store. The front of the place was dark. There was a sign listing their hours in the window. The place was supposed to be open until midnight every night. I tried the barred glass door, and it was locked.

I stepped back and checked out the stores on either side of the place. To our right was a laser tattoo removal shop that was closed. To the left, in the corner spot, was an unoccupied retail space.

"Check if there is an entrance around back?" asked Bree.

I nodded and we walked around the empty store to the back of the building. There was a poorly lit alleyway behind the buildings that didn't look inviting. I called on my Electrical powers and readied them. "You see, smell, or sense anything in there we need to worry about?"

Bree shook her head but then closed her eyes and inhaled. "The alley smells of urine and rotting food but there is also an odd musty decaying smell there too. There is nothing in the alley other than rodents and a stray cat farther down."

We entered the alley and stopped at the back door of the payday loan place. The heavy grey steel door was featureless with no lock or door handle on it. I assumed the back door must just be an emergency exit.

Bree leaned close to the door and sniffed deeply. "I'm getting blood, sweat, and stale cigar smoke from inside. The same odd musty decaying scent is here too and stronger."

With the place locked up, I pondered what to do next. Blue could enter from the shadows and unlock it and let us in. With the victim dead, we didn't need to rush in. Detective Little had been good to us, so I decided to play this by the book to pay him back for his kindness.

I was just about to call him when I noticed that Bree was clenching her hands so tightly her knuckles were white, and her jaw was tightly locked. "You okay?"

Bree nodded. "Yeah, just not liking this feeling of death and fear all around us."

I could relate, as I wasn't exactly enjoying the ambiance either. I knew, though, that it hit Bree harder than it did me and felt for her. "If you want to go home, I can have Blue open a portal. You don't need to suffer here on my account."

"No. I'll stay."

I kicked around arguing with her but knew if I pushed this, she'd get mad, so I just nodded. "Let's move around front."

We walked back out into the lights of Ferguson, and it felt better to me just being out of that alley. I stopped us on the corner. The closer we got to the payday loan place, the stronger the dark feelings got, so hanging back here made it easier on both of us. We could see the front door of the business easily from here, so there was no need to get closer yet.

I called Detective Little and told him what we'd found. I offered Blue's services to get him inside the place and he took me up on it. He also said he'd call EIRT and hung up.

Five minutes later, Detective Little opened the door from inside the payday loans shop and stepped out. Liv came out behind him with Alteea's rainbow aura atop her shoulder. Both Liv and Detective Little wore protective coverings on their hands and feet.

Two cruisers came up King Street with lights flashing and stopped in front of the building as Bree and I approached. The officers got out and started putting up police tape around the front area, keeping the small crowd that was gathering back.

Detective Little handed me a bundle of protective gear and then frowned. "I'm sorry I didn't realize another of your teammates was here. I didn't bring any extra gear for her. She'll have to wait until my partner gets here with the car."

"Your partner didn't want to shadow travel?" I asked with a knowing smile.

"Understatement of the year there. I won't get into his exact words, but they weren't meant for polite company."

His partner being a friend of Murdock's made me suspect that he wouldn't use a shadow portal. Murdock liked to pretend that Enhanceds didn't exist, and I assumed the detective would be of the same mindset. Teleporting through shadows made denial a much harder road to travel.

The detective pulled me from my thoughts. "Once you are suited up, we can examine the victim."

I nodded but a hard shudder from Bree pulled my attention to her. "Bree, I'll call Blue and have her open you a portal." She was about to protest but I held up my hand and added, "EIRT is only going to want two of our team on site anyways. As Liv is a vampire and we are the English Court's representatives, she has to be here and I'd like to be the other one, okay?"

Bree nodded and I said, "Look, you did great. The only reason we are here now is because you were able to detect something that I completely missed. You'll be more useful at home helping Blue and Stella."

Bree straightened her shoulders at that and seemed satisfied.

As she wandered off to meet Blue, I spotted two more cruisers down the street blocking off King to traffic. Thankfully, traffic was reasonably light at night. Closing off one of the main arteries to the core during the day would have made traffic a nightmare.

I put on the plastic boots and Liv helped get the elastics over the bags around my hands and we went in. The front lobby of the building was tiny, with probably less than six feet from the door to the plexiglass-enclosed cashier's window. There was a counter off to the left with a pen chained to it and a single chair in front of the outside window. There were also two video cameras mounted on either side of the lobby. Both had green lights on them.

I hoped that this time we might get lucky and get a shot of the lich and the vampires entering the place.

The door on the right to the cashier's cage was wedged open. I assumed Detective Little had done that to stop it from closing and locking behind him.

Liv and I followed him through the door to the cage. It was a small area about six feet deep. Another camera was mounted in the corner.

We went through another door to the back of the store.

The moment we entered the room, I was hit by the same stench of stale cigar smoke that Bree had mentioned.

In front of us on the right was a small kitchenette. To the left against the far wall was a twin-sized bed with a badly stained mattress, rumpled blanket, and a grimy pillow that needed to be burned rather than washed.

Just beyond the kitchenette and bed was a chair with the victim tied to it. There was a desk in the corner with an old PC on it that at one point had been cream-colored but now was yellowed by smoke. There was an ashtray filled with cigar ends sitting on the desk, which had an old, battered file cabinet on the far side of it.

At the back of the room was a small room on the left which I assumed was a bathroom and the emergency exit door to the right of it.

By the dirty dishes in the sink and the bed, I was willing to bet that Boris didn't just work here but lived here too.

I focused on the victim. Boris had been a big man and I guessed he was at least 250 pounds, if not heavier. It was harder to tell his height, but he was at least six feet tall by my estimation.

Boris's head was tilted back and his mouth, full of yellowed teeth, was open in a permanent scream like all the other victims. His right eye was swollen shut and the area around it badly bruised. The rest of his face looked just as bad. Boris hadn't gone easy and had been worked over badly before they killed him.

There were matching neck wounds where both vampires had fed. The gold chains around his neck and the large gold and diamond rings on his fingers ruled out robbery as a motive for his death.

Detective Little said, "The victim is Boris Semenov. We looked into him a couple of years ago, as we had intel that he was running an illegal sports betting operation out of this place but couldn't find anything to make that stick. There were also rumors of him running an escort agency here, too, but once again we couldn't prove it. We had a couple of witnesses, but both recanted before we could press charges. Pretty sure Boris or one of his associates got to them."

I smiled to myself, as it looked like Stella had been right about the guy. We spent a few more minutes looking around the body but nothing new popped out at us.

Our luck improved as I hit the space bar on the computer and it came to a desktop with no password. Detective Little sat down in the swivel chair in front of the PC and found the monitoring software. He brought up all three camera feeds and began rewinding the videos. I cursed to myself, as all three turned to static at one point.

He kept going until the static stopped. All three now showed a brightly lit lobby and cashier's cage. The time on the video was 8:03 p.m. He fast-forwarded to the end of the static and the time stamp was 8:10 p.m. Now all three cameras showed dim areas with the lights off. I could also see that the bolt lock on the front door was engaged.

"By this, it looked like they must have arrived just after eight. There is no static or video of them leaving, so they probably went out the back via the emergency door. What time did you and your teammate get here?" asked Detective Little.

"I'd have to check the recording on my visor for an exact time but probably around 10:15 p.m. Blue spied on the place from the shadows just after that and there was no one here but the victim."

"You could have waited until I got here," said the older detective as he entered the room.

Detective Little shrugged and said, "You could have shadow traveled with me . . ."

The older detective gave him a dismissive wave and said, "Frank, bring me up to speed."

I stepped away as Detective Little went over what we'd found. I went deeper into the room and opened the door to the bathroom. I was surprised to see a small upright glassed-in shower unit in the corner of the room in addition to the toilet and sink. There was a glass on the sink with a toothbrush in it and a hairbrush beside it. The shower and the toiletries confirmed my suspicions that Boris had been living here in addition to working here.

I pushed the bar on the emergency exit, and it opened easily. I took a quick look out into the alley and then stepped back inside as the door closed itself. I heard the clunk of the lock reengaging. That confirmed that the lich and vampires probably exited here.

A voice from the front of the store yelled that EIRT had arrived.

A few minutes later, Bobby Knight and the mage walked in. We exchanged greetings and the mage said, "I've been giving more thought to your lich theory. I still don't think a lich is a possible suspect, but I have a spell that will confirm, at the very least, that a necromancer is involved."

"What does the spell do?" I asked.

"It will confirm if someone has used blood or death magic in the area."

I perked up at that and followed the mage closer to the victim. He pulled out a small wooden board from a bag and a couple of bottles of powder. He sat down on the floor and placed the board in front of him and poured out a small amount of white powder from one bottle onto the board. He resealed the bottle and then carefully added some brown powder. He closed the bottle and then took a deep breath.

The mage looked at me and said, "You may want to stand back. If the spell detects blood or death magic, a small cloud of black smoke will appear. If it doesn't, it will be a small cloud of white smoke."

The detectives, Bobby, and Liv had also crowded around the mage. We all stepped back to give him some room.

The mage got a serious look on his face and stared down at the board. He brought his right hand up and made sharp gestures and began casting. He said a few words in a language I didn't recognize but assumed was probably Latin, as that tended to be the most common language used in spellcasting.

The moment he finished, a loud *poof* filled the room and a huge cloud of black smoke erupted from the board. The mage coughed as the cloud of smoke engulfed him and everyone hastily stepped back again to avoid the growing smoke cloud. I called on my Air powers and formed a small cyclone in the air and used it to suck up the smoke. "Liv, open the back door for me?"

She blurred over to the door and had it opened in under a second. I walked the smoke-filled cyclone towards the open door then released it out into the night. I thanked Liv for her help and then turned my attention back to the mage.

He was coughing and shaking his head. His face, etched in concern, had gone ghost white.

"That shouldn't have happened," the mage said between coughs.

"You said if it detected blood or death magic, there'd be a cloud of black smoke. Looks like your spell worked perfectly," said Bobby.

The mage shook his head. "I said a small cloud of smoke; that was a ton of smoke. I've only cast this spell once before and that was back when I was at the Magic Academy. Our professor had cast a very simple blood spell and then we all cast this spell to detect it. None of the smoke clouds were bigger than a couple of inches high and were barely a wisp in width."

"You've obviously grown in power since the Academy, any chance you put a bit more gusto into the spell than you meant to?" I asked.

The mage shook his head but then a thoughtful look appeared on his face. "No, I used the correct amount of power, but your idea about power might be the answer. I need to make some calls to confirm, but I suspect the size of the cloud might be related to the amount of power used in the blood or death magic spell itself. I hope, though, that isn't the case."

Bobby frowned. "Why not?"

"Because if that is the case, whoever or whatever cast that spell is an immensely powerful magic user."

Chapter 13

Wednesday, October 12

By the time we left that night, the mage had yet to hear back from one of the instructors at the Academy, but he had consulted with some colleagues about the spell. The consensus was that he was correct in believing that the size of the cloud was proportional to the power of the blood or death magic cast. The mage still hadn't been willing to accept we were dealing with a lich but agreed that it had to be a very powerful and dangerous necromancer at a minimum. He planned on bumping his concerns up the chain to hopefully get more resources shifted to this case.

My guess was that it wouldn't be enough to get GRC13 involvement. It probably meant that they'd put an EIRT team up in a hotel here in town to allow better response times.

I thought about going to Acting Director Cooper directly, but I still felt that I didn't have enough evidence to prove my lich theory. It was a shame that none of the cameras at any of the scenes had caught a picture of the lich. A shot of a skeleton carrying a magic staff and a glowing ruby would have done wonders towards proving my theory.

Stella and Blue had been busy last night and this morning. While we were at the crime scene, they'd updated the map with blue pins, indicating where any crimes or odd incidents had occurred. The problem was the map didn't tell us much. The blue pins ran across the map from Stoney Creek in the east to Westdale in the west. They also went north right to the shores of Lake Ontario and south along the edges of the escarpment of Hamilton Mountain.

The only area it did eliminate was Hamilton Mountain proper, as there were only a few blue pins on in that area and those numbers seemed in line with the numbers from last year at this time. Based on this information, I was leaning toward the theory that the lich's hideout was somewhere down the mountain in the main area of Hamilton, which was a sizable area and not narrowed enough for us to search effectively.

Blue and Stella were out the door at nine that morning and had taken another fourteen businesses off our list. The twenty-eight they'd been to in the last twenty-four hours were all the ones that were directly between the dry cleaners and the pizzeria. As that had been the area the lich had been operating in, it had also been our best hope for finding the headpiece. Unfortunately, none of the owners had any knowledge about the artifact.

The only slim bit of good news I could take out of that was if we hadn't found the headpiece there, he wouldn't either. That good news was tempered by the fact that the lich would still be adding more victims to his list until he found the headpiece.

Scratching twenty-eight names off our list was a nice start but we still had more than double that left to visit. Worse, the farther we got away from the downtown core, the more spread out those remaining businesses were.

Blue's holographic disguise had drained its batteries, which was why they were now back. After lunch, I would take Stella and continue visiting businesses on the list.

The afternoon turned out to be just as dreary as the weather. It was a typical overcast fall day in the Hammer with the occasional light showers thrown in to add to the misery. Stella and I managed to visit another ten businesses before stopping for dinner. These ten were on the outer edges of the core. Most of the people we talked to had no idea about the headpiece and had never seen anything like it before. The ones who recognized it were worse, as their reactions were either mirth or disbelief that we were searching for it. One business owner joked that he had it in the back room along with Excalibur and the Holy Grail. It made for a long day.

Dinner was a quiet affair for two reasons. The first was Stella, Blue, and I were discouraged about our lack of results in canvassing the businesses. The second was due to Olivia's absence. The moment she'd arisen, she came upstairs all excited and asked Blue to portal her to a local car dealership. It seemed she got a message that her new ride was in.

After dinner, Bree suggested that I take her out on patrol again this evening and added that starting sooner than later might be a good idea.

"Why earlier?" I asked.

"The lich seems to go out early. If we'd been downtown at this time yesterday, we might have caught him in the act."

Bree brought up a good point. The pizzeria attack had been later, but the last two did happen around this time. I'd realized that I let my own personal biases cloud my judgment. Back in the day, when I was patrolling as a hero, the crime and issues in the city usually happened closer to midnight or in the wee hours of the morning. Going out just as it got dark was normally a big waste of time. But these days my reason for patrolling wasn't to stop crimes, or save people from accidents or fire, but to catch the lich.

I told Bree to give me five minutes and headed upstairs to get my armor and get ready.

I'd just gotten dressed when a call came in on my visor from Liv.

"Have everyone out front in the next minute. Bye," said Liv in an excited tone.

She ended the call before I could respond. I kicked around the idea of just leaving on patrol with Bree but figured a couple of minutes to check out her new ride wouldn't hurt. I also knew that if I did leave, she'd be annoyed with me.

I gathered the troops and we stood out front.

We didn't have to wait long. Bree got a look of concentration on her face and said, "I think I hear her coming."

She turned east and starred off into the distance. I couldn't hear anything like a car, but I wasn't going to doubt Bree's enhanced hearing and faced the same direction. I picked up the throaty rumble at the same time as I spotted two headlights off in the distance, heading towards us at a high rate of speed.

The highly illegal speed the vehicle was traveling at left no doubt in my mind I was watching Liv approach. While I didn't drive or even have a license, I'd gotten quite good at recognizing makes and types of vehicles, as it was a useful skill to have. On many bounty cases, we'd end up searching for a suspect's car to try and find them.

Even though I'd gotten decent at identifying motor vehicles, I was frowning, as I had no idea what I was looking at. The only two things I knew for sure were that it was big and loud. It wasn't just the vehicle's exhaust that was obnoxiously loud, but its oversized off-road tires were equally noisy. My jaw dropped as the vehicle got closer and I spotted that it had six wheels instead of the usual four. The front grille and the headlights on this thing looked like an evil grinning skull.

Liv locked up the brakes and left six-foot-long skid marks on the pavement and a cloud of tire smoke in her wake. She gunned the engine a few times which rattled the neighborhood's windows. I groaned to myself. If the neighbors hadn't hated us for drow and robot attacks, then whatever goodwill we had left had just been destroyed by the monstrosity currently sitting outside our house.

I looked at the vehicle, and my first thought was, *Mad Max called, and he wants his truck back.*

I studied it and was pretty sure that this thing had started life as a Jeep but had been drastically modified. The hood had been extended and heavily modified, as had the rear bed of the truck. The extra two tires at the back had probably been the main reason for extending the bed.

I glanced over at Bree's 4-Runner in the driveway, which I thought was a sizable vehicle, and then back at Olivia's new truck, which made the 4-Runner look like a kid's toy in comparison.

A small part of me was willing to admit that it looked badass. If you needed a vehicle to navigate around in after nuclear Armageddon, this would be it.

Mercifully, Liv stopped revving the engine and turned the truck off. The silence was welcomed.

I turned to Bree and said, "If a guy had pulled up in this thing, I would swear he was trying to compensate for having the world's smallest wiener." Bree turned to me and nodded, and I added, "I didn't think this was an issue women suffered from. Do you think Liv is trying to overcompensate for, um . . ." I mimed a small chest with my hands.

Bree smiled and said, "Maybe, I have no idea."

Liv got out of the truck and immediately started looking under it.

We moved closer and I asked, "Whatcha doing?"

Liv giggled and said, "I felt a bump on my way home and worried I might have run over a small compact car. I'm just checking to make sure there isn't one lodged under here."

I rubbed my temples, as I felt a large headache coming on. I wasn't entirely sure if Liv was making a joke or not.

She stopped looking under the trunk, turned to us, and said, "Well? What do you think of my new beast?"

The four of us stood speechless and looked at one another. I mentally groaned as all eyes fell on me and realized I'd been nominated to speak for the group. "You won't lose it in a parking lot."

Liv's face fell a little and she said, "You guys don't like it?"

"It's, um, cool, we are just trying to get used to it," I said and then added, "Can I ask why you got this particular vehicle?"

Liv perked up again and said, "After robots destroyed my last car, I wanted something that could take a licking and keep on ticking. Also, I wanted something more practical than a two-seater."

My eyes bugged out at the term 'practical,' and Bree and Stella turned their heads to hide their laughter.

I mentally cursed them as Liv was looking at me to say something more. "How is this practical?"

Liv tapped the side and said, "First, the paint is mixed with Kevlar, so things like exploding houses shouldn't even scratch it." She blurred over and opened the driver's door and added, "There is ample seating for five, so the whole team can comfortably fit in her. It has off-road capabilities so I can go anywhere in this."

She blurred to the back of the vehicle and said, "Come see the best part."

As a group, we walked around the back of the truck and Liv reached up and rolled up what sounded like a metal shutter that covered the top of the bed and then lowered the tailgate. "Ta-da!"

Mounted in the back of the bed was a full coffin.

Before any of us said anything, Liv said, "Let's say Bree and I are out and having a good time, and we lose track of time and the sun comes up. I can pop into the back, pull down the shutters, and lock myself in. I can then get in the coffin and sleep the day away in safety without worrying about burning to a crisp in the sunlight."

I had to admit that a mobile safe and secure sleeping area wasn't the worst idea for a vampire. I also doubted there were many vehicles that would have the cargo space to store a full coffin. I still wasn't sure I'd class the vehicle as practical, but Liv had brought up some good points.

Blue saved me and said, "It seems like an impressive mode of transportation."

Liv grinned at that and then turned to Bree and said, "Can you move your truck over a bit so I have room to park?"

Bree smiled and said, "You sure you can't just park over my truck?"

Liv eyeballed the 4-Runner and said, "I can try."

***

Bree and I ended up patrolling once she and Liv got the parking arrangements figured out in our driveway. Bree ended up having to back her vehicle in on the left side of the driveway. Liv got her monster parked on the right side but there was less than a foot between the two trucks. I had a feeling that one of these days, Liv would get to test out how scratch-resistant her paint was when she parked a bit too close to Bree's truck.

We did a couple of slow laps above King Street and then the return route along Main Street but there was no sign of the lich or its presence. A part of me hoped that meant we wouldn't be looking at another victim this evening. Another part of me, though, was disappointed that we hadn't gotten a shot at the lich.

Just after ten, a call came in via my visor from Dave Collins.

"Hurricane, I'm on sight at the main steel foundry for Steel Co. We had reports of two or three creatures lurking around the place. An officer just spotted them and has called for SWAT and EIRT, but both are thirty minutes out."

I pondered that statement and then asked, "'Creatures' covers a wide range of things, any chance you can narrow down what you are dealing with?"

"The officer that spotted them called them 'really fast zombies.' He also reported a bad smell of rot."

I groaned, as they sounded like ghouls. *"Try and keep an eye on them but don't corner or confront them, and we'll be there shortly. Also, get any workers out of the plant."*

I ended the call. I gained some altitude and banked us north and headed for Steel Co. I knew Bree had heard the call and was waiting for more information from me. I ignored her for the moment and called Stella. *"There has been a sighting of two or three creatures that sound like ghouls at Steel Co. They are around the main foundry building and police are on scene. Grab Blue and Liv and meet us there."*

"Will do."

I ended the call.

"What's the skinny on taking down ghouls?" said Bree.

"They are part of the undead class, so the same as zombies: behead or burn them. Silver also hurts them."

She nodded. "Okay, why did you groan earlier?"

"They are killed the same way as zombies but are much more dangerous. Unlike zombies, ghouls can think and speak. They are cunning and vicious. They are also faster and stronger than zombies."

"How much faster and stronger?"

I pondered that for a moment and said, "For both speed and strength, right between zombies and vampires for both. They can't move at a vampire's blinding speed, but they can move quite quickly when they want to. I will land us on the roof so you can change when we get there."

"Standing or beast form?" asked Bree.

I kicked around the two options. Her beast form was faster but her standing one was stronger. "Standing. Your speed and theirs will be the same but you'll have the advantage of strength over them."

Dave's timing had been good, as we'd been fairly close to Steel Co. when he called. We were already coming up on the main building and I spotted four cruisers circling around the building. Two were stopped at the main entrance and a couple officers were directing a steady stream of employees out of the building. I recognized Dave's tall lanky form as one of the two officers.

I landed us on the roof and Bree was already peeling off her grey sweats. After a quick look around the roof to make sure no ghoul was lurking, I turned my head away to give her some privacy to change. Dave and the officer were beneath us and I looked around to down to make sure there were no ghouls lingering around them.

I tried to ignore the sounds of bones snapping and muscles tearing behind me as Bree morphed into her hybrid Werepanther form. Every time she changed, I cringed at how painful the experience must be. Bree, though, had never once complained about it.

A deep growl shattered the quiet night sky as Bree finished her change. I turned around and picked up her clothes and stuffed them into the compartments of my armor. I lifted us both into the air and descended to where Dave and the other officer were.

I smiled when the workers coming out of the building gave us a wide berth. I assumed Bree's near-seven-foot dark, snarling form was the reason.

Dave smiled as he saw me and said, "There are three of them inside the building."

"The rest of my team will be here shortly. Send them in when they arrive."

He nodded.

I turned to Bree and said, "Let's go hunting. Their smell should lead you to them."

As we entered the building, that task of finding the ghouls instantly seemed harder. The heat of the place was intense. Worse than the heat, though, was the smell. I was terrible at identifying scents but was overwhelmed by an oily burnt one as we entered.

Bree let out an unhappy growl, too, but immediately headed deeper into the foundry, obviously tracking something.

Thankfully, the building was tall, so I had plenty of room to fly. I took to the air and followed Bree. I instantly felt safer being airborne knowing I'd be a harder target for the ghouls to ambush. I scanned the rafters for auras. Ghouls were nimble and I had no doubt they could get up there if they wanted. The last thing I need was one dropping on me from above.

The tricky part was not overreacting to movement, as there were still workers in the building. Frying a Steel Co. employee with lightning probably wouldn't have gone over well. Thankfully, most were heading for the exits, but they were another thing we had to be careful of.

Bree and I had made it about midway into the building when Blue's voice came over the comm channel. *"We've arrived at the main entrance. Olivia just entered."*

I shook my head as Liv blurred up and appeared beside Bree just after that; vampire speed was impressive.

"Stella and I are standing by. I am using the shadows to search for the creatures, and we will join you once we have spotted them."

I noticed that Alteea wasn't on Liv's shoulder. "Where's Alteea?"

"Enclosed space with too much metal, so we left her at home," said Blue.

Pixies were better than most fae about metal but even they had their limits, and a steel mill certainly wouldn't be comfortable for her. "Roger that."

Bree growled and began running forward, Liv keeping pace beside her. I scanned up ahead and spotted three blood red, brown, and black auras lurking in the shadows of some machinery. Bree snarled as she tackled one and the other two ghouls tried to help their companion out. Liv just missed beheading one that ducked at the last second. It turned its attention to her and lashed out with its lethally sharp nails. Liv easily darted back, and I used my Air powers to lift the third one into the air and away from Bree's exposed back.

It hissed as it left the ground and I pulled it closer to me but didn't let it touch the ground or come close enough that it could strike at me.

"Elemental, release me or feel the Night Lord's wrath," said the ghoul in a gravelly tone.

I perked up at that. "Tell me where the Night Lord is and I'll release you."

It flashed me a grin of rotted teeth and said, "The Night Lord is all around us. He is the night."

I rolled my eyes. "Any chance you can narrow that location down a bit? I'd like to pay him my respects."

"Wise to respect the Night Lord. You and everyone will meet him soon enough."

Bree growled off in the distance and I worried she might be in trouble. I needed to end this. "Last chance, point in the direction where he is, and I'll let you go."

My heart beat with excitement as the ghoul slowly raised his right arm and pointed to my right. My excitement faded as he slowly panned his arm in a 180-degree arc and laughed.

"Well, a promise is a promise, I'll release you now."

The ghoul's smile grew at that. I called on more of my Air power and hit him with a powerful gust that sent him flying to my left. The ghoul's smile disappeared as he began to curve towards the open furnace of molten steel.

"NO!" it screamed as it plunged towards its demise.

The ghoul ignited before it even reached the molten lava. The moment it touched the river of hot metal it burst into ashes.

A triumphant growl echoed around the foundry, and I spotted Bree toss the severed head of the ghoul she'd been fighting to the ground. I grew concerned at the sight of deep gashes in her black fur but watched in astonishment as the wounds healed before my eyes.

I glanced around and spotted Liv wiping the black blood off Mr. Slicey on the dirty, ripped pants of the ghoul she'd beheaded.

Blue and Stella in her Hyde form popped out from the shadows behind Liv and Bree. Stella's large bulbous right eye looked around and she grunted in confusion.

I popped my faceplate to my armor and yelled, "It's over, Stella."

Before I could blink, Stella's monstrous form shifted and changed back to her smaller human form.

Stella's young-looking face bunched up in disgust. "My, those are quite potent."

She held her hand out to Blue and Blue handed Stella's phone to her. Stella turned and snapped pictures of the two ghouls for a bounty claim and then looked around. "Where is the third one?"

I pointed at the furnace and said, "Ashes to ashes . . ."

Stella shook her head at me. "You better have it on video so we can make a claim."

***

It was past one in the morning before we got home. Steel Co. management weren't happy with me for using their steel furnace as a crockpot to cook a ghoul and were bitching about impurities in the metal. Thankfully, after I pointed out the possibility that ghouls might have converted their entire workforce to undead carrion eaters, they let the matter drop.

At least we had bounty claim numbers for the three ghouls and that would add a sweet tax-free forty-five grand to our bank account. It was also a blessing that no one, other than the ghouls, had been hurt.

This evening had erased any of my previous doubt that we were dealing with a lich. The Night Lord references were one reason, but the presence of the ghouls was another. In my entire hero and bounty hunting career, I'd only come across two ghouls, and both of those had been in cemeteries. Three in a steel mill of all places made no sense. Ghouls feared fire so there was no logical reason for them to be there unless something had stirred them up or disrupted their routines. I was betting that the lich's presence in the city was that catalyst.

Bree and I on our earlier patrol hadn't detected even a whiff of the lich and I hoped that meant he'd taken the night off. My biggest fear now was that there was a body tied up in a chair in a store somewhere that would be discovered by some hapless employee or relative tomorrow morning.

The long days had caught up with Stella and Blue and both were now in bed getting some much-needed rest. They were planning on getting an early start tomorrow in getting more names off our list of businesses.

Liv, Bree, and Alteea were downstairs on the couch watching movies, so I had the upstairs office to myself. I found myself at a loss. I wandered over to Stella's map and idly stared at it. There was a nice cluster of green pins in the center of the map representing businesses that we visited but there were a lot of red ones we had to get to.

I shifted my attention to the blue pins that marked crimes and unusual incidents. They seemed slightly denser in the northeastern part of the map but not by enough to make any serious conclusions.

I debated going back out on patrol but nixed the idea for two reasons. The first was between my earlier patrol with Bree and the combat with the ghouls, my power levels were half empty. The second was that the lich's pattern so far was to attack during early evenings and around midnight, so the chances of me coming across him were remote.

Charlie popped into my mind, and I was overcome with profound sadness. I knew it was time for me to deal with her loss. I closed the door to the office and took a seat at my computer. I plugged in some headphones and opened my music player, selecting some suitable slow, meaningful songs, and then found the two pictures I had of Charlie on my iPhone.

I smiled at the first one, which had Charlie in her full Curveball gear and standing in a classic hero pose with her hands on her hips. I swiped across the photos until I found the second one. The moment I saw it, I felt the tears run unabashedly down my cheeks. This one was of Charlie after one of our more intense training sessions. Her short blonde hair was plastered against her head with sweat, but she had a satisfied grin on her face and that twinkle of life in her blue eyes that I loved.

A part of me was still angry at her for not calling us that night. I knew that anger was misplaced. Even if she had called, we wouldn't have made it in time to save her. I also knew from the video that she had no time. She did what any hero would do; people were in trouble, and she acted.

I cursed into the air and tore some tissues from the box on my desk and tried to clean myself up. It was a pointless act, as I couldn't stop crying. I hated being this weak but knew I had to work through this.

It had been a long time since I'd lost someone I cared about this much. It hit me that the last person I'd lost was my mother and that had been fifteen years ago. Rob being in a coma a few months ago was probably a close second but, thank Odin, he'd recovered.

An hour and a box of tissues later, I started to pull myself together. I switched the music to a song with a powerful metal guitar riff and let its energy and rage fill me. I bobbed my head and exhaled deeply and gathered my resolve. I couldn't bring Charlie back, but I sure as hell was going to make the creatures responsible for her death pay.

Chapter 14

Thursday, October 13

My phone buzzed and woke me up. I answered it without looking at who was calling.

"Mr. Stevens, it's Diane Peters, Charlie's mom."

I winced at the small hitch in her voice when she said, 'Charlie's mom.' Her voice also fully awakened me. *"Please, Diane, call me Zack. Is everything okay?"*

"As well as can be expected, I guess. I'm calling as we are having a service for Charlie this Saturday. You and your team are invited."

I thanked her and said we'd be there and got the details of where and when.

I was surprised that she hadn't asked about the status of the case and if we were close to bringing Charlie's killers to justice. I remembered that it had been Charlie's grandmother that had been the one looking for vengeance and not her mom. I suspected that Diane knew that whatever happened, it wouldn't bring Charlie back.

I quickly sent a group text to the team and my foundation members to let them know about the funeral service and the details.

With that out of the way, I had some breakfast and a shower and was ready to hit the streets with Stella when she and Blue returned from their morning canvassing of businesses on our list.

By the end of the day, we'd eliminated twenty-two more businesses off our list, bringing our total to sixty. While I was happy that we were making good progress, another part of me was beginning to worry that we might be wasting our time. The sixty were in the downtown and surrounding areas and had been our prime candidates, as this had been where the lich was operating. Unfortunately, we still hadn't found a solid lead on the headpiece.

The remaining thirty-eight businesses left on the list were in the outlying suburbs of Hamilton, including Stoney Creek, Dundas, Ancaster, and Hamilton Mountain. I had much less hope about finding the headpiece in those areas but kept my doubts to myself.

Dinner that night ended up being a quiet affair. Stella was unusually silent, and I wondered if she, too, was beginning to question our tactic of searching for the headpiece at a Russian-owned business. Of course, I could have just been transferring my worries onto her and it was possible that she was just deep in thought.

Liv was in a snit, as she wanted to go deer hunting in the woods and take her new ride off-roading, but Bree had shot her down. Bree made it clear that she was going patrolling with me this evening and now they were both giving each other the cold shoulder.

My biggest concern was that we'd find another body tonight. The lich hadn't struck last night, and by his pattern so far, that meant he would this evening.

We were just starting to clean up dinner when all our phones went off at once. Stella perked up and said, "I forgot to mention, I modified the monitoring program we used to track for signs of the Acolytes to screen for local emergencies, anything vampire or lich related, or any local Enhanced Individual activities."

I nodded as I read the texts that were appearing on my phone. The first one read, *Officer down, vampire attack*, which started my adrenaline pumping. The subsequent ones provided more details. The address was in Westdale and sounded familiar.

Stella said, "Blue and I visited a jewelry store in that plaza this morning."

I nodded as that explained why I'd recognized the address. I'd seen it on the list when the three of us updated the map earlier this afternoon.

"Gear up, people," I said as I got to my feet.

Liv blurred off to fetch her sword and comm visor. Bree was already peeling off her clothes to change before I'd even finished speaking.

Stella and I dashed up the stairs to my room to get my armor. Blue was already ahead of us, heading to her room to get her comm visor and whatever extra instruments of death she felt would be appropriate for tonight's encounter.

As we snapped on pieces of my armor, I weighed the odds in my head that this might be the lich and his two vampire lackeys versus just a random vampire attack. In my gut, I believed this was the real deal. It was too much of a coincidence that the crime took place at one of the businesses on our list.

The good news was that if it was the lich, then we didn't need to pull any of our punches; no one in their right mind tried to capture a necromancer, never mind a full-blown lich. With an officer down, the authorities also wouldn't be holding back. The only thing that would limit us was that area of Westdale was a fairly busy place and that meant there'd be lots of civilians around that we'd have to be mindful of.

My gut knotted a bit at that last part. We might temper our response due to the presence of civilians but that wouldn't hamper the lich. We needed to take him down quickly or the casualties could be bad.

Stella and I joined the rest of the team in the living room. Blue was in a trance looking into the shadows but blinked and looked our way as we entered.

She had a confused expression on her face and said, "I can see the plaza from the shadows across the street but cannot access any of the shadows in the plaza directly."

I frowned at that. The only time Blue hadn't been able to access the shadows was during our last case with the Master. He'd stolen some tech from the Chinese military the blocked shadow traveling and teleportation in a preset area when the device was employed. The tech he stole had been prototypes and there was no way one of those was sitting in a strip plaza in Westdale.

Stella said, "The lich must have cast some sort of anti-scrying spell to prevent anyone from tracking or spying on him."

I thought about that and couldn't argue with Stella's logic. "Can you still get us close?"

Blue nodded. "I can open a portal across the street without issue."

"Great," I said, and then shifted my attention to the rest of the team. Bree was in her standing hybrid Werepanther form, Liv had her silver-edged sword in a sheath on her back and her comm visor on, Alteea had already engaged her glamor, Blue, too, had her visor on, and Stella was still just in her human form, but she could change in a blink of an eye. "If this is the lich, we hit him hard. Magic users are exceptionally dangerous, and his use of blood and death magic makes him even more so. Go for the ruby he'll be carrying—that is the source of his power. Either destroy it or take it away from him. Try to keep him off balance to prevent him from casting spells. Also, watch for the two vampires with him. Questions?"

I was met with silence and said, "Blue, open the portal. We go in heavy formation."

Blue turned to the shadows and made a sharp gesture with her hand. "It's open."

Stella moved in front of the shadows, changed into her massive Hyde alter ego, and stepped through. We all followed closely behind.

The second I stepped out from the shadows behind a coffee shop in Westdale, any doubts that the lich was here evaporated instantly.

"By Odin's beard!" I said as I tried to deal with the wave of fear and death that assaulted me.

I staggered on my feet due to the sheer intensity of it as I tried to move away from the portal. Every fiber of my being was urging me to flee. My primitive fight or flight response had been triggered big time. I gritted my teeth and thought of Charlie and chose to fight.

Having hardened my resolve, I focused on my surroundings. The night was bright with the three-quarter moon in the cloudless sky above us. The air was cool but not unseasonably so. It being a nicer night, I'd expected to see more people around, but the area was a ghost town, at least for foot traffic. I suspected I had the lich's shroud of death and fear to thank for the lack of people. Vehicles, though, were still going by at a steady pace on King Street to my left.

I glanced across the street and spotted the jewelry store on the corner of the plaza. There was a police car stopped in front of it in the parking lot. Its headlights were on, and the motor was running but its light bar wasn't flashing red and blue. I could see the driver's side door was open and the car was unoccupied.

The store itself was dark inside other than the display cases next to the windows which were lit up and showing their glittering wares.

Stella was already lumbering towards the police car in the parking lot. Liv was just behind her and had her sword out. Stella's Hyde form didn't feel fear and Liv being undead meant she, too, was immune to the aura of death and fear around us.

Bree was trailing behind Liv and her whole form seemed to be shaking. She growled loudly with each step but kept going.

I was concerned about Bree as she seemed to be more sensitive to this shroud of death and fear than all of us. Each step seemed to be like torture for her. I was barely able to put one foot in front of the other to follow them and couldn't imagine how bad Bree must be feeling this.

I smiled, as she didn't hesitate and just kept moving forward. That girl had a spine of steel, and I was proud to call her a friend and teammate.

Alteea's rainbow aura shot by me and up into the night sky. I knew she'd have her phone out and would be filming everything that happened tonight.

Blue stepped out of the shadows. She shook her head and drew her sword, and without a word fell in behind me. I knew Blue wouldn't let something like overwhelming fear get the better of her; she was too disciplined to let that happen.

I drew strength from my teammates' attitudes and willpower and the fear in me receded.

Sirens were closing in on our position from what sounded like every direction of the city. We were on our own, though, as SWAT and EIRT would be at least thirty minutes out and probably longer for the latter. The best we could hope for was the police to keep the area clear of civilians.

As we crossed the street, a police cruiser with a siren blaring and its red and blue lights flashing drove up King Street to the next intersection and skidded to a stop, blocking the intersection. Another one did the same at the nearby intersection and I nodded in approval. The fewer vehicles around the better. The police were doing their part; it was time for us to do ours.

Stella walked around back of the cruiser and stopped. Liv blurred forward and crouched down and disappeared from view and I wondered what the two of them were doing. Bree let out an angry growl as she walked around Stella's massive form. I thickened the air around me as a precaution and rushed to catch up, dashing around Stella before stopping dead in my tracks.

On the ground was the downed police officer with his throat torn out, staring lifelessly into the night sky. I spotted that his holster was open, but his pistol was still inside of it. By the look of it, the vampire had jumped him the moment he'd exited the vehicle. He'd had no chance. Liv removed her hand from the undamaged side of his neck where she'd been looking for a pulse and shook her head at me.

I staggered suddenly as the aura of fear and death mounted, and I was barely able to stay on my feet. The door to the jewelry store swung open and the redheaded vampire who had blood smeared across his chin stepped out. The lich came out right behind him in a cowled black robe, clutching a dark wooden staff in his skeletal hand. An ominous crimson glow shone from under the robe around his upper chest. Two burning red eyes peered out from within the dark hood of the robe. Its gaze flicked over us with disdain and no concern.

My knees trembled at the black and bloodred aura around the lich; it had to be three feet in diameter. The only aura I'd ever seen that was remotely as large was Elizabeth's, Master of the English Vampire Court. The power that aura represented was truly frightening.

The dark-haired vampire came out last.

Bree let out a challenging growl that shook all the windows of the plaza and set off two car alarms in the parking lot. She sprung towards the lich but before she'd barely left the ground, the lich pointed his staff at her and muttered something short and sharp. Bree was suddenly thrown back, as though an invisible hammer of force had hit her. She shot across the parking lot and went clean through the side of a minivan. The entire van lifted up on its far two wheels before crashing back down and rocking back and forth.

The lich said in a hiss, "Get the horseless carriage; I will deal with these insects."

Stella grunted and lumbered towards the lich like the unstoppable force she was. Blue was directly behind her. Liv, though, stood catatonic, mumbling to herself. I defensively moved closer to her to protect her.

As I got close, I heard her say, "Pretty shoes!" in a happy, far-off voice.

The lich said something sharply in Russian and waved his staff. Instantly, everything around me went pitch black.

The fear that I'd been fighting from the lich's presence became unmanageable, as I was suddenly blind. I lifted my hand until it was almost touching my face but couldn't see it. Standing completely blind less than twenty feet away from one of the most dangerous things to walk this earth, waiting for the next blow to fall, had me close to losing it.

This so not good, I thought in near panic as the ground started to tremble under my feet.

I frantically felt around in the darkness to the last place I remembered Liv being. My gauntlet touched up against what I hoped was Liv. I stepped closer, wrapped my arm around her, and called on my Air power. The expression 'flying blind' popped into my head, as if to warn me that what I was about to do was probably a very bad idea.

The rumbling under my feet got stronger with each passing second so I didn't have a choice. I pushed a huge amount of air under me and Liv and shot us in the air in what I hoped was straight up.

I exhaled in relief as the bright lights of the city appeared and my vision returned. I glanced down and the lich was still standing in front of the jewelry store. He was moving the staff around with precise gestures and I knew he was casting another spell.

A thick black fog covered half the parking lot, including the area I'd stood moments before. That fog had been the reason for my blindness. Blue's Keetiyatomi blade suddenly ignited in the center of the dark fog and the darkness seemed to retreat from it. Blue waved the sword around her and more of the fog dissipated. I assumed the magic of her blade was dispelling the magic of the unnatural cloud.

An angry grunt came from somewhere in the fog below me and I knew that was Stella. Stella was nearly indestructible, so I suppressed my concern for her for the moment. Bree was also in that fog, and I had no idea if she was even conscious or not after her impact with the minivan earlier.

I spotted a small rainbow aura about twenty feet off to my left, which meant Alteea was okay and still filming.

The screech of tearing metal, followed by a loud growl of a severely pissed off Werepanther cut through the night, and I smiled knowing that Bree seemed to be okay.

A faint chant pulled my attention back to the lich. His motions with the staff were getting more intense and my gut knotted as I knew he was close to finishing whatever spell he'd been casting.

I called on a short, sharp burst of lightning and fired it at him.

I cursed as a faint pick bubble briefly surrounded the lich and the blue electricity seemed to fork around him. He had some sort of energy shield around him that protected him from my attack.

A white van backed up out of a parking spot at the far end of the lot with a squeal of its tires. I spotted the redheaded vampire in the driver's seat and knew I had to stop that van to prevent the lich from leaving.

I just started calling on my Air powers again, planning to send a powerful gust of the wind under the one side of the van to flip it, when Liv screamed out, "GET OUT OF MY HEAD!"

She thrashed against me, and her arm hit the center of my chest armor hard enough to break the grip I had on her. Liv slipped out of my grasp and far enough from me that she was no longer held up by my Air power and started falling back to Earth.

I used the Air power I'd been summoning to catch her and bring her back up to me.

As she got close, she shook her head and blinked a couple of times as if awakening from a dream.

"You okay?" I asked.

Liv nodded. "He tried to bribe me with shoes . . . wonderful shoes, but no shoes are more important than my friends. What happened?"

It dawned on me that the lich had tried to influence Liv. I should have seen that coming. The creature was a master of the undead and Liv was a young vampire. The good news was that he tried and failed. I hoped that meant going forward, Liv would be able to more easily resist his call as she'd recognize when he was trying to influence her.

Tires squealed below us, and I saw the van heading out of the lot. The lich was no longer anywhere to be seen. I assumed he must be in the van. I was about to go after them when I noticed the tarmac of the parking lot was buckling and shifting violently like an earthquake was occurring.

I spotted Stella, Blue, and Bree being tossed around at the edge of the lot, but they were all running away from the epicenter of it. I flew us lower and towards them and started calling on my Air power again in case I had to lift all of them off the unsteady ground.

By the time we'd reached them, Blue and Bree had reached solid ground across the street and Stella was lumbering her way closer. Stella bent her legs and leaped the last twenty feet towards us. Bree and Blue dove to the side as Stella's massive Hyde form landed hard on the sidewalk where they'd been standing.

I lowered Liv down to join the rest of the team. I was about to yell that I was going after the lich when the pavement in the center of the lot exploded up into the sky in a cloud of dirt, dust, debris, and asphalt.

Two small lights in the same malignant crimson that matched the lich's ruby hovered in the dust cloud about twenty feet off the ground. A deep angry roar echoed through the night and came from the direction of the cloud.

A primal part of me was triggered by that roar and screamed at me to flee.

A large dark shadow began to appear from within the dust cloud. As the dust began to settle, I got a better look at what was hiding in there.

"No fucking way!" I said as my sphincter tightened so badly I wasn't going to be able to crap for a week.

A fully formed Tyrannosaurus rex skeleton stood there looking at us with glowing red eyes. It opened its jaws, crammed full of deadly teeth, which made it seem like it was giving us an evil smile.

It swung its long tail around behind it and hit an overturned compact car. The impact sent the car tumbling back into the ruined lot like it was a child's toy.

Oddly enough, my mind began wondering what the bounty would be for a zombie T. rex and I quickly decided that whatever it was, it wasn't enough.

Its evil gaze locked on to us. The zombie T. rex roared again and snapped its massive jaws shut before it began moving towards us like someone had rung the dinner bell and we were the main course.

Normally I didn't worry about Stella's impervious Hyde form but I wasn't sure her form could handle a bite from those teeth. She was also the slowest of all of us, which meant if she couldn't take the punishment that T. rex could dish out, she was a sitting duck. "Stella, change! The rest of you, run!"

Blue turned and dashed towards the back of the coffee shop. I assumed she was going to use the shadows to disappear. Liv blurred off towards the T. rex and Bree was right behind her.

The moment Stella appeared back in her small human form, I sent a blast of air under her and lifted the both of us into the night sky.

The T. rex couldn't seem to follow Liv's inhuman speed and instead focused on Bree. Bree veered off to its right and it snapped out with its deadly jaws at her. She dove past them and kept running, nimbly leaping over the T. rex's whipping tail.

The dinosaur zombie stopped and turned, and then lumbered after Bree's retreating dark-furred form.

"Why did you have me change?" asked Stella.

"Your Hyde form is too slow to outrun that. I wasn't sure if even your Hyde could withstand a bite from that thing."

Stella glanced down at the T. rex and slowly nodded. "How do we kill something like that?"

"Technically it is already dead," Stella glared at me, and I added, "but I get your point. Theoretically, it should be the same as taking down any other zombie: we cut off its head or burn it. We just need an eight-foot machete or a big ass flamethrower . . ." I tossed the suggestion out jokingly.

Liv and Bree had reached the far side of the parking lot and the T. rex was charging after them. I had no clue how to stop this thing but seeing the houses and apartments behind Liv and Bree, I knew we had to at least keep it contained to the parking lot.

I opened a channel to Liv, *"Liv, let Bree know I need the two of you to play tag with this thing. Keep it in the parking lot."*

"Roger."

The police cruisers at each intersection at the ends of the parking lot had wisely got back in their cars and were laying rubber to get out of there. I assumed they would widen the perimeter to keep civilians and traffic out of the area. They would also report what they'd seen, so at some point, EIRT or even GRC13 would arrive, but that would take time that we didn't have.

"Zack?" asked Stella, pulling me from my thoughts. "Can you get Blue to open a portal for me?"

"Sure, why?"

"I have an idea but need some things from the lab."

I thought about asking more but I watched Bree narrowly miss getting turned into a T. rex snack and decided she and Liv needed help.

I called Blue and had her open a portal. I flew us behind the coffee shop and landed. The ground shook a bit as the T. rex headed towards us in hot pursuit of Bree and Liv.

The moment Stella disappeared into the shadows, I launched myself into the air. I opened a channel to 911. The moment the operator came on the line, I gave my hero ID and the description of the van, including its license plate number. I explained that it was occupied by a lich and two vampires who were responsible for the death of a Hamilton police officer. I warned them not to stop the van if spotted but to follow and wait for SWAT or EIRT. Before the operator could even respond to that, I ended the call.

I flew towards the T. rex to assist Bree and Liv. I called on my Electrical powers and tossed a powerful blast of lightning at Barney the Unfriendly Dinosaur.

To my surprise, the lightning stopped it in its tracks, and it shook a bit as the voltage poured through its massive frame.

The moment the lightning ended, though, it roared, and its eyes tracked me. I pushed some air under me and not a moment too soon, as the freaking thing actually leaped up at me. I tucked my legs up as its jaws slammed shut less than a foot below me. The loud snapping sound as its jaws crashed together left no doubt about the power they possessed. My armor was supposed to be fang- and claw-resistant, but I was pretty sure forty-foot-long dinosaurs weren't covered.

The law of gravity kicked in and Barney was pulled back to Earth.

The pavement buckled under its weight as it landed, and it let out another ear-shattering roar at me.

A sharp whistle cut the air the moment the roar ended. Both Barney and I looked to the far end of the lot.

Liv stood there with a big grin on her face. She brought her hands up to her chest and started waving them around like they were short little arms and said, "Look at me, I'm a T. rex *Growl, roar.*"

I face-palmed at Liv's antics but it worked and the zombie T. rex roared and began charging towards her.

My concern grew as Liv continued stomping around, laughing and waving her hands as the undead dinosaur closed on her position. Only Liv could ignore Odin-only-knew how many tons of T. rex charging at her while she made fun of it.

I cursed and poured on the speed and readied another blast of lightning to save my undead comedian. I extended my hand to launch a blast at Barney when Liv suddenly became aware of the threat and blurred off.

Barney roared but my lightning slammed home and cut it short. The zombie dinosaur stopped moving forward and shook slightly as the electricity poured through it. I banked away and headed back to the opposite end of the lot where Bree was now waiting.

The T. rex turned, and its tail shattered a window of the bakery at the far end of the plaza. It lumbered towards Bree, and she growled loudly at it.

For the next few minutes, the three of us kept up this deadly game of tag with Barney, but while we were keeping it contained to the parking lot, it was showing no signs of slowing. Worse, the lightning I was throwing around was seriously draining my power. I knew I couldn't keep this up for much longer.

Stella's voice came through on the comms. *"Blue and I have a plan. We are just about ready but need Liv to execute it. Blue has opened a portal behind the coffee shop."*

Liv was quicker in her response than I was and said, *"Roger."*

She blurred past Barney who was still charging at Bree, and she disappeared into the shadows. Bree started right and waited until the T. rex shifted its approach, and then cut hard left and sprinted around it.

The zombie T. rex skidded to a stop, turned, and ran after Bree.

I popped the hatch on my right arm and hit the red button for the built-in Taser. I moaned as its sweet juice flowed into me, boosting my lagging power levels. Normally, I avoided using these as to get replacement cartridges I had to fill out a report with the RCMP. They would determine if I used them in an emergency situation or not. If I had, they would issue a replacement. Today, though, I figured if a forty-foot-long zombie dinosaur didn't qualify, then nothing would.

The boost helped but ended way too soon for my liking. I was barely back up to half-power and needed more. I opened the hatch on my left arm and used my final boost.

Charged up, it was time to get back in the fight. I flew towards Barney and laid some lightning into him, which gave Bree the moment she needed to dodge around him and dash to the other end of the lot.

I pushed some Air under me to get out the T. rex's leaping range, banked around, and headed towards Bree.

I tried both Liv and Blue on the comms but got no response. I prayed that meant they'd be here soon.

Chapter 15

Thursday, October 13

Bree ducked under the snapping jaws of death, but it was so close that I was surprised that Barney didn't have Werepanther fur stuck in its teeth.

I exhaled in relief at the near miss. I hadn't shot lightning at the zombie T. rex this time, as I was running low on juice again. I had one, maybe two more blasts of lightning left, and then I'd be drained. My decision to withhold it this time had almost cost Bree her life.

I tried the comms again for the third time in as many minutes, but once again, I only got silence in response. I assumed that meant Blue, Liv, and Stella were at the underground lab, as reception there was extremely limited. I prayed they'd get here soon.

I flew after Barney who was chasing Bree to the far end of the lot again.

As the distance between them narrowed, I lashed out with another blast of lightning but cut back on the power to leave me just enough juice for one final blast. It was enough to stop Barney in his tracks and freeze him long enough for Bree to duck by him.

I banked around to fly after Bree and heard a loud engine noise echoing in the night sky. Out of the shadows of the coffee shop, Liv's new six-wheel beast emerged like a bat out of hell. It chewed up the grass and flattened a small sapling as it launched off the curb towards the parking lot.

Bree dove to the side as Liv laid on the air horn and rumbled by her, heading directly for Barney.

Barney roared in challenge and ran straight at Liv's truck.

I cursed and banked around, reaching the dinosaur ahead of Liv. I had no idea what Liv was up to playing chicken with the undead dinosaur but figured she could use help. Once again, I lashed out with lightning, which stopped Barney in its tracks.

Liv gained more speed with each passing second and I kept pouring lightning into the undead monster.

There was a horrific bang below me as Liv's new truck rammed into Barney's left leg just as I ran out of juice. The leg bone shattered like a tree getting hit by an artillery shell. Smoke and a bit of flame erupted from the now-crumpled front end of Liv's truck.

The momentum carried the truck deeper into the lot and Barney toppled over and crashed hard onto the pavement.

I'd have liked to seen more but I had my own problems. I was sixty feet off the ground and had almost no power left. As gravity started to pull me back down, I needed to do something fast. I spied a small tree off to my right. I reached deep and used the last wisps of my Air power to push me towards it.

I was pleased that I was now heading directly for said tree but knew this part was going to suck. Time seemed to slow down. All at once, I saw the tree coming, Liv's truck roll to a stop, Barney trying unsuccessfully to get back up with one leg, and even spotted Blue and Stella in her Hyde form appear out of the shadows.

Blue had Stella's homemade holy water cannon on her back with the nozzle pointed at Barney. The water cannon was made up of two nineteen-liter water cooler containers on a frame, a compressor, a battery to power the compressor, and a hose. It could shoot the water about thirty feet and had been useful against the demon we'd hunted months ago with GRC13.

I frowned. While holy water was great against demons, it wasn't ideal for the undead. To use holy water against the undead, you needed to have faith in God. I somehow doubted that our blue alien had strong Judeo-Christian beliefs. Her absence of faith meant she would just be hosing Barney down with plain old water, which would be like throwing spitballs at him.

My internal debate about the value of holy water used by a crazy blue alien came to a crashing halt as I impacted the tree.

The next few seconds were a blur of pain as I snapped and bounced off tree limbs before landing with a solid thump on my back in the grass at the base of the tree. I may have blacked out for a moment.

I groaned as I came to. I could taste blood in my mouth and throat, which I assumed was from having bitten my tongue at some point. It could also have been from my nose which throbbed. I'm pretty sure it was the impact of my nose into my faceplate that caused me to blackout temporarily and now had me seeing stars.

Slowly everything started coming back to me. Lying prone while there was a forty-foot man-eating zombie dinosaur lurking probably wasn't the best plan. As much as I desperately wanted to get back on my feet, I wasn't even sure that was possible. I did a quick check to see which parts of my body were still working. Being able to wiggle my toes and fingers was a good sign that I seemed to be in one piece, but I was pretty sure I was bruised everywhere.

I cursed in pain as I rolled over and used my arms and legs to get up on all fours and then to a kneeling position.

A soft *whoosh* and a bright light to my left caught my attention. I glanced over to see Blue holding her ignited Keetiyatomi blade near the nozzle of the water cannon, which was now spraying liquid fire out over the prone zombie dinosaur.

Barney roared as the flames coated his skull and upper body.

In my dazed state, it took me a moment to comprehend what was happening. I was puzzled how holy water was flammable and then realized it wasn't holy water that was in the tanks but gas or some other combustible fluid. Stella had taken my semi-humorous suggestion of a flamethrower to heart.

The door to Olivia's wrecked truck opened and she got out and seemed to be in one piece. She shook her head sadly as she walked around the front of the vehicle and surveyed the damage. I was no mechanic but even I could tell the thing was a total write-off.

The zombie T. rex let out another angry roar, but it seemed to lack the intensity of its previous ones. Liv looked over at the flaming dinosaur with a concerned expression. She blurred off in a wide circle, avoiding the growing fire.

Bree and Liv appeared beside me and helped me to my feet. We stood there and watched Blue hose down Barney with a steady stream of fire.

About a minute later, trouble started as the nozzle to the improvised flamethrower had caught alight and the flames began travelling up the outside of the hose. Blue said something to Stella, and Stella's Hyde form stepped closer and grabbed the tanks of the flamethrower. Blue hit the release button on the chest straps of the device and yelled, "Clear!"

Stella heaved up the entire flamethrower and then tossed it towards Barney. Blue dove behind Stella and I suddenly realized we had an 'oh shit' moment on our hands.

Bree and I must have realized the danger at the same time, as we both tackled our flammable undead friend to the ground and covered her with our bodies.

I groaned as my bruised body hit the ground. I barely had time to release the sound before a large *kaboom* echoed in the air and the night sky briefly lit up like it was noon as the two fuel tanks exploded.

Bits of flaming debris and pieces of dinosaur bones rained down on us a few moments later. I groaned when Bree's paws slapped down on my armor as she attempted to put out the small bits of fire clinging to me. The moment she stopped, I did the same thing for her.

I blinked at the smoldering T. rex tooth lodged point-first into the ground beside me. Bree got to her feet and helped Liv up. The two of them then hauled me to my feet.

Blue stood and dusted herself off behind Stella's slightly charred Hyde form.

There was a small blackened crater where Barney had fallen. Just behind that were the charred remains of its lower half and tail. Of the upper body and head, there was no sign.

There were small fires all around us but none of them seemed that serious. I'd barely finished that thought when another explosion went off at the end of the lot. Liv's truck lifted itself into the air by a good six feet and then crashed back to Earth.

The blast shattered any remaining intact windows in the plaza and then the blast wave hit us and knocked me clean off my feet.

I hit the ground hard enough to knock the wind out of me. As I lay there gasping for breath, a flaming coffin arced overhead and came down with a small crash on King Street.

Liv sighed beside me and said, "Well, there goes my good driver discount."

From my position on the ground, I took stock of our situation. We were all battered and bruised, and we'd lost the lich, but stopped a zombie T. rex. I wasn't sure if that was a win or not, but we were all alive, so I'd take it.

***

Twenty minutes later, I was standing with Blue outside Marion's apartment. She opened the door and was wearing a pink bathrobe and tie-dyed bunny slippers. Her normally braided silver hair was loose, and I'd guessed we'd caught her just as she was getting ready for bed.

Marion looked at me through her glasses, which made her eyes look huge, and said, "Sorry, robot repair is the next apartment down."

"Har, har. It's me, let me in," I said.

Marion nodded and stepped back. Blue helped me into the apartment and put me on the couch and said, "Call me when you need transport. I am going to return to the crime scene and assist Stella and Liv with law enforcement."

I nodded and winced at even that small movement.

Blue left me to Marion's care. I popped the faceplate to my helmet and Marion shook her head at me. "You look like a cross between a boxer and a raccoon."

I pondered that for a second and realized she was referring to my broken nose and probably my two very black eyes. I didn't reply.

Marion helped me get my armor off which was in surprisingly good condition, all things considered. Grundy's might be expensive, but they built things to last.

Once I was armor-free, I sat back down on Marion's orange couch while she examined me.

"Do I want to know what happened?" she asked. I groaned as she found that my right pinkie was broken.

The sad thing was I didn't even remember breaking it. "We were hunting a creature of legend that has been murdering people with Russian ancestry. It's looking for a piece of a magical artifact that can turn day into night. We confronted the creature at a strip plaza in Westdale and it summoned a zombie T. rex. We beat the T. rex by using a vehicle from *Mad Max* to run it down and then torched it with a homemade flamethrower that exploded, which caused the vehicle to blow up as well. Oh, before that happened, I ran out of juice sixty feet in the air and saved myself by falling into a tree, which kindly broke my fall by bruising every part of me on the way down."

Marion numbed the area on my hand and reset the finger before using her powers to heal it and said, "If you don't want to tell me, don't; you don't have to make up crazy stories."

I was going to argue that I wasn't telling stories but just said, "Blue got carried away with her training exercises again."

Marion nodded in satisfaction and began working on fixing my face. "See, was that so hard?"

***

Blue took me back to the plaza thirty minutes later, healed and pain free, but not before we made a stop at our secret lab. I wolfed down some much-needed food, which, thanks to Marion's healing, my body was begging for. I also got a solid ten minutes up between the Tesla coils to recharge enough of my power so that I wasn't running on empty. My body was also looking for sleep, but I knew that wasn't happening anytime soon and had to settle for filling a thermos with coffee.

EIRT, the Hamilton Police Department, and the Hamilton Fire Department were on scene when Blue and I arrived. The fire department was wrapping up after putting out the flaming remains of what had been Liv's new truck.

Stella was talking to a detective that I didn't recognize and there was an EIRT agent taking notes as well. The EIRT agent had no aura, so he wasn't Enhanced, but I was pretty sure he was one of the agents on Bobby Knight's team.

Liv was nowhere to be seen.

There was a news van parked off the nearby intersection of King Street and a cameraman and local reporter were filming the area, which now looked like a warzone rather than a quiet strip mall in Westdale. There was yellow police tape around the entire plaza.

Two EIRT agents and two uniformed Hamilton police officers stood in front of the door of the jewelry store.

Blue said, "Olivia is inside acting as the English Vampire Court's representative."

I nodded and Blue and I parted ways. She headed over to be with Stella and I made my way over to the front door of the jewelry store.

The downed officer was still on the ground beside his cruiser but now had a tarp covering his body. I was a bit surprised that both the officer's body and his cruiser were still in one piece after our battle with Barney. Crime scene techs were erecting a tent around the body as I walked past.

After getting some protective gear on, I headed inside. The plastic bags on my hands made carrying my thermos awkward, but there was no way I was surrendering it.

Just inside the door was a deceased man in a security uniform with his throat torn out. I noticed he had a blank expression on his face rather than the death scream expression the other victims had had. I assumed that this job had been rushed and that the vampire attack killed him outright, so the lich hadn't had time to drain his soul.

Detective Little and his partner were deeper inside the place as were Bobby and the mage. Liv was there, too, but was spending her time eying all the display cases. I made a mental note to warn her about taking souvenirs and joined the rest near the other body.

This victim was in her mid-forties, well dressed and groomed. She was tied to a chair but had minimal facial bruising. Her head was tilted back, and her perfect white teeth were displayed, as her mouth was open in a final scream. She had a deep neck wound but only on one side, which meant that only one vampire had fed from her and not both. The lack of damage to her face also showed that the lich rushed this job and they hadn't interrogated her anywhere near as long as the others.

It was a small comfort that she hadn't suffered as long, but I'd been hoping that we'd get lucky and there wouldn't be a victim in here at all. Instead, I had two victims and a dead police officer. My anger grew. We'd had the lich right here and let him get away. I took a deep breath, and corrected myself. We hadn't exactly let him get away; it was more like we'd been forced to make an impossible choice. The zombie T. rex would have killed a lot of people if we hadn't taken it down and had gone after the lich instead.

I could have gone after the van by myself and had my team deal with the T. rex, but that plan wasn't practical either. The lich had gone through my entire team with ease; me going after him solo would have been suicide.

I couldn't change the past and focused on dealing with the here and now.

The other disappointment of the evening was that even though both Alteea and I filmed the encounter, neither of us had a picture of the lich. Where he had been standing just showed up as a blurred image on the recordings. At least all five of us had witnessed him. The fact that he'd summoned a freaking dinosaur might add more weight to our case too.

I moved closer to Detective Little, "My condolences on the loss of a fine officer. Any idea what happened?"

"He radioed in that he might have a possible sighting of the redheaded vampire. I listened to that recording from dispatch and by his tone, he didn't sound very confident. I assumed he must have pulled into the lot and gotten out of the car to take a closer look. He was attacked by the vampire the moment he left his vehicle."

"The officer looked young; had he been with the force long?"

Detective Little shook his head, "Less than a year."

I mentally winced at that. A rookie cop made sense. Likely anxious to earn points but not confident enough to trust his gut. A veteran probably would have waited until backup arrived before taking a closer look to see if they'd been right or not. "Any sightings of the van?"

He frowned at that. "A patrol car got a sighting on Main Street near the core, but his car got hit by a spell that completely shut everything down. It was like something drained all the power out of it. No engine power, no communications, even his personal cell was dead. By the time he found a phone at a local business to call it in, the van was long gone. The plate also came back stolen. It was taken from a rental car place last Friday."

I mentally sighed, as I'd been hoping that the police might have been able to spot and follow the van back to wherever the lich's lair was. Main Street was a one-way street by the core and that meant they were fleeing east. Stella's crime and odd-incident map were denser in the eastern part of the city, which fit with the direction they were heading, but that was still a lot of territory to cover. We were narrowing its location down, but the cost of that information was getting way too high.

I thanked the detective for his help and made eye contact with Bobby. He pointed to the back area of the store, and we headed over with his mage in tow.

"We are dealing with a lich. My entire team witnessed it."

The mage, to my surprise, slowly nodded his head. "I saw the footage of the zombie T. rex; no necromancer is powerful enough to summon something like that in such a short period of time. The lack of a clear image of the lich in your videos also sealed it for me."

I blinked at that. "The *lack* of an image?"

"There are spells that can be used to mess up electronics and blur or distort a person's image, but they are tricky and have limited range. Your video was taken from about twenty feet away and that should be about the maximum range of a distortion spell. However, your drone video was easily fifty feet away and that was blurred too. We just got in some footage from a bank on the other side of the street on the far corner, and the image of the creature was distorted there too. That is over a hundred feet away. A spell like that shouldn't even be possible."

For a brief moment, the drone comment threw me, but I realized he was talking about Alteea's footage. The drone, though, was a good idea, and I made a mental note to get one to help disguise Alteea's presence.

"So does that mean we'll have a GRC13 team on standby to deal with the lich?"

The mage shook his head. "Normally you would, but we got an alert yesterday that one of the two GRC13 teams has been deployed out west. There were no details about why, but I have to assume that it is something big. That leaves them with one team. With the prime minister's office and the Mint in Ottawa, they are going to be reluctant to pull that other team away from the capital."

I was going to ask what could be more dangerous than a lich but stopped myself. I had a lot of respect for Acting Director Cooper, and he would have been the one to make that call. In hopes of ever being able to sleep again, I didn't want to know what GRC13 was dealing with out west.

The irony of his statement was that we were one of the reasons they'd be hesitant to pull GRC13 away from the Mint. Until we'd robbed it, it hadn't been successfully robbed since the nineties. "So, we have a 400-year-old lich that is trying to assemble a major magic artifact of untold power and we're on our own? That's just great."

"I didn't say that. If I had to guess, they will probably assign a couple of EIRT teams to the area. GRC13 also has a reserve group of agents and I suspect a couple of them will join the EIRT teams to bolster their rosters. I will make my report and we'll see what happens. I'm also going to file a report with the Mages Council. They, too, might be able to send some people in to help."

I felt a bit better at that. "The good news is that Stella and Blue interviewed the owner here earlier today. She didn't recognize the picture they showed her of the headpiece which, unless she was lying to us, means the lich is still missing the final piece to the Staff of Darkness."

We chatted for a bit more and by the end, the mage promised to keep me informed about any extra resources that would be shifted to this case. Bobby also cut a bounty claim tag number for Barney the Undead Dinosaur.

I asked Bobby if he could speed up the review for my replacement Taser cartridges. The idea of being without a backup power reserve while confronting the lich again didn't sit well with me. To my surprise, he had me follow him out to one of the two EIRT SUVs. He popped the back hatch and opened a black case. He fished out two cartridges and handed them to me. "I'll need the two spent ones, and I'll handle the paperwork."

I removed the old ones and installed the replacements at the same time. "Thanks, Bobby. I really appreciate this."

"No problem. With a lich out there, it's all hands on deck."

An hour later, we were done at the crime scene, except for Olivia and Alteea who would stay until dawn in case any of the victims were reborn as vampires.

The rest of the team gathered at home in the office. The mood in the room was somber. Everyone was down about letting the lich get away. I needed to change that. "Look, I know tonight could have gone better, but it wasn't a total loss. We saved a lot of lives tonight; if that zombie T. rex had gotten out of the parking lot and began traipsing around the city, the death toll would have been horrific. Also, I have no idea what the bounty is on a zombie dinosaur, but I suspect it will be a good-sized one."

Blue and Stella perked up a bit at that last part and I continued, "We also provided enough proof to EIRT that they are convinced a lich is present in the city and they'll be shifting more resources to help stop it."

Stella frowned. "Does that mean they are taking over the case and we've lost our shot at the bounty on the lich?"

I shook my head. "No. I suspect that this will work the same way as it did when we worked with GRC13 to take down the demon. Law enforcement can't claim a bounty. So, if we spot the lich, we can call it in, wait for their assistance and take it down together, which means we can still claim the bounty."

Stella smiled at that, and the Blue said, "It might not be in our best interest to work with EIRT."

Now it was my turn to frown. "Why's that?"

"When you were discussing liches the other evening at dinner, you mentioned that the last two were taken down by cannon fire and artillery. It seems that liches are not that aware of modern firepower. I still have a Javelin Anti-Tank Missile in my inventory . . ."

My gut knotted at the pointy-toothed grin Blue flashed as she finished. I rubbed my temples as I felt a headache coming on. Normally, I had a firm no-rocket-launcher rule with Blue, but the situation was dire enough that I was strongly considering allowing her to use it.

The lich's energy shield had protected it from my lightning attack. That shield spell was our biggest issue; if we couldn't crack it, the lich would be able to just stand and cast spells at will, and we were going to be toast.

Blue's missile might be enough to shatter that shield and give us a chance to bring it down. Even if the missile didn't break the shield, the sheer force of its impact and explosion would at least knock the lich back or off its feet.

The issue was if we were caught using it, we'd be looking at criminal charges. Using the missile would create a nightmare of a shit storm, but if that's what it took to take this thing down, I owed it to Charlie to do just that.

I exhaled and said, "If we are in an unpopulated area, and you can get a clear shot, do it."

Bree's ice blue eyes went wide at that, and Blue's smile got even bigger.

Chapter 16

Friday, October 14

The next day turned out to be another overcast dull fall day that made it hard to get motivated. Despite the gloomy day, Stella, Blue, and I were productive and eliminated another twenty businesses off our list. Once again, none of the business owners had any knowledge of the headpiece to the Staff of Darkness.

The whole business list was looking more and more like a waste of time. Today's businesses were in the Stoney Creek, Ancaster, and Dundas subdivisions of Hamilton. The remaining eighteen businesses on the list were all on Hamilton Mountain. I wasn't holding out much hope on those, as none of the increased crime or odd incidents had been in that area, which meant the lich hadn't been even remotely near there.

Stella and I had wrapped up our canvassing for the day and just arrived home when my phone rang. The caller came up as B. Stanley.

"Hey, Brock, what's up?" Brock was a powerful Earth elemental and member of my foundation. I'd been expecting a call from him.

"Zack, I'm the proud father of a healthy baby girl."

I was ashamed to admit that my first reaction was one of disappointment, as I'd been hoping to pull Brock's Earth elemental talents into our fight with the lich. Brock was the only veteran in my foundation and the only one of its members that I would have been comfortable bringing into the fight. My three Werewolf members were teens, and after losing Charlie to the lich, there was no way I was risking anyone that young. Blink, the remaining hero in my foundation was twenty, but his teleport power would be of limited use against the lich, so I'd written off his involvement too. "Congrats! I thought Megan wasn't due for another couple of weeks?"

"What can I say? My amazing wife is always an overachiever."

"That's great. Have you picked out a name?"

"Yup, Madison Charlie Stanley."

My eyes welled up the moment I heard the middle name. Brock and his wife were good people, and I was touched by their dedication to Charlie. *"That is a beautiful name for what I'm sure is a beautiful little girl."*

"Thanks. Megan and Madison are being kept overnight for observation but are expected to be released first thing tomorrow morning, so I should be good for the service tomorrow afternoon."

We chatted for a few more minutes and then I congratulated him again and ended the call.

Stella lifted a curious eyebrow at me, and I explained about Brock's new addition. When I told Stella the baby's name my voice cracked a bit but I kept it together.

We had time before Liv was up and we'd all have dinner together, so I made another call.

"Walter, any progress on the magic finding device?"

"I seriously underquoted on this project. It is much more challenging than I expected it to be. I'm making progress but need at least another day," said Walter, frustration evident in his tone.

I made the mistake of asking what snags he'd run into and spent the next five minutes listening to him rant about the issues. Half the things were complex magic matters that I barely understood. It reminded me of listening to Stella when she got into deep computer hacking discussions, as in both cases some phrases and terms were industry-specific and meaningless to me.

Once he was done with his rant, we ended the call.

I exhaled and hoped that Walter came through and had that device done by tomorrow. With the businesses leading nowhere, that device might be our only chance at stopping the lich.

Dinner that night turned out to be more drama, as Liv was in a foul mood.

"Stupid insurance company. They won't pay out for my truck because quote 'zombie dinosaurs aren't covered under my auto policy.' What is the point of paying insurance if when you need it, they don't pay?" said Liv in a huff.

While I, too, wasn't a huge fan of insurance companies, I didn't think purposely driving your vehicle into a forty-foot-long prehistoric monster was something that they should be expected to pay out on. "Call Bobby after dinner. The damages might be covered by the Emergency Enhanced Damage Fund. If they aren't, the bounty on

Barney should be easily large enough to cover the cost of replacing your vehicle."

Stella nodded and added, "We'll be able to expense the damages as a tax write-off."

Liv cheered up at that, and I asked, "Are you going to replace it with the same model?"

Liv shrugged. "Not sure. While I liked having a mobile bed, it lacked the speed of my old car. I was thinking that a sport bike might be fun."

The idea of Liv on some high-end motorcycle with the type of acceleration and speed one of those things was capable of was terrifying. My mind being what it was, I suddenly got an image of Olivia in formfitting motorcycle leathers, and a part of me warmed up more to the whole bike thing.

Unfortunately, Bree poured cold water on my hot biker chick fantasy. "Um, you know it's October and we are only a month or so away from snow being on the ground."

"If I get a payout for the truck, the money will easily be enough to cover a bike and something with a roof to get through winter."

I tuned Bree and Liv out as they started kicking around car ideas.

My thoughts turned back toward how we were going to hunt this thing down. Bree and I were planning on going out on patrol again tonight. Extending our patrol to Westdale would more than double the territory we'd previously covered. I wondered why the lich had strayed so far from his prior hunting ground. There were still plenty of Russian-owned businesses in the core, so lack of targets couldn't have been the reason.

The more I thought about it, the more I realized that there were too many variables in the equation to come up with an answer on why the attack occurred in Westdale.

I changed my focus from how to find the lich to what we'd do once we did. He'd dealt with my team like we were nothing last night. That shield spell around him was our biggest issue. While I'd approved Blue using her rocket launcher if we were in a relatively unpopulated area, the chances were that we wouldn't be. That meant we needed another way to take that shield down. The only two ideas that came to mind were having me hit it with enough lightning that I overpowered it and made it collapse or Blue striking it with her magic blade.

It hit me that trying to solve this problem on my own wasn't the best solution. Stella was easily the smartest person on the team and Blue was no slouch either. I shared my concerns about the lich with them and my two ideas about taking down the shield.

I smiled as Stella tugged on one of her braids and got a faraway look on her face, Blue's tail began moving in short sharp motions behind her, which meant both of them were thinking of solutions. I had faith that between the two of them they'd come up with something, I just hoped it would be in time.

***

Bree and I had been patrolling for a couple of hours when a call came in from Detective Little.

"Hurricane, we have another victim. A Red Line cab driver."

I cursed to myself and said, "When and where?"

"Within the last hour. An abandoned lot in the north end."

"What's the address?"

Detective Little gave me the address and I told him that we'd be there soon and ended the call. Bree and I were over in Westdale at the moment which put the crime scene a fair distance away from us. I called Blue and had her open a portal nearby.

Less than three minutes later, Liv, Alteea, and I stepped out of the shadows behind an old rusty shipping container on the abandoned lot. I gritted my teeth as I immediately felt the lich's lingering aura of fear and death. I shook my head at Liv who seemed bored more than anything, and I envied her lack of awareness of the dread-filled shroud around us. I left Bree at home for that very reason, as there was no need to subject her to this.

The lot was fenced in and empty, other than the shipping container beside us and three more up against the west side opposite us. I could just make out the foundation lines to whatever building had originally been there. I assumed the old building had probably been condemned and demolished.

To our south, there was a parked Red Line cab with detectives and a bunch of EIRT agents around it. By the number of EIRT agents, I could tell there were more than two teams onsite. The cab was on the other side of the fence where a small part of the lot had been carved out as a front entrance. Yellow police tape was already around the entire front area.

I spotted three auras among the EIRT agents. The first was a multicolored one that I recognized as Mac's, the mage on Bobby's team. The second aura had a purple core with a brown and silver outline and was a good six inches in size, which meant an experienced Werewolf. I cursed at the shifter being a part of the group. The Werewolf would be able to smell and hear Alteea, which meant her glamor here was useless.

I opened a channel on the comms to Blue. *"Open another portal. I'm sending Alteea home. One of the agents on site is a Werewolf."*

"Roger that."

As Alteea disappeared into the shadows, I continued studying the group of EIRT agents at the crime scene. The last aura was the biggest surprise, as it was bright red, which meant Fire elemental. This close, I should have been able to sense it before even seeing it. I closed my eyes and nodded as under the overwhelming fear and dread around me I could just detect the Fire elemental's presence.

The aura around the Fire elemental was a good seven or eight inches in size, which meant this was one of the more powerful elementals I'd ever encountered.

I assumed that I was looking at the improvised team that Mac had mentioned was filling in for GRC13. A mage, a Werewolf, and a Fire elemental were pretty decent choices for going up against a lich. I wasn't feeling so bad now about not having Brock's Earth elemental talents to use.

I used my Air power to lift Liv and myself into the air. I put us down just outside of the yellow police tape. Bobby came over and lifted the tape to let us through.

The moment we stepped onto the scene, the Fire elemental came over like he was on a mission. His expression of almost pure rage took me aback and I wondered what I'd done to deserve that look. He was wearing an EIRT vest but on his sleeve was a GRC13 patch. The patch marked him as a member or a reserve member of GRC13. All GRC13 members had a rank of lieutenant, other than GRC13 team leaders, who were captains. That meant the Fire elemental was the ranking federal agent on scene. I also spotted a name patch on his vest that read, 'Chambers.'

"Sergeant, why are you letting civilians on my crime scene?" the elemental asked through clenched teeth.

The nice thing about wearing a helmet with a face shield was that the angry elemental couldn't see my eye roll.

Bobby said, "The Hurricane and Miss Dick are here as the English Vampire Court's official representatives and, therefore, have full access to this scene and all files pertaining to the investigation."

Olivia frowned at Bobby using her last name. The last name wasn't one she was born with, more like reborn with. As a favor to Stella, the English Vampire Court had created new identities for both her and Bree after they'd been turned into a vampire and Werepanther respectively. Sarah, the English Court's enforcer, and Elizabeth's right hand, had picked the last names. Sarah and Liv got on like oil and water, and the last name Sarah assigned to her was just another shot in the ongoing cold war between them.

The Fire elemental stood there gaping like a fish out of water. The angry shade of pink of his face darkened further.

After a good ten seconds, he turned and stomped off, barking orders at other EIRT agents who all suddenly tried to look busy.

I opened my faceplate and leaned into Bobby and asked, "What is his problem?"

Bobby, in a soft voice, said, "He was the active Enhanced GRC13 agent on scene when you and your team robbed the Royal Canadian Mint."

I groaned at his answer. During our case against the Acolytes, Bree had been kidnapped by them, and they used her as leverage to force us to rob the Mint. In the end, we took down the Acolytes, recovered and returned the gold we'd stole, and were cleared of all charges. That said, I'm sure being the Enhanced agent on scene while we stole the gold out from under him hadn't done wonders for Agent Chambers' career.

Bobby handed us some protective gear and we headed over to the cab. Detective Little and his partner were there examining the body in the open trunk of the cab.

I greeted both of them and asked Detective Little for the details as I looked over the body in the trunk. The victim was an older man in fairly good shape. Bald with a thick dark-dyed mustache. He was on his side in the trunk facing towards us. His head was tilted back, and his mouth was open in the familiar last scream of agony that we'd seen on the faces of the other victims. His throat had a large wound where a vampire had fed, and I spotted the barest hint of a similar matching wound on the other side of his neck but with his position, it was hard to tell. I assumed both vampires had fed. His hands were tied behind his back.

"Lev Pavlov, 63. Red Line dispatch got a call from him at 8:03 p.m. He said he was going offline for thirty minutes. A driver will go offline if he's grabbing a bite to eat or taking a break. More often than not, it means that they are doing private fare off-book. We think that is what happened here. We asked for his phone records to confirm that but probably won't get them until tomorrow at the earliest."

I nodded and Detective Little continued, "We believe his cab was hit by the same spell that drained one of our patrol cruisers the other night on Main Street, as everything in the cab was dead. No power, the engine won't turn over, and even his cellphone is drained and won't power on."

Cabs were a favorite target for robberies, as the drivers usually carried cash. Due to this, licensed cabs had many anti-theft and emergency features. A single button in the cab would send out a distress signal, activate a flashing yellow light on the back trunk of the cab to indicate the driver was in trouble, and a camera in the front of the cab recorded the interior. The draining spell would eliminate all of those measures.

"We think he pulled into the lot. The lich and his crew pulled in behind him, cast the spell, and boxed him in with their vehicle. At that point, they pulled him out of the cab, tied his hands, and sat him on the back bumper while they interrogated him."

Detective Little pointed at the blood spatter on the pavement and continued, "Once they were done questioning, they killed him and stuffed him in the trunk, closed it, and left. We have no witnesses. Officers are canvassing the neighborhood, but . . ."

He let that last part hang and after one look around it was obvious why. The area was made up of empty industrial lots and warehouses. The place was like a ghost town. If we'd encountered the lich on this lot, I'd green light Blue's rocket launcher.

I nodded and a thought occurred to me. "The lich has been hitting business owners, why change to a cab driver?"

"He is technically a business owner. He owns the license medallion for this cab, and the cab itself. He is self-employed and is just under contract with Red Line."

I mentally groaned at his answer. We'd been defining business owners as those who leased or owned retail space, as that's where all the previous attacks had occurred. Self-employed business owners expanded our definition substantially. Real Estate agents, tradespeople, computer consultants, consultants in general, and many more fit this extended list. I'd been hoping to narrow down targets for the lich, but this new information easily quadrupled our existing list.

Detective Little's voice pulled me from my thoughts. "The coroner and the crime scene techs will be here shortly. As this is an outdoor environment, they will probably take photos and document the scene quickly and then move the body the moment they are done. Olivia will probably spend the rest of the evening at the morgue."

I gave Liv a questioning glance and she shrugged and said, "Better than standing in this lot all night."

I wondered why they weren't keeping the body on site until dawn as they'd done with the others but remembered that rain was expected later this evening. Being indoors also made things less risky for Liv as she needed to stay with the victim in case he rose as a vampire. At least this way if Blue was delayed, Liv wouldn't be in direct sunlight.

I thanked Detective Little for his help and gave the body one last look over before joining Bobby and Mac who were standing off to the side on their own.

Mac the mage said, "They've assigned our team and another EIRT team to the case full-time. Agent Chambers and a two-man GRC13 sniper team are also part of the group. The Mage's Council is also sending some equipment to me to help. It should arrive first thing tomorrow."

The equipment part of his statement puzzled me. "What type of equipment?"

"Three dispelling grenades. They work on magic like an EMP device does with electronics. When one of these grenades goes off, any active magic within a thirty-foot radius of the blast is cleared."

My excitement grew at that. Those grenades would wipe out the lich's energy shield, which would give us a shot at the lich itself.

The enthusiasm must have been displayed on my face as Mac added, "They are useful but limited. They are only good against active magic, so wards, runes, and other passive magic devices aren't affected. They also don't stop the lich from casting new spells the moment the blast has finished. We also are only getting three, so we need to make each one count."

"How long does the blast last?" I asked.

"Three to five seconds."

That wasn't much time. We'd need to strike almost the moment the dispelling grenade went off. "You mentioned a blast. Is that a figure of speech or is there actually an explosion when one of these things goes off?"

"Figure of speech. They go off with a small popping noise, which is all non-magic users will notice. To a mage, or a lich, in this case, they will be temporarily disoriented for a second or two as they adjust to the lack of magic around them."

I liked his answer. We could work with these grenades, and they might just be the edge we needed to take the lich down. I made a mental note to mention them to the rest of the team.

I spent a few more minutes chatting with Bobby and Mac. I found out the EIRT teams were working out of the central police station and staying at a downtown hotel. That information would be useful if we came across the lich, as we could use Blue's shadow traveling abilities to get them onsite quickly.

Bobby and Mac were called away by another EIRT agent, which left me on my own. There wasn't much more for me to do here.

My gaze fell on Agent Chambers and his bright red aura, and I pondered what to do about him. A Fire elemental was an amazing asset to have because fire was a very effective way to deal with the undead. The problem was his hostility towards me and my team meant that cooperation was going to be difficult.

I strongly suspected that if they came across the lich, we wouldn't get a courtesy call to assist with the takedown. I also worried that if we called this improvised GRC13 team for assistance, Agent Chambers would try to sideline us. Both of those were bad things. We were trying to take down a very dangerous creature; not hitting it with everything we had would cost lives.

I needed to clear the air with Agent Chambers or get him removed from the leadership role. "Agent Chambers, can I have a word in private please?"

He glanced over at me and shook his head. "I have nothing to say to you."

I mentally sighed at his answer. "You can either talk with me now, or we can have this conversation later with Acting Director Cooper involved, your choice."

I hadn't wanted to name drop but we needed to get this resolved. I cringed at the number of EIRT agents who were covertly staring at Agent Chambers and the look of concern and anger that appeared on his face. He nodded and stomped over to me.

He stopped a few feet from me and said, through gritted teeth, "Talk."

My concern grew when I saw the small flames dripping from his fingertips. He followed my glance down and exhaled as if centering himself and the fire stopped. My visor was recording video, but as my faceplate was up, the video would just be of the night sky, but all I needed was the audio portion of this conversation. I took a deep breath and said, "I'm sorry for the difficulties the heist at the Mint may have caused you and your career."

He seemed to be a bit taken aback at that and I continued, "We can't change the past, but we can make things better for the future. There is a lich lurking out there and leaving a trail of innocent victims in its wake. Taking it down is going to require all of us to work together, and I need to know if I can count on you going forward."

He stood straighter and said, "My team will deal with the lich. We don't need civilians getting in the way."

I sighed and shook my head. "Wrong answer. GRC13 doesn't recruit stupid people, so check your emotions and start using your brain."

Agent Chambers' face darkened at that, and he was about to speak, but I held up a hand to cut him off and continued, "In the last year, my team has taken down a full demon, the Master, and the Rose. We have worked with GRC13 on multiple occasions. We trained against Dmitri's team when he was rebuilding it after the losses inflicted against it by the demon. My team beat Dmitri's team as often as we lost. If we can beat a full GRC13 team half the time, how do you think we'd do against your improvised team?"

He looked around at the agents off in the distance and his shoulders slumped. "What are you proposing?"

"That our teams work together to take down the lich. Full cooperation between us."

A look of disdain appeared on his face. "You just want the bounty. Typical."

"I don't give a fuck about the bounty. The lich killed a seventeen-year-old girl who was my friend. That girl was a hero who rushed in to save a couple that was being tortured by the lich and his two vampires. She died trying to save them."

Agent Chambers looked surprised by that and said, "I'm sorry for your loss and my comment about the bounty."

I nodded. "Thank you. So, can we work together?"

"Yes. How about we start over? I'm Doug," he said as held out his hand.

I shook it and said, "Zack."

"How's this going to work?"

"I have a few ideas . . ." I said and then the two of us went over details of how our teams would work together going forward. We spent the first ten minutes going over the logistics of working together from an overall case perspective and then twenty minutes quickly covering team tactics for dealing with the lich if we encountered it again.

At the very end, we exchanged contact information and I gave him the frequency of our comms so both teams could coordinate in the field. He said he'd be in touch and then excused himself to deal with the coroner who had just arrived on scene.

As he walked away, I hoped that I'd made the right decision and Doug would hold up his end of the bargain. A Fire elemental would be a strong ally against the lich, but if his grudge against me came up at the wrong time, it could be a disaster. I prayed that his commitment to GRC13 and their standard of professionalism would be enough to keep him in line.

Chapter 17

Saturday, October 15

Stella and Blue had gotten an early start and had eliminated eight more businesses off our initial list, leaving us with only ten left. After the attack on the cab driver, Stella and Blue had begun putting together a second list that consisted of self-employed business owners. Filling this second list with names was turning out to be a challenge, as it was harder to find them without an associated retail building. Stella had put a call in to the Russian community center to help fill out the list. They agreed to help but needed time to get the data.

Charlie's funeral service that afternoon had turned out to be a happier affair than I expected. A member of Charlie's high school baseball team spoke at the service and got a few laughs talking about Charlie and the team's antics. The place was packed. It wasn't just Charlie's friends and family that attended but also prominent members of the community, police officers, and people Charlie had saved or assisted during her short but productive hero career. The mayor and the chief of the Hamilton Police Department were in attendance. The mayor was also one of the speakers at the event, and while I wasn't a fan of his politics at times, his tribute to Charlie was touching and poignant.

All five members of my foundation attended too, including Brock. He looked happy but tired. His wife and new baby daughter were both resting at home.

The outpouring of support from the community made me proud to be a Hamiltonian. Hamilton at times got a bad rep as a tough blue-collar steel town. The truth was the people of Hamilton were tough, but they all had big hearts. They'd be the first to rally around a community member that was sick or having a hard time. Even if times were tough and they were struggling, they'd still find a way to donate a little bit or volunteer their time. Curveball had embodied that spirit and had been well-loved by the community.

By the end of the service, I was more determined than ever to take down the lich.

We'd just got all the foundation members home when my phone rang, and I saw Walter's name was on the display.

"The device is done, but there is a small problem; the best it can do is a half-kilometer range. I can keep working on it and try and boost the range, but that will take another couple of days."

At first, I wasn't too concerned about that, but then I realized that while the range was half of what Walter had quoted, it meant it would take four times as long for us to search the city. *"How confident are you that you can boost the range in a couple of days?"*

The line went quiet for a moment. *"This is more an art than a science, so while I feel fairly confident, I can't guarantee it."*

I weighed the pros and cons of having him keep working on the device and said, *"I'll take it now as is."*

"I'll be there within the hour."

We ended the call and I brought Stella and Blue up to speed on what was going on. Bree had already ditched us and was in the kitchen making herself a pre-dinner snack. I had no doubt that Bree heard every word of my conversation with Walter with her Were hearing.

"You made the right choice, Zack. Better to have the device now than to wait another couple of days, especially if the device might not be improved in that time," said Stella.

I nodded and hoped she was right.

Less than an hour later, Walter knocked on my door. He handed me something that looked like a battery tester with a wooden drumstick sticking out the top.

My lack of excitement over his handiwork must have shown on my face as he said, "Yeah, it won't win any awards for craftsmanship, but the important thing is that it works."

"How does it work?" I asked.

Walter moved closer and pointed to a switch on the base and said, "Turn on that button there. To use it, all you have to do is turn slowly in a circle. The indicator will swing to the right when it detects magic. How much it moves to the right determines how powerful the magic signature is. Try it out. I'm wearing a fairly powerful medallion that I borrowed from a fellow wizard."

I turned it on and did a slow circle as I watched the narrow indicator. Sure enough, when I pointed the device at Walter, the indicator jumped around halfway to the right and bobbed around. The indicator shot back to the left the moment I pointed it away from him.

"Look, I know I quoted a one-kilometer range and only delivered half that, but I put a lot of time and magic into that device, so I really don't want to discount the price. I seriously underestimated how much work was involved with this project."

We haggled over the new price and ended up at sixteen grand versus the original twenty he'd quoted. Neither of us was overly happy with our new agreement so that probably meant it was fair.

"The device has a brand-new battery in it and that should be good for months, as I don't believe it draws much power, but if it suddenly stops working, a new battery should fix it."

Walter then showed me where the hatch on the bottom was to change the battery. I thanked him and we said our goodbyes.

I joined Stella and Blue up in the office and showed them the magic-detecting device. I was anxious to get out now and start searching but Stella had other ideas and pointed at the grid lines she'd added to the map. "Hamilton is approximately twenty-five kilometers wide if we include Stoney Creek and Dundas and it's roughly fifteen kilometers deep from the harbor to Hamilton Mountain. That means we have 375 squares to search. Doing that one at a time is going to take a lot of time but I have a better idea."

"What idea is that?" I asked.

"We use the crime and odd-incident pins on the map to prioritize which squares we search first. The squares with the highest volume of pins are the first ones we search and work in descending order."

I pondered that and realized Stella had something here. We'd theorized that the lich's presence caused the uptick in crimes and odd incidents. It made sense that areas with the greatest number of pins likely meant he was close by. Hitting those areas first should speed up the search and certainly was better than trying to work through hundreds of locations in a block-by-block search. "Great idea, which ones have the most pins?"

Stella shook her head. "Look, Zack, I know you want to get started on this right away but give Blue and me the rest of the day to put together a list. We'll start first thing tomorrow morning on the search."

I wanted to argue but knew that Stella was right. Getting things organized would be a better use of our time. The sun would be down in an hour anyway. It would be safer if we found the lich's lair during the day, as that would eliminate his vampire companions and prevent him from calling any more zombies as well. "Fine, get the list together and I'll join you and Blue in the search first thing tomorrow."

***

After dinner, Bree and I took to the skies of Hamilton to patrol. It was a cool, crisp autumn night, and the clear sky was filled with stars. Between my resistance to cold from the minor amount of Ice elemental power I had in my blood and my armor, it was comfortable. Bree was also bundled up warmly and seemed to be having no issues.

An hour into our uneventful patrol, it dawned on me that Bree had been unusually quiet. "What's up?"

Bree blinked at me as if being pulled from deep thought and said, "Shawn called me this afternoon after the service."

Shawn Woods was the Alpha of the Barrie pack that Bree was a member of. The full moon was weeks away, so I was curious about why he was calling Bree. "Are he and the pack okay?"

"Yeah, they're fine. Great actually. Are you aware of the Were Alliance?"

The Were Alliance was an organization that all packs in North America were a part of. It came into being just after World War II when Enhanced Individuals were exposed to the world. Originally, it was just a loose association of packs that worked together to lobby for rights. Over the last few decades, its mandate had changed, and it became more formal. The group's goal shifted to improving the lives of Weres, dealing with rogue Weres, and acting as a court to settle disputes among the packs. "What about it?"

"For the last fifteen years, the Alliance has done annual anonymous surveys of all Weres in North America. The survey asks them about their pack life and their lives in general. The results are then tabulated to form a ranking of the packs from best to worst. The Barrie pack was rated one of the top five packs in North America."

"Hey! Congrats! I knew Shawn ran a tight ship. It's nice to see him and your pack get some well-deserved recognition."

Bree smiled. "It's more than that. Finishing top five means Shawn will be added to the Council of Eleven this year."

I lifted my eyebrow at that. The Council of Eleven was the group that ran the Alliance. It made Shawn one of the most powerful and influential Alphas in North America. A few of those Alphas would also attend the annual worldwide and secretive Master-Alpha summit between vampires and Weres. It was at one of those summits that was hosted in Canada that Liv and Bree got turned. They'd been hired as serving help for the event. The event had gotten heated and turned into a bloody brawl between some of the Masters and Alphas and Bree and Liv got attacked. I hoped that if Shawn did get to attend this year's summit, that it would be much more peaceful than that one had been.

Bree pulled me from my thoughts. "Being rated top five also comes with some responsibilities. One of those responsibilities is to send out delegations to visit the bottom twenty-five packs. Those delegations put together reports on how to improve on the packs they visit and submit them to the Council of Eleven for review. The idea is to raise the standards and living conditions in the lower-rated packs to make them more stable and enjoyable for members."

This was new information to me, but I liked what I was hearing. In the pack structure, the Alpha was like a king or queen in that his or her rule was absolute. With someone like Shawn, who was a fair and strong leader, this was beneficial for the pack. A bad or cruel Alpha, though, could make members' lives a living hell. The Alpha literally had the power of life or death over their members. They could make dominance duels to the death. An Alpha could also declare a member rogue, which was also a death sentence, as rogue Weres were a danger to everyone. Law enforcement let the Were packs manage their own affairs and were reluctant to get involved even in the worst cases. It was good to see the Alliance was trying to weed out these bad Alphas. "That seems like a worthy goal."

Bree nodded. "Shawn has asked me to be a member of our delegation. It is important that the delegations be as diverse as possible. As Sabina and I are the only two cat-type Weres in the pack, one of us has to go. Sabina has a course booked next month which is important to her medical career. Completing that course gets her a promotion and a major salary increase, so she has begged me to take her spot."

I sensed that I was missing something. "This sounds like a great learning opportunity for you. What am I missing?"

"The trip lasts for three months and leaves next Saturday."

That last part hit me like a hammer blow. It put a deadline on us taking down the lich or we'd be without Bree's services when we went after him. It also meant we'd be living without Bree for three months. Another thought occurred to me. "Have you talked to Liv about this?"

Bree shook her head and got a forlorn expression on her face. "No. Not yet. I was planning on talking to her about it tonight."

"I'm sure she'll take the news in a mature and thoughtful manner." I tried to say that with a straight face but couldn't and burst out laughing.

Bree chuckled at my comment as well.

When we both stopped laughing, I said, "What about you? Do you want to go on this trip?"

Bree shrugged. "I'm torn. Thanks to my extended Were lifespan, I'm going to be one for a long time. Learning more about Were culture can only be an advantage in that regard. I believe strongly in what the Alliance is trying to do to improve conditions for all Weres and helping the bottom packs get better is a major step towards that goal. I'd also like to travel and see more of this country and other places, so that too is a plus."

We reached the jewelry store in Westdale on our patrol route, so I banked around in the air and headed south to Main Street for the return leg of our journey. "I sense a 'but' coming . . ."

"Yeah. Now with the lich out there, it isn't a great time for me to be leaving. Liv is not going to be happy with me gone for three months. The Alliance pays each member of the delegation a weekly salary, but it is a pittance compared to what we make bounty hunting. I'm also a little nervous about what we might find."

I frowned at the last part. "What is there to be nervous about?"

"You know how badly run the Mississauga pack is, right?" I nodded and Bree added, "They were in the bottom half of the pack ratings but aren't one of the bottom twenty-five. That means the packs we are visiting are even worse than them."

"Are you concerned about your or the delegation's safety?"

Bree shook her head. "No. No Alpha is going to be stupid enough to attack or harm an Alliance delegation. The firestorm that would bring down on them would be insane. I'm more concerned that I will find pack members suffering and that I won't be able to do anything there and then to help them."

I smiled mentally at Bree's last concern. There was no doubt that Bree had the biggest heart on our team, and this was another example of that. "Look, Bree, that may be the case. Change takes time. At least your report will bring help at some point, which is better than no help at all."

Bree gave me a thoughtful look that let me know she was pondering my last statement. As much as I wanted Bree to stay, I knew this would be a great opportunity for her and something she should do. "Look, we have a week to take down the lich. That should be enough time; all of us want to take him down sooner than later or the body count is just going to keep rising. As for Liv, she'll get by without you around for three months. This might actually be a good thing for her."

Bree lifted a questioning eyebrow at me, and I added, "I sometimes wonder if Liv is doing enough to embrace her vampire nature and learn about her situation. Maybe some time apart from you and seeing you learning more about Were culture might inspire her to do the same." Bree gave me a slow nod and I added, "As for your last concern about the money over the next three months, the lich's bounty should leave us with enough cash that your lower earnings as a delegation member won't be a problem. Don't forget we'll also be getting payouts for the zombie dinosaur, the zombies from the cemetery, and the ghouls we took down as well."

Bree stayed deep in thought until we approached the downtown core and then said, "Are you really okay with me going on this trip?"

I exhaled and considered my words carefully. "I won't lie, I'll miss you and would prefer from a selfish perspective that you stayed here with us. That said, I think this is a worthy goal and a great learning experience for you. I also know that Sabina has been like a big sister to you and has done a lot for you since you joined the pack. Helping her out by taking her spot on this trip would be a nice way to repay her kindness to you."

Bree gave me a soft smile and went back to her thoughts.

As we continued hovering down Main Street looking for signs of the lich I got lost in my thoughts. Bree's departure put more of a hard deadline on taking down the lich. We had one week. I also figured that if the delegation was driving to each of the packs that we probably could push back Bree's departure a day or two if worst came to worst. We could use Blue's shadow traveling to get Bree to the first pack and that would still keep them on schedule.

Whether it was a week or a week and a bit, either way, we needed to take down this lich and do it soon.

Chapter 18

Sunday, October 16

Early the next morning, I found myself hovering in a slow circle with the magic detector in the center location of the first one-kilometer square that Stella had on her list.

It was a bright, cool sunny day and made a wonderful change from the dull overcast days we'd been having recently. The sunshine lifted my spirits, and I took it as a positive omen for our search for the lich.

The neighborhood was in the northeastern part of the city, and none of the homes I was seeing around me would be featured in *Better Homes and Gardens* anytime soon. Most of them were small War World II-era homes that sat on postage-sized lots that were crammed tightly together. Rusty chain-link fences and peeling paint seemed to be the popular look around here.

I completed my circle and was disappointed that the indicator hadn't so much as twitched. I double-checked that I'd turned it on and did another circle to be sure and got the same result.

One down, three hundred and seventy-four more squares to go, I thought with a mental sigh.

Stella and Blue had been busy last night and had built an extensive search list. For each entry, they had the number of crimes and odd incidents that occurred and had Googled the addresses nearest to the center of each kilometer square.

I opened a channel to Blue. *"No luck, flying to the next location."*

"Roger that."

The first twenty squares on Stella and Blue's list were all in the northeastern part of the city and it was quicker for me to fly to each one rather than Blue opening a portal back to home and then opening another one to the next location.

The second location was a bust like the first and the two areas were so similar that you could have swapped the houses around and nobody would have noticed.

The third location was similar to the others, but to my right, there were some three-story apartments. I turned in a circle and my heart beat faster as the indicator suddenly jumped three-quarters of the way to the right. Walter's borrowed medallion had only caused the indicator to move halfway, so there was some very powerful magic nearby.

"I've got a hit. Flying towards it now to narrow down its location."

"Roger."

The magic signature came from the direction of the apartments and I flew over towards them, keeping my eyes locked on the indicator.

It stayed fairly steady until I flew over one of the three-story apartments. I stopped in the air and slowly turned. The moment I was pointed back at the apartment, the indicator jumped back to the right. I spotted an address on the building and relayed that information back to Blue so she could spy on its interior from the shadows.

"Roger that, hold on."

While I waited for Blue, I checked out the building. It didn't look like anything special. These types of three-story walk-up apartments were pretty common in the city. I'd lived in a number of them during my hero days when I was hurting for cash.

I didn't think I was looking at the lich's hideout, as I hadn't felt the shroud of despair that would have indicated its presence. I was puzzled, though, about what could be producing that much magic. These apartments were usually occupied by low-income residents. Magic users were usually on the wealthier side, as magic services were always in demand. Powerful magic items were also of high value, which didn't fit with this building.

Blue's voice came over the comms and pulled me from my musings. *"The apartment building is not what it seems. The entire interior has been gutted and turned into a single residence. The first two floors are an upscale living area, but the third floor has been set up as a museum display of magic artifacts. There is no sign of the lich. The residence is occupied by an old man and his personal servant."*

My eyes widened at Blue's report. As a single residence, this place was huge. These apartment buildings usually had six apartments per floor, which meant eighteen units total. The owner must have some serious wealth. It was a bit odd that he was living in this area, but it didn't get us closer to the lich and while my curiosity was piqued, I didn't have time to investigate things further.

"Roger. Moving to the next address."

I took one very low and slow pass over the roof of the building, making sure I couldn't sense the lich, and then set a course for the next square on our search.

The next three search squares were a complete bust, and the indicator didn't so much as twitch when I did my circle. The seventh stop, though, yielded much more promising results. To my north were industrial areas and warehouses and to the south were more small wartime houses. I'd barely started my turn when the indicator jumped all the way to the right.

I glanced in the direction the indicator pointed and there was nothing there but worn or abandoned warehouses and empty industrial lots.

I frowned in confusion, as those areas didn't seem like a logical place for the amount of magic the detector was picking up, but then my hopes soared as I realized this sparsely populated area would be a perfect hiding spot for the lich.

"The detector just went off the scale. Flying towards where it's pointing."

"Roger that. Be careful."

I'd barely started moving forward when at the very edges of my mind I felt the aura of death, fear, and despair creep into my awareness. Oddly enough, that cloud of fear had the opposite effect on me and my excitement grew knowing I'd found the lich or at least a place where he'd been recently.

Directly in front of me was what looked like an abandoned warehouse. The few windows it had were boarded up, there was graffiti covering most of its grey walls, and there were No Trespassing signs on the tall rusty chain fence that ran around the property.

I gave the place a wide berth and circled around it. Once the warehouse was south of me, I lifted the detector again and smiled as the indicator jumped fully over to the right, confirming that the place was the center of the magic.

I kept my distance but did a slow lap around the warehouse to look for an address. I exhaled in disappointment when I completed my lap but couldn't spot a building number. Farther down the street was another warehouse and I flew towards it. This one had a building number on it. I relayed the address to Blue via the comms and told her the warehouse was the one south of it.

If the lich was in that warehouse, I didn't want to spook him. I flew farther back and landed on the roof of another warehouse in the area. From there I could just see the front of our target building.

Blue's voice came over the comms, *"I cannot access the shadows inside the warehouse."*

For a brief second, I was puzzled and then I smiled. "Same issue as the jewelry store?"

"Exactly the same. I can access shadows around the outside of the building but nothing on the lot or inside the building itself."

I fist-pumped at her answer and was now convinced that the lich was inside that warehouse. *"I'm east of the building on the roof of another warehouse, can you see me?"*

"Hold on."

Now that we knew where he was, my mind began considering how to take him down. It was just coming up on 9:00 a.m., which meant we had plenty of time until nightfall. My first instinct was to gather up Bree, Stella, and Blue and hit the warehouse immediately. We wouldn't have Liv's services but that put the lich's two vampires out of play as well.

When dealing with a magic user, the first rule was to never hit them on their home turf. I had no idea what type of protection spells or traps might be around that warehouse. The lich had dealt with us easily on neutral ground; hitting him in his lair would be suicide.

I briefly considered Blue's rocket launcher. The warehouse was fairly isolated and blowing it up, or at least a good portion of it, would probably take care of any wards, spells, or traps the lich had set. The snag was we had no idea what was inside the warehouse. The lich or the vampires could easily have some innocents imprisoned there for sustenance. If that was the case, not only would we be screwed for using a military-grade explosive device but we'd also be on the hook for manslaughter, if not murder, charges.

It suddenly dawned on me that I had other resources and we didn't have to do this alone.

"I have found your location."

"Can you open a portal nearby?"

"Yes. Proceed to the shadows on the west side of the air conditioning unit on the roof you are on. The portal will be open and waiting for you."

"Roger that."

I spotted the industrial-sized AC unit at the far end of the roof and headed for it and home.

***

An hour later, we and most of the entire EIRT taskforce were in our hangar in our secret underground lab in London, England.

We'd moved our modular training building out from the back wall of the hangar to the center of the room and used eight of its modules to represent a smaller-scale model of the warehouse.

At the front of the hangar, we'd set up a projector that was connected to the now-disconnected visor of my armor and was currently looping the video of my flybys of the warehouse. Stella and Blue and most of the EIRT team were studying it, looking for possible entry points and weaknesses.

Agent Chambers, Bobby, and I were off to the side studying the blueprints to the warehouse on Agent Chambers' laptop.

Bree and the EIRT Werewolf were in the main lab chowing down food to fuel their upcoming change.

Liv was at home in her daytime death trance, and we'd left Alteea with her. The Were on the EIRT team would have been able to detect Alteea and as we'd be fighting inside the warehouse, her presence to film things wasn't required.

The only missing member of the EIRT task force was Mac the Mage. He was currently being driven around the warehouse by a detective in an unmarked car. Mac was using passive spells that wouldn't alert the lich to our presence to try and detect wards, spells, or traps around the fence line of the warehouse.

Without the lich's shroud, Agent Chambers' Fire elemental presence was certainly more noticeable than the first time we'd met. Thankfully, our elements weren't opposing ones, so his presence registered more as a distracting tingle than the nasty discomfort I got around Brock's Earth elemental powers. That said, I'd have been happier with more than three feet between us.

"I really don't like the idea of going in blind," said Bobby as we studied the plans.

"Agreed. Also, the basement on this place really complicates things," I said. "It is probably safe to assume that's where the vampires are resting at the moment, but the lich could either be on the main level or in the basement."

Agent Chambers nodded and said, "We also have no idea if there are any hostages inside the building either."

A sharp distant ringtone pulled my attention from the plans on the laptop to Blue who immediately headed for the main part of the lab where the phone was, as it was the only area down here that got reception.

The ringing stopped just as Blue slipped into the hallway and I assumed Bree had answered it.

I turned my attention back to the laptop. "Hopefully that was Mac calling for a pickup. Once he gets here, we'll know more about what we are up against."

A few minutes later, Mac and Blue emerged out of one of the hallways from the main lab and they both joined us.

"I have good news and bad news. The bad news is that the place is heavily warded. The entire fence line is warded, as is the main entrance to the warehouse on the east side and the two loading bay entrances on that side as well. The emergency exit on the north side is also warded."

I cursed mentally at that. "I'll bite, what's the good news?"

"The six windows high up on the east and west sides aren't warded."

That *was* good news. But all six of the smashed windows had been boarded up from the inside. Getting in that way wasn't going to be quick or easy.

Bobby got an excited look on his face and said, "Looking at your flyby video, I'm pretty sure there is a small gap in one of the boards on the middle window on the west side."

I wondered if EIRT secretly had a swarm of pixies they hadn't told me about, as a small gap didn't sound like something we'd be able to enter from.

Agent Chambers perked up at Bobby's statement.

"Okay, what am I missing?" I asked.

Bobby said, "We have a small pinhole video camera in our equipment back at Central. We can have you fly up to the window, slip the camera inside, and then we'll have eyes on what is on the main level of the warehouse. The camera is attached to a small screen, but that screen can also broadcast the video in real time."

We'd still be blind as to what was in the basement, but if the lich was on the main floor, knowing where he was would allow us to hit him harder as we entered the building. Another thought hit me, and I turned to Mac and said, "There looked to be an access hatch on the roof of the warehouse, any idea if that is warded?"

He shook his head. "No idea, that hatch wasn't visible from the ground when I drove by. If you can fly me above it, I can scan it for wards. You're thinking that if the lich ignored the upper windows, he might have also ignored the hatch?"

I nodded. We still had plenty of daylight left but the clock was ticking. It was time to get more information quickly.

***

Mac and I and the two-man GRC13 sniper team stepped out onto the roof of the building I'd been on earlier. The sniper team hustled off and headed for the end of the roof that was facing the warehouse to set up a position.

I had the tiny camera and screen in one of my pouches in my armor and a knapsack filled with explosive devices over my shoulder. The latter was making me a touch nervous, but Bobby assured me they were perfectly safe to transport.

Mac had a pair of brass goggles with green lenses perched on his forehead. These were what allowed him to see wards. He also looked a touch nervous.

"Relax, flying with me is perfectly safe. I haven't dropped anyone that I didn't mean to yet," I said with a grin, but then realized with my visor down he couldn't see it.

He nodded and lowered the goggles. I called on my Air power and slowly lifted us both into the air.

"You only need to get me to the road in front of the building. From that distance, I'll be able to see the hatch and any wards with no issues."

I did just that and then stopped and hovered us in the air.

"Good news, the hatch is ward-free. Now get me back to solid ground."

I laughed to myself at Mac's lack of enthusiasm towards Air elemental travel. I slowly spun us around and returned us safe and sound to the roof. With Mac on the roof, it was time for the next part of the plan.

I opened a comm channel to Blue. *"The hatch is ward-free. Open a portal for Mac and let me know when you are ready."*

"Roger that."

I pushed a gust of air under me and took to the skies. I looped around until I was facing the south side of the building and waited in the air across the street from the warehouse. I spotted a cruiser off in the distance blocking access at an intersection. It was one of many doing the same thing to keep the area free of civilians.

I spotted Stella walking with Agent Chambers in civilian dress rather than the tactical gear he'd been in earlier. The two of them looked like a father and daughter out for a walk. They were heading towards the front gate of the fence. They were on standby in case my recon went sideways. If I was spotted or attacked, Stella would go full Hyde and charge the gate. Hopefully, her impenetrable form would be able to soak up or deal with whatever nasty surprises the wards on the fence tripped. Agent Chambers would then go full Fire elemental and take to the sky to assist me.

The rest of the team was standing by in line at the hangar. There would be an open portal that came out just across the street in the shadows of the building there. They, too, would move in if things went south.

"Portal open. You are good to proceed," said Blue over the comms.

I took a deep breath and made a beeline towards the south side of the building. I landed gently on the gravel ground a few feet from the side of the warehouse. I exhaled in relief as nothing seemed to happen. Mac had assured me that there were no wards in this location; it was nice to know that he'd been right.

I slipped the black knapsack off my shoulder and placed it on the ground carefully. I unzipped it and fished out the first of the four explosive devices. My hands shook slightly when I gently placed it on the side of the warehouse about six feet up the wall and pushed the button in its center. Pale blue lights flashed around it, and I slowly moved my hand away. The button had both armed the device and activated an electromagnet that kept it secured in place.

One down, three more to go.

I took another one out of the bag and placed it at the same height as the first but four feet farther along the wall and hit the button. Lights flashed on this one and it stayed in place as I moved my hand away.

I repeated this with the last two explosives devices, placing them directly below the first two but about a foot off the ground. The moment the last one was in place, I called on my Air powers and got the heck out of there. "Breeching explosives in place."

As the door had been warded, we were going to use the explosives to blow a new door into the side of the building.

I flew around the back of the building and up to the windows where the two-inch gap that Bobby spotted was. That opening was much larger than we needed, as the camera tube wasn't much wider than a thick plastic straw.

I fished the camera and the screen out of the pouch on my armor while I hovered in the air just outside the window. I turned on the screen which activated the camera and then slowly fed the tube into the hole.

At first, I was worried the camera wasn't working, as all I could see was a blank black screen on the display. The glare of the sunlight didn't help matters.

Bobby's voice came over the comms, *"You have the camera pointed towards the ceiling, rotate it slowly."*

I carefully turned the stem of the camera tube and a clearer image appeared on the screen. My heart rate picked up as a white van suddenly appeared on the display. From this angle, I couldn't see its license plate, but it matched the make and model of the one I'd seen at the jewelry store.

I panned past the van and more to the center of the warehouse. The interior was fairly dark but there was enough light to see most things. There were a few empty wooden crates around the place. My interest grew as the camera reached the center of the main floor. Near one of the walls, there was a large wooden crate on its side with what looked like stacks of old books and parchments on top of it. The crate was being used as an improvised desk. The image in front of the crate was blurred and fuzzy.

"Are you guys seeing this?" I asked softly over the comms.

"We see it. The distorted image matches the videos you took at the jewelry store. Looks like we've found our lich. Keep panning and check the north end of the warehouse," said Bobby.

I slowly twisted the camera around and watched the screen. There were more empty and rotting wooden crates but not much more of interest. At the far north end of the warehouse was a piece of machinery. I stopped and focused on it and then realized it was a broken forklift on its side. Behind the forklift were two small rooms and the emergency exit door beside them. The one room had a chipped and worn blue and white sign with the outline of a man and woman on it, which I assumed was a bathroom. The other room had a similar blue and white sign with a staircase icon on it. The stairs to the basement reminded me of one other thing.

With the camera back in the center of the room, the blurred image and the crate desk came into view again. I pulled down on the camera tube to pan it eastwards. It slowly crept along the dusty and dirty concrete floor until I found what I'd been searching for. Close to the east wall, there was a five-foot square metal hatch in the floor that led to the basement. I assumed there must be a ladder down but with the hatch shut, I couldn't confirm that.

The image on the screen shook as Bobby's voice over the comms startled me. *"You've covered the entire floor. The vampires must be in the basement unless they are risking sleeping in one of those crates. Move the camera back to the lich's location and get out of there."*

I pushed the camera forward until the image blurred and the crate desk came back into the picture. I gently placed the display down on the window ledge, screen side up. I pulled some double-sided tape out of one of my armor pouches and used it to secure the camera tube in place. Satisfied that it wasn't going anywhere, I pushed some more air under me and flew off.

A minute later, I was back in the lab. The image up on the projector was now the feed from the camera.

Agent Chambers and Stella arrived a minute later, which meant everyone was here, minus the two-man sniper team. They were staying in their rooftop position to keep a visual on the warehouse and were also watching the camera feed.

Bree was already in her standing hybrid Werepanther form, as was the EIRT Werewolf.

Agent Chambers immediately took charge. "Alright, people, gather round. Here is the plan . . ."

Chapter 19

Sunday, October 16

We spent almost until noon gaming out entry scenarios to take down the lich using the modular training model in the center of the hangar until we settled on our best plan. As we were attacking a creature of darkness, it was no coincidence that we were going in right at high noon when it should be at its weakest.

I was now on the roof of the warehouse where the sniper team had set up with two EIRT agents and Agent Chambers. Both of the EIRT agents had grenade launchers, submachine guns, and rappelling gear on them. One of them also carried a three-foot-long crowbar, which we might need to gain entry to the roof hatch.

Agent Chambers threw me a curveball when he started stripping off his clothes and stopped once he was down to a pair of small bright-orange briefs. The coarse, thick material of the underwear caught my attention. They honestly didn't look very comfortable.

Even though I was wearing my armor with my faceplate down, Agent Chambers must have guessed where my attention was. "They are Mad Scientist tech. Fully heat- and fire-resistant. Not the most attractive things but better than the alternative."

I nodded in understanding. Fire elementals had to ignite themselves completely to generate enough heat and thrust to fly. The downside of that was any clothing they were wearing when they did so burned up, so when they turned off the flames, they were left naked. If I had the choice between wearing bulky uncomfortable underwear and being left with my junk flapping in the breeze, I would have made the same choice. That meant, though, that Agent Chambers wouldn't be on the comms either, which was why he was going to be my shadow during this operation.

The two of us working together meant we were going to rain both fire and lightning down on the lich, and that thought gave me a warm fuzzy. I was honestly impressed at Agent Chambers' complete attitude change since our discussion; he'd been nothing but straightforward and professional. I'd expected at least some lingering resentment but none had popped up so far.

After completing a comms check with the entire team, we were ready to go.

I turned to the two EIRT agents and said, "Brace yourselves. The shroud of death and despair you felt at the cab driver's murder scene is nothing compared to what it feels like when the lich is actually present."

The one agent gave me a solemn nod, but the other just flashed a cocky grin at me like I was pulling his leg. I honestly wasn't sure which reaction concerned me more. I told myself that both were highly trained law enforcement personnel with years of experience and would be able to handle it. "Ready?"

"Good to go," they said in unison.

I called on my Air powers and lifted the three of us into the air. Out of the corner of my eye, I saw a bright flare come from the roof beneath me, and I spotted Agent Chambers in all his flaming goodness launch off the roof and head towards us. All my prior experiences with Fire elementals were on the receiving end of their powers; it was nice to know those fireballs and flames would be on my side for a change.

I flew us across the road towards the warehouse and gritted my teeth as we entered the shroud of despair. Both officers stiffened as it hit them.

As we approached the roof, the sensation got much worse and a large part of me wanted nothing more than to just turn around and fly away. I fought that urge and lowered the two EIRT agents onto the roof by an old air conditioning unit. The moment they touched down, I pushed some air under me to gain some altitude.

I tried telling myself that the altitude was to get a better tactic perspective on the area and not to get a break from the lich's aura, but deep down I knew that wasn't true.

I ended up circling in the air about forty feet above the roof and Agent Chambers was directly behind me doing the same pattern.

I watched with concern as the EIRT agent who'd flashed me the confident grin just stood there frozen while his partner had begun tying himself off to the AC unit. The second agent, sensing something was wrong, stopped what he was doing and approached his partner. He tapped him on the arm and said something to him off the comms.

The first agent shook himself out of his stupor and then nodded and got to work.

Once they were both tied off to the air conditioning unit, they turned and ran out their lines towards the roof hatch. I frowned when one of the agents pulled out a small blue can from the pocket of his vest. He shook the can and sprayed it along one edge of the roof hatch. As he put the can back in his pocket, I spotted the logo on the can and realized he'd greased the hatch hinge to lessen possible noise.

The other EIRT agent reached down and slowly turned a handle on the hatch. The first agent took up a position to his right and aimed the grenade launcher towards the closed hatch.

"E6 and E7 are in position. Hatch is free and ready."

I smiled and took it as a good sign that the crowbar had been unnecessary. The EIRT team was using E1 thru E11 as their call signs. 'E12' and 'E13' were Agent Chambers and the Werewolf respectively but neither of them had comms. I was given the call sign 'H1,' and Blue was 'H2.' Stella was 'H3,' and Bree was 'H4,' but they, too, wouldn't be on the comms.

"Assault team is in position and ready," said Bobby over the comms.

I spotted Stella in her Hyde form lurking in the shadows beside a building across the street. Behind her were Bree, the EIRT Werewolf, and the rest of the EIRT team. The only person not in that group was Blue who was still back at the lab. Blue would spy on the operation from the shadows, and if needed, would portal herself in once the lich's magic was disrupted.

"E10 and E11 ready," the sniper team reported.

I began calling on my Electrical powers and building up a charge. With everyone set, I opened a channel. *"On my mark."*

I held my hand out with my fingers and thumb extended for Agent Chambers' benefit and began counting down *"Five—,"* I said.

I spotted Stella's massive Hyde lumbering out from the building across the street.

I continued my countdown over the comms and with my fingers. *"—Four. Three. Two. One. Breach, breach, breach!"*

The moment I finished, Stella hit the fence like a bulldozer and plowed through it like it was made of paper. The hatch was thrown open and a small *pop* came from below as the first EIRT agent fired in a flashbang grenade. A loud rumble came from the far end of the building as the breaching explosives detonated.

A deafening bang and a bright light issued from the roof hatch of the warehouse as the flashbang went off inside.

I banked and dove at top speed towards the open hatch with Agent Chambers hot on my heels. I gritted my teeth as the feeling of fear and despair rose in me.

The second agent fired his grenade launcher into the hatch and quickly stepped back. This one was the more important of the two, as it was the magic-dispelling grenade.

I sighed in relief as the intensity of the lich's shroud of death diminished.

The hatch was coming up very quickly, and I tried to make myself as small and narrow as possible as it was going to be a tight fit. I silently cheered when I cleared the hatch without hitting it and flew inside the warehouse. A quick banked turn to left got me out of Agent Chambers' way.

The lich stood still in front of his makeshift desk. His glowing red eyes gazed up at me from within his cowl. As I extended my hand to release a blast of lightning at him, his boney hand lifted the staff he held and tapped it hard on the floor. A cloud of black smoke suddenly engulfed him.

I released a blast of lightning towards the cloud in the direction the lich had been. A bright light to my right lit up the warehouse again and an enormous fireball streaked in towards the cloud.

The lightning hit the cloud and seemed to dissipate some of its mass. The fireball hit next, and the cloud appeared to absorb it for a moment before the cloud disappeared. Flames licked across the makeshift desk and the concrete floor where the lich had been standing, burning everything in its wake.

I readied another blast of lightning but held my fire, as the lich was nowhere to be found. *"Does anyone have eyes on the target?"*

I circled in the air with my eyes frantically searching for any sign of the lich. My heart pounded in my chest as my fear grew to panic. Losing track of a creature that could kill you in a blink of an eye was never a good idea.

I spotted the two EIRT agents rappelling down on ropes from the roof hatch.

The warehouse darkened as the sunlight that had been streaming in from the new entrance we'd blown into the side of the building was suddenly blocked. I raised my hand in that direction to release a blast of lightning but stopped at the last second as I recognized Stella's Hyde form as the reason for the mini solar eclipse.

She grunted and stepped through, and Bree's dark Were form dashed in behind her. Right behind Bree was the silver-and-brown-furred Werewolf. They were followed by a steady stream of well-armed EIRT agents.

I pulled my attention away from the south side of the warehouse, as the additional manpower meant it was secure. It dawned on me that the shroud of fear and despair had lessened in intensity to much more manageable levels. I took that as a sign that the lich was gone. I circled the warehouse one last time to make sure it wasn't hiding somewhere but came up empty.

Agent Chambers landed beside the flaming desk and instantly reverted to his human form. He held out his hands towards the fire and I wondered what he was doing. My eyes went wide as he pulled the raging fire towards himself and seemed to absorb it all. He sucked in all the fire like some sort of human vacuum, and a few seconds later, it was completely gone. It was an impressive display of his powers.

I flew over and landed beside him. The spell books and parchments on the desk were now mostly a charred mess but a couple hadn't completely burned up and might be salvageable.

I turned towards the north of the building as a loud crash filled the warehouse and spotted that an EIRT agent had kicked in the door to the bathroom. His partner shined the tac light mounted on his submachine gun into the room and said, "Clear!"

Two other agents had taken up positions in front of the door to the basement stairs. They didn't breach and just stayed in there, pointing their weapons at the door.

The two EIRT agents that had been on the roof stood slightly back from the hatch in the floor to the basement with their weapons pointed at it. Stella, Bree, and the EIRT Werewolf were on the opposite side of the hatch, waiting to go.

Bobby and Mac joined us, but Mac's attention was on the charred floor behind the makeshift desk.

"There are runes here," said Mac in a warning tone.

He took out his goggles from earlier and put them on. He shook his head and said, "They are no longer active. I think the lich used them to teleport out."

I cursed under my breath at that. Mac lifted the goggles and crouched down to take a closer look at the charred runes on the floor.

After a few moments, Mac said, "Runes and wards aren't my specialty, but I recognize one. It's the rune for travel."

I opened the comms. *"E10 and E11, any sign of the lich from your vantage point?"*

"Negative," was the reply from the sniper team.

Bobby's voice came across the comms. *"Be advised the lich has escaped. Alert local officers to be on the lookout."*

I turned my attention to Mac. "Any idea how far the lich might have teleported?"

He shook his head. "The distance you can teleport all depends on the power behind the spell. We know the lich doesn't lack for power, so he could be anywhere by now."

I popped the faceplate on my armor to rub my temples, as I felt a headache starting to come on. We had had him dead to rights and missed. If he teleported to a new location, all my team's data was meaningless now. That meant we were back to square one in our search.

Agent Chambers interrupted my thoughts. "Shall we search the basement? If we are lucky, both the lich's vampire accomplices are down there, and we can deprive him of their services." I nodded and he turned to the group of EIRT agents that guarded the south entrance that we created. "Vickers, Robinson, get outside and take up positions on the northwest and southwest corners. The lich might decide to return and hit us again. I want some warning if that happens."

"Roger," replied the two agents as they left the building.

An inhuman scream of anger and rage came from beneath us that almost seemed to shake the building. I put down my faceplate and called on my Electrical powers. I didn't recognize that cry but knew whatever had made it wasn't human. It looked like our work wasn't done yet.

***

Another scream rocked the place as we gathered around the closed hatch to the basement. Stella crouched down at the hatch and looked at me with her misshaped eyes. I nodded and she tore the hatch off and tossed it to the side. The moment it was opened, Bree and the Werewolf jumped into the dark abyss below. Stella gave them a moment and then jumped into the hole after them. The place shook a bit as Stella's massive Hyde form crashed down on the floor below.

Two EIRT agents cracked tubes of chemical lights and began tossing them into the hole.

I took a deep breath and called on my Air powers and lifted myself and Agent Chambers into the air and then lowered us down.

We touched down on the concrete floor and I looked around. Stella was in front of us facing west, Bree was to our left facing south, and the Werewolf was to our right towards the north. Agent Chambers called a small amount of fire to his hands, which helped light up the place.

Around us was a maze of metal shelves, stacks of old car tires, and metal industrial drums with warning stickers on their side. The shelves were mostly bare but there were some old paint cans, empty boxes, and other odds and sods on them.

I spotted the staircase off to the north. On the opposite end, there were two small rooms with both of their doors closed. I assumed that if the vampires were here, they'd be in those rooms.

A scream of challenge came from the south end of the warehouse from behind a stack of tires, but I couldn't see anything.

A flash of bloodred, silver, and black went by us in front of Stella. She let out a questioning grunt and toppled over on her side, knocking over a nearby shelving unit with a crash. Stella's Hyde form lay on the ground and tried to get back on its feet. But only her right arm and leg were moving. Her entire left side seemed to be immobilized.

It dawned on me that the flash I'd seen was an aura. The bloodred core meant it would be something from the undead class, but I'd never seen the silver and black outline before and had no idea what we could be dealing with.

A blur of bloodred, silver, and black came back from the north end. The EIRT Werewolf let out a howl of pain and went down. He had four long bloody gashes on the left side of his furred stomach. He, too, didn't seem to be able to move his limbs on his left side.

My sphincter tightened as it hit me what we were dealing with—a wight. Wights were similar to ghouls in that they could operate during the day, unlike vampires and zombies. There was speculation that wights were ghouls that had evolved. Wights had vampire-like speed but weren't anywhere near as physically strong as vampires. What made them exceptionally dangerous was their paralyzing touch.

Another angry scream from the south end of the warehouse shook the place.

Stella caused my heart to almost stop as she changed back to her normal and very vulnerable human form. She got to her feet and quickly morphed back into her Hyde form.

"We have a wight down here. Chambers, get up the ladder now. Bree, grab the Werewolf and go. Stella, hold your position and we'll cover them."

"I can go full flame. That will stop it from touching me," said Agent Chambers.

"No. This place is like a tinder box. Just go."

His gaze flicked over the industrial drums covered with warning stickers and he nodded. He extinguished the fire in his hands and leaped onto the ladder. The place instantly darkened with only the odd green glow of chemical lights on the ground, casting deep shadows on everything. Bree lifted the Werewolf over her shoulders in a fireman's carry and moved to the ladder.

I thickened the air around me, hoping that might prevent the wight from making contact, and took a position opposite to Stella to protect the base of the ladder.

Bree growled unhappily behind me as she hauled herself and the EIRT Werewolf up the ladder. I wasn't sure if she was annoyed about leaving the fight or from trying to haul hundreds of pounds of Werewolf up a ladder.

A flash of the wight's aura went by again and Stella let out an annoyed grunt as she went down again.

"Don't change yet," I said to her as I shifted over to cover both her and Bree.

The undead blur came back from the north, and thanks to my Air shield, it only managed to brush its claws against the front of my armor as it passed by. I wiggled my fingers and was relieved that they were working; my theory about my armor protecting me from the wight's paralyzing touch had been correct.

"Stella, change back to human," I said as I called on my Air powers.

The moment she was human, I sent a blast of air under her and shot her up and out of the hatch. I watched one of the EIRT agents pull her out of the air and to safety.

"Close the—" I started to say but was slammed hard from behind into the metal rungs of the ladder.

I cursed as the impact caused me to bite my tongue and I tasted blood. I would have loved to spit it out but doing that inside my helmet would be a bad idea. The only thing worse would be opening my faceplate to spit and exposing myself to the wight. I grimaced as I swallowed it down and tried not to gag.

I turned and hastily erected another Air shield. I was just in time, as the wight had come back for another pass at me. It let out a deafening scream as it went by, probably unhappy that it hadn't managed to hit me hard again.

"Close the hatch!" I yelled up.

I caught a glimpse of Stella's massive Hyde form as she dropped the hatch cover back into place with a resounding crash, leaving me alone in the almost-darkness with the wight.

Chapter 20

Sunday, October 16

There were times where I wished I had a normal life. Sitting at home watching a football game with a plate of nachos and a cold beer like most people were doing sounded pretty sweet.

Instead, I was unsuccessfully dodging a hyper-fast undead creature that wanted to crack me out of this armor and have its own version of a lobster dinner.

I picked myself up off the floor for the third time and tried to figure out what to do. "Yo! Tall, dark, and screechy, you want a grab a beer and watch the Bills with me?"

The creature screamed its displeasure at me from deeper in the room.

"Don't tell me you're a Cowboys fan . . . it's bad enough your ugly and dead, you could at least have some taste!"

I just managed to move the Air shield behind me as it blurred by and I avoided the full impact of its hit. The wight screamed its displeasure at me again as it disappeared deeper into the darkness.

The wight and I were at a stalemate. It couldn't penetrate my armor and paralyze me, and I lacked a way to take it down. To kill the wight, I'd need to decapitate it, drive something made of silver through its blackened heart, or burn it to a cinder. I didn't have the strength or the right tools to decapitate it, and I had nothing silver on me, so the first two options were out. I could burn it to a cinder using a massive blast of lightning like I'd done with Waldo, the zombie back at the cemetery. The problem was I had no idea what was in those industrial drums with the scary warning stickers on them. If any of them were close to full and were flammable or explosive, they'd be scraping charred bits of the Hamilton Hurricane off the walls and floor.

I guessed wrong again and the wight's impact as it passed by knocked me off my feet again. While the armor protected me from getting shredded by the wight's claws or getting paralyzed by its touch, it didn't do much to lessen the impact of the hard concrete each time I face-planted on it.

The wight let out more of a taunting cry this time as it disappeared into the darkness.

I groaned and got myself back on my feet. I wasn't sure how much more of this abuse I could take. I also realized that if I hit the floor hard enough, there was a chance I could get knocked out. If that happened, I was screwed, as I had no doubt that with some time, the wight would find a seam or a release latch on the armor and I'd be done for.

I readied my Air shield again and waited.

C'mon, Zack, think! There has to be a way to take this thing down.

It blurred by again and I silently cheered as I guessed right where the attack would come from and got my Air shield in place in time.

The vampire-like speed gave me an idea. I dropped my Air shield and called on my Electrical powers. This was going to be tricky, as I needed to hit the wight and avoid all of the drums.

I caught a flash of movement to my right and lashed out with a narrow burst of lightning. The wight shrieked as the electricity slammed into it. My smile grew as the wight's speed slowed to almost a normal run.

At that speed, I got my first good look at it. With its pale mottled skin and red eyes, the thing looked like an albino ghoul. It had long black nails and blackened pointed teeth. As it was moving at a slow speed, I managed to move back and out of its swipe range as it ran by. My lightning attack, though, was disrupted when it managed to get a metal shelving rack between us before blurring off into the darkness.

I mentally cheered. While my lightning hadn't stopped the wight, it had disrupted its speed. My lightning did the same thing to vampires, which was why I had tried it to see if it would do the same to the wight. Since it had, I now could try my plan.

I opened a channel. *"When I say go, have Stella lift the hatch and have Agent Chambers ready to, um, do his thing."*

There was a pause before a *"Roger that,"* came back over the comms.

I purposely kept my communication vague. My fear was that wights were like ghouls and understood speech. I didn't want to tip it off to what I had in mind. Hopefully, my team upstairs would figure out what I needed.

I faced south where the wight has gone and readied my Electrical powers and waited.

The seconds ticked by and there was no sign of the wight. I frantically scanned the near-darkness and listened for the slightest sound of movement, but everything remained dead still. For a brief second, I worried the wight might have escaped from the basement but dismissed that thought. The hatch above was closed and the staircase was at the other end of the room. Even if it snuck by me and went up the stairs, I knew there would be a host of EIRT agents pointing a crap load of guns at that door. They'd also have switched to silver bullets by now. The moment that door even twitched, they'd open up with enough rounds to take down an elephant.

My head snapped back as the wight plowed into me from behind and drove me hard into the floor. The impact was hard enough that I saw stars. Thankfully, it ran over my prone form and kept going.

Son of bitch! I thought angrily as I forced myself to my feet.

The wight had snuck around behind me on that last attack. I took the change in its tactics as a positive, figuring it had done that because it hadn't liked my lightning attack earlier.

I shifted until my back was firmly against the ladder and readied my Electrical attack again.

I caught movement off to my right and lashed out with the lightning. The wight managed to swerve away from the lightning but ran straight into a stack of tires. The tires and wight both crashed to the floor. I shifted my lightning towards it, but the wight nimbly rolled to its feet and vanished into the darkness again.

I readied my lightning once more and waited. While I was facing forward, I kept my attention glued to my left. I was betting the wight would try and be tricky and attack from this direction.

My bet paid off. I lashed out and nailed it as it came screaming in. The wight slowed down again and I called on my Air power and lifted it off the floor. It screamed at me as I held it suspended in mid-air.

"*Open the hatch*," I yelled over the comms.

I moved back and, using my Air power, pulled the wight forward until it was almost directly under the hatch. I'd purposely kept it back enough that it was out of reach of the ladder.

Everything almost went to shit as Stella removed the hatch suddenly and the bright light from above streamed down, blinding me. I managed to keep the wight in the air until my eyes adjusted.

"Is Agent Chambers ready?"

Whatever the reply was, I missed it, as the wight chose that same moment to let out an ear-splitting shriek.

The moment it ended, I said, *"Say again?"*

"He's ready."

I opened the comms to reply but the wight once again screamed. I was really starting to hate this thing.

When Mr. Screams-a-lot finally shut up, I said, *"Get everyone back from the opening."*

"Roger that."

I sent a huge blast of air under the wight and shot him up through the hole like a ping-pong ball in a vacuum tube. My heart almost stopped when the wight barely missed grabbing one of the support beams in the ceiling before tumbling back to the ground. I used my Air power to catch it about five feet from the top of the hatch and held it there.

I smiled as a gigantic fireball streaked in and engulfed the wight. I didn't mind hearing his last ear-shattering scream as he burned.

A minute later, the wight was reduced to a smoldering, unmoving skeleton. Stella's Hyde form reached out and batted it to the side. Pieces of blackened bones fell to the floor beside the hatch.

I used my Air power to fly out of the gloomy basement and into the warehouse proper. Off to the side was a naked man being bandaged up by an EIRT officer while Bree's Were form hovered over them. I realized the man was the EIRT Werewolf back in human form.

My concern grew as I watched blood soak through the bandage. His Were healing should be dealing with the wounds. I wondered if the wight's paralyzing touch was also hindering his healing ability. I tried remembering everything I could from reading about wights. I was pretty sure that the paralysis was temporary but couldn't recall how long it lingered. I had to assume that whatever the time period was, it would be shorter for a Were due to their enhanced metabolisms. At least the wounds, while serious, didn't seem life-threatening.

Agent Chambers interrupted my thoughts. *"Is the basement clear?"*

I popped open my faceplate and said, "I didn't spot anything else down there but there are two small rooms on the south side whose doors are closed."

"Okay. Good work down there."

"Thank you for the assist at the end."

Agent Chambers smiled. "My pleasure. Now if you'll excuse me, I'm going to clear the basement."

I nodded and watched him gather up five EIRT officers and head for the basement stairs. Bobby caught my attention when he turned to Stella and said, "Can we get your help in clearing a path outside so vehicles can get through?"

Stella nodded and transformed into her Hyde form again. I followed her over to the hole in the south wall and we stepped outside. I froze as I looked at the fence line. Just inside the fence, there were rows of wicked-looking white spikes. I moved closer and noticed that the spikes all had a light coating of a green substance on them.

"Yeah, nasty bit of work there. They shot up from the ground the moment Stella breached the gate. Thankfully, the ones under her feet just shattered and never penetrated and the poison on the spikes didn't have any effect on her," said Bobby behind me.

I glanced over to the front gate where Stella was heading. There was a gap in the spikes about three feet wide. I assumed Stella must have marched through on her way in and cleared a path for the rest of the team.

Snapping noises filled the air as Stella stomped through the spikes and widened the gap at the entrance. There were two EIRT SUVs with their red and blue flashing lights just outside the gate waiting for her to finish.

Stella used her feet to sweep the broken bits of spikes to the side and cleared a path. She moved out of the way and the two SUVs pulled into the lot. An ambulance came screaming up the street and pulled in just behind the SUVs.

Two paramedics got out and retrieved a gurney from the back of the ambulance. Bobby excused himself and rushed over to the paramedics, I assumed to guide them to the hole in the wall rather than having them use one of the trapped entrances.

Agent Chambers' voice came over the comms. *"We have the vampires in power blocking cuffs. I need two body bags for transport."*

"*Roger.*"

An EIRT agent opened the hatch of the SUV and pulled out two thick black bags. I directed him to the only safe entrance into the warehouse.

Stella's crisp English accent cut through the air beside me. "We didn't get the lich but at least taking the two vampires out of play will weaken him."

"Hopefully we'll get lucky and one of them might have a clue where the lich went." I looked down at her and added, "You okay? No lingering issues from the paralysis?"

Stella shook her head. "You know me, a quick change from one form to another and I'm as right as rain. How about you? It sounded like you were taking quite the beating down there."

"I'm fine. Sore, a slight case of whiplash, and I'm probably covered in bruises. I'll swing by Marion's after this and get her to fix me up."

We watched silently as the paramedics wheeled out the gurney with the injured Werewolf. I tried to think positively and remind myself that we accomplished something here. We'd taken down a wight and two vampires and taken on the lich. The Werewolf was our only casualty, but I figured he'd make a full recovery the moment the paralysis wore off. One injury considering what we'd been up against was a minor miracle; it could have been much worse.

The problem was the lich was in the wind and we had no idea how to find him.

***

After debriefing with Agent Chambers and the rest of his team, I visited Marion's to get some healing. This time I didn't mention the lich when she asked what happened and I just told her it was another training accident. She tutted at me and then went about healing me.

Dinner that evening with the team was a quiet and sullen affair. I think we were all wrestling with the fact that we had the lich in our sights and missed him. The bigger issue was that it put our search for him back to square one. The crime data plotted out on the map upstairs was now useless. We didn't even know if the lich was still in the city, though I suspected he was lurking out there somewhere. I couldn't see him giving up on his search for the headpiece.

The one upside, though, was that we knew Walter's magic-detecting device worked and could be used the find the lich. But it would take us time to search the entire city. We needed to find a way to narrow down the area of the search.

Bree, towards the end of dinner, said, "Have you thought about our patrol route for this evening?"

I blinked at that, as I hadn't been planning on patrolling tonight. I'd figured since the lich had lost his two vampire minions today and the van that they used, he wouldn't be out tonight. A part of me was tempted to skip patrolling for that reason, and because Marion's healing had taken a lot out of me. I was tired.

It dawned on me that Bree was doing the right thing. Rather than sit around and mope about not taking down the lich, we needed to buckle down and keep going. Sure, the chances of the lich being out tonight were slim, but it was possible. After losing his base of operations today, maybe the lich needed to harvest more souls to recover some of the power he lost. I sat up straighter and said, "Probably the full route between all the attack sights. I will have to hit the lab first to recharge my powers."

Bree nodded at that, and I turned my attention to Stella and said, "What is the plan for tonight and tomorrow?"

Stella tugged at her braid for a moment. "Tonight, I want to look over the map upstairs and see if the warehouse the lich was using should have been obvious from the crime and incident data. The cemetery where we fought the zombies wasn't that far away from the warehouse. Tomorrow, we have ten businesses to visit to finish our list."

I frowned at that. "What does it matter if data should have told us where he was hiding? He's gone from that location now. Ditto for the zombies."

"The zombies could help us narrow down his new location." My confusion must have shown in my facial expression as Stella added, "What if the lich didn't intentionally raise those zombies? What if just his presence nearby was enough to bring them back to life?"

My excitement grew as I understood what Stella was getting at. If the zombies did rise from his presence alone, then if his new location was near a cemetery the same thing could happen. Another zombie uprising might allow us to narrow the search of the city to a much smaller location.

Stella continued, "As for the map data, I wanted to check the early reports and see if there is any sort of pattern that we could have used to triangulate the warehouse's location."

I nodded at that. If there was some sort of pattern, that same pattern might start appearing around the lich's new location, which would be another way to narrow it down. "Okay, that all makes sense, but what is the point of hitting the last ten businesses? They are on the mountain. The lich hasn't been near the mountain and none of the incidents have occurred there."

Stella pointed out that it was almost as important to find the headpiece as it was to find the lich. At least if we got the headpiece, it would keep the lich's power in check. She also added that if we did find the headpiece, we might be able to use it as bait to bring the lich out to a place of our choosing. I argued that our time would be better spent eliminating squares of the grid using the magic-detecting device to locate the lich. Stella pointed out that it would take us at least four days to search the grid.

In the end, I decided that Stella's plan of finishing the list was fine. Hopefully, over the next day or so, either we'd get a zombie uprising or Stella would find a pattern in the crime and incident data that would allow us to drastically narrow the area of the search.

After dinner, I had Blue transport me to the lab so I could spend time between the Tesla coils to recharge my powers. Once I was topped up, Bree and I went out on patrol.

We'd barely started our patrol when Bree said, "I talked to Shawn this afternoon and accepted the invite to join the Weres from our pack as part of the delegation. We're on track to leave this Saturday."

We had less than a week to take down the lich before we'd lose Bree's services. "Did you talk to Liv last night?"

Bree nodded. "She wasn't happy but took it better than I thought she would. I think she understood how important this trip is for me. Oddly enough, the part about learning more about Were culture seemed to really resonate with her."

There were times I underestimated Liv, and this was one of them. I'd have bet money that she'd have been in a snit over Bree leaving and would have been in a mood for days. Tonight at dinner, though, she was just quiet and introspective more than anything else and didn't seem to be in a bad mood.

My thoughts returned back to Bree and her leaving, and I wondered if that was why she had been so keen to patrol this evening. A part of me was also unhappy about losing Bree for three months, even if we did take down the lich before she left.

It dawned on me how much my life had changed in the last year. A year ago, it was just me bounty hunting and now I was upset at losing one member of a five-person team, six if I included Alteea. Even without Bree, we were still a formidable group. I also had my foundation members I could call on if we needed extra help. I'd miss Bree while she was gone but realized that we'd do fine in her absence. The bigger issue was taking down the lich before she left.

Chapter 21

Sunday, October 16

The patrol with Bree turned out to be a bust, as we didn't get even a trace of the lich's presence. We also didn't come across any regular crimes or emergencies. The city seemed strangely quiet.

The next morning when I got up, I was relieved to find no messages on my phone from Hamilton police or EIRT about another victim. The lack of activity had me worried that the lich might have left the city. I pushed those doubts to the side. I still felt there was no way the lich would leave until it found the headpiece.

Even the house was quiet. Stella and Blue were out visiting the last ten businesses on our list. Bree and Alteea were sleeping, and Liv was in her daytime death trance.

I ended up at a loose end and spent the morning on the computer doing paperwork and looking over yesterday's crime reports online, killing time until Stella and Blue returned.

They showed up around lunchtime. We had a quick bite to eat, and Stella said, "We have only two businesses left but Blue's holographic disguise needs recharging. Do you mind going out with me this afternoon to finish up?"

I still felt this search on Hamilton Mountain was a waste of time, but I could tell it was important to Stella to finish the list so I agreed.

Blue opened a portal. Stella and I came out in the shadows behind a small strip mall. Looking around, I recognized the location as a southeastern part of the city. The strip mall had been around for decades, and I'd been here before. We walked to the front of the mall and found our target business sandwiched between a paint store and a shawarma restaurant.

The windows were blacked out and the red and white illuminated sign above the place had Russian writing on it. The door to the business just had 'Members Only' written in huge white letters. Overall, the place had an inhospitable appearance.

"I thought you said this was a Russian sports bar," I said.

Stella shrugged. "That is what it was called on my list from the community center."

I tried the door and it opened, so we went in. My confusion grew as we entered a small room that had an old wooden desk with a monitor, mouse, and phone on it. In the far corner, there was another blacked-out glass door that I assumed led to the main part of the building. I also spotted a small black video camera just above the door.

A large man with jailhouse tats and a shaved head sat behind the desk. He wore a black T-shirt that was stretched tightly across his pecs and had 'Security' written on it in white lettering. He glanced up from the Russian newspaper he was reading and in heavily accented English said, "Members only. Fuck off."

Well, at least the greeting explained why there wasn't a Better Business Bureau logo on the front door, I thought to myself.

"We need to speak to the owner."

"He's busy. Fuck off," said the man without even looking up.

I took a deep breath and said, "It is a matter of life and death."

The man glanced up this time and said, "It will be if you don't leave."

I tried the nice way. I thought about it and then said, "Stella, change."

In the blink of an eye, Stella's harmless little girl form was replaced by her monstrous Hyde form, which barely fit between the door and the desk.

"*Bozhe moy!*" said the security guard as he looked up at Stella's new form in shock and fear.

"Now that I have your complete attention, we need to see the owner."

The guard started to reluctantly shake his head when the phone on his desk rang. He picked it up, listened for a few seconds, and then simply said, "*Da*," and hung up. "Owner will see you now."

"Thank you," I said and then turned to Stella and gave her a small nod.

She grunted then changed back to her normal human form.

As we approached the inner door, the guard with shaking hands reached under the desk and the door in front of us buzzed.

This whole setup had me on edge and I called on my powers to thicken the air in front of me as I reached for the door.

It's only paranoia if people aren't out to get you.

I opened the door and was greeted by the sounds of sports fans chanting. There were soccer games playing on the multiple large screen TVs around the place. I wrinkled my nose as I was hit by the smell of stale cigarette smoke. The smoke scent caught me off guard, as Hamilton had banned smoking in public places almost two decades ago now. I wondered if that was the reason for the elaborate security arrangements. It seemed like overkill just to avoid bylaw enforcement officers and I suspected that there were other illegal activities happening here.

The place was dimly lit, and it took a second for my eyes to adjust. The room was empty other than two large guys sitting at a table watching the game. The area was quite small and held just five tables, chairs, and some bench seating. At the back, there were neon beer signs and a bar. There was a small hallway to the right of the bar which had a restroom sign at the entrance.

An ember glow of a cigarette heater pulled my attention back to the bar. The smoking man was in his late forties or early fifties, medium height with a slightly heavyset build. I assumed he was the owner and I approached the bar.

As I got closer, I spotted elaborate tattoos peeking out from the collar of his black T-shirt. He glanced up from the glass he was drying with a worn bar towel and gave us a quick once over before turning his attention back to the glass. The two guys watching TV gave us long glances, sizing us up.

I stepped up to the bar and pulled out the picture of the headpiece from the folder I was carrying and dropped my Air shield. I placed the picture on the bar and said, "We are investigating murders of Russian business owners and believe the killers are interested in finding this. Have you seen or know of this object?"

He glanced down at the picture and nodded.

I waited for him to say something, but he just picked up another glass and started drying it. "Do you know where it is?"

"*Da.*"

My frustration turned to excitement. "If you have this object, you are in grave danger. We can take it off your hands and protect you."

His dark eyes looked up at me and he studied me for a moment and then said, "One thousand dollars."

I blinked at the short answer, and it took me a second to realize that he wanted money for the headpiece. "I don't think you understand how much danger you are in having this. The killers have murdered more than half a dozen people already and would kill anyone here without breaking a sweat."

He shrugged. "One thousand dollars."

I was about to argue with him when Stella tugged on the back of my shirt. I turned to her, and she said, "Just pay him."

I looked at Stella like she had lost her mind. Paying to take an item that was death to anyone who had it seemed nuts to me. "I don't have the money on me."

Stella just smiled and pointed behind me. I turned and the man was entering digits into a credit card payment machine. He put the terminal down on the bar and it had a thousand dollars as the transaction amount listed on the screen.

I sighed, fished out my wallet, and got my credit card out. I entered my pin. A few seconds later, the transaction was approved.

The man picked up the terminal and nodded. He moved over to the draft beer and began unscrewing one of the pull levers.

I stood there open-mouthed in shock as he removed it and placed it on the bar. It fit the description perfectly, other than the beer logo that had been stuck on the back. My heart beat faster as I turned it over and saw the infinity symbol etched into the brass. There was an indent in the center with four small claws where the ruby would be mounted. It was the headpiece to the Staff of Darkness.

By Odin's hairy balls! I thought as I picked it up. A piece of a major magic artifact had been used as a draft beer pull lever for years. I shook my head. Next, I'd probably find Excalibur being used as a tomato stake in some garden in England or the Spear of Destiny being used as a tent pole in Oregon.

As I held it in my hands, I was a bit disappointed, as I couldn't sense anything special about it. It weighed a decent amount and the craftsmanship was nice but that was about it. I handed it to Stella who beamed at me as she took it.

The man behind the bar had a smug grin on his face. I had no doubt he was thinking he just sold a used draft pull to a couple of rubes for a grand. I was inclined to agree with him, but it was a perfect match, and I was pretty sure it was the headpiece.

Stella and I turned and headed for the door.

As we entered the small room at the front, I heard Russian being spoken behind me, followed by deep laughter and I wondered if we'd been had.

***

Once we were back at the house, relief filled me when the needle on Walter's magic-detecting device shot over to the right as I pointed it at the headpiece that Stella was holding. "It's the real deal."

Stella's smile got bigger at that.

Blue eyed the headpiece with curiosity as she stood beside Stella. "What should we do with it?"

I frowned at Blue's question. "What do you mean?"

"I can attempt to destroy it with my Keetiyatomi blade."

Blue's magic sword did seem to be able to cut through just about anything and might be able to demolish the headpiece. If we smashed it, that would prevent the lich from reassembling the Staff of Darkness. It was tempting, but Dmitri's story about the Night Lord and the Staff of Darkness flashed into my mind. "No, there was a great explosion when the staff was disassembled during the battle that killed everyone around it. Odin only knows what could be released if you destroyed it."

Blue's tail began swinging happily behind her and she said, "We could use explosives in a remote location."

I mentally rolled my eyes at Blue's penchant for things that went *boom*. Destroying the headpiece might stop the lich from reassembling the Staff of Darkness, which was an advantage. Or destroying it might actually help him. The lich was the one who crafted it in the first place, so rather than coming to Canada and spending all this time searching for it, why not just build a new headpiece? That question had bothered me since finding out about the Staff of Darkness. The headpiece didn't appear that special and seemed to be made out of common brass. Surely, it wouldn't be that difficult to make another one.

Maybe there was some sort of magic bond between the staff, the headpiece, and the ruby. At least that was the only explanation that made sense to me. Maybe the other two pieces would reject a new headpiece if the old one still existed. If that was the case, we might help the lich by destroying the headpiece, as it would free him to create a new one.

I told Blue my concerns and Stella advised that I call Walter and get his opinion.

Ten minutes later, I had an answer—sort of. Walter got deep into magic theory and techno-jargon and lost me for most of our conversation. In the end, I asked him to simplify things for me. He answered that was there was a fifty-fifty chance that destroying the headpiece would either end the threat of the Staff of Darkness for good or it would allow the lich to build a new headpiece and reassemble it.

I'd barely finished going over Walter's answer with my teammates after ending our call, when Stella said, "Well that settles it then. We can't risk helping the lich, so destroying the headpiece is out."

Blue seemed disappointed at that, but I agreed with Stella. Risking the fate of the world on the same odds as a coin flip didn't make sense to me either.

Stella was also quicker than me in thinking about the next step and said, "So, if we can't destroy it, do we keep it with us at all times or put it someplace safe?"

I smiled as the answer came to me. "Give it to Blue to put in her room at the lab." I turned to Blue and added, "Rig it up to something that will explode if it is touched."

Blue's purple eyes gleamed at my suggestion and her tail started doing happy movements again.

She took the headpiece from Stella and started heading towards the living room to use the shadow there when Stella said, "Wait!"

Blue turned and gave Stella a questioning look.

"What if the lich can sense the headpiece? If we move it out of Hamilton, he will leave."

A small part of me liked the idea of the lich leaving Hamilton; at least that would end the trail of dead bodies he was leaving across our city. However, the lich would still be out there somewhere in the world and wouldn't stop killing. It also meant that at some point in the future, we'd have to deal with him again, as he wouldn't end his search for the headpiece.

"I find it highly unlikely that he can sense the headpiece, or he would have found it by now," said Blue.

I frowned at that. "If he can't sense the headpiece, how did he know to come to Hamilton?"

"Research. He found the names of the two people Peter had given the staff and the headpiece to and traced their lineage to find the logical heirs."

I spotted a flaw in Blue's claim. "If he knew the heirs, why not go straight to the person here in Hamilton who had it? None of the victims seemed to be related, so it doesn't seem like he is targeting a certain Russian family."

Blue's tail made a couple of sharp motions and she said, "Many records from the Russian Revolution were destroyed. Even more were ruined during the Second World War. It could also be that the heir purposely changed their name when they came to Canada to protect themselves from any reprisals from the old country."

I pondered Blue's statement and thought it made sense. "Go hide the headpiece in your room at the lab." Stella was about to object, and I turned to her and added, "If there is no activity from the lich in a couple of days, we can always bring the headpiece back here."

Stella gave a reluctant nod and Blue disappeared into the living room.

Knowing the headpiece was secure in Blue's room at our underground lab made me feel better. It didn't end the threat of the lich, but it did stop him from reassembling the Staff of Darkness and drastically increasing his power. But having it wouldn't stop the lich from killing more Russian community members in its effort to find it.

"Having the headpiece is good but letting the lich know we have it would be better," said Stella.

I mentally smiled at that, as Stella had already jumped ahead of where my thoughts had been going. It was nice having smart teammates but at times it was annoying that they beat me to the punch. "I doubt that the lich is hanging out online in Internet forums, but we could try posting messages to users with aliases like DeathDealer69 and such."

Stella rolled her eyes at me and shook her head. It was odd seeing Stella's eye roll, as that was more of an Olivia and Bree thing to do. While I'd hoped Olivia and Bree would pick up more of Stella's and Blue's habits, it seemed like influence worked both ways.

"No, we need to go a more old fashioned route to contact him."

"A stone tablet in Gore Park that reads, 'We haz ur headpiece,'?" I grinned and added, "We could sign it with five stick figures that represent our team. Maybe a lightning bolt for me, and we'd make your stick figure really big, give Blue's a tail, Bree's a happy cat face, and Liv's a sword . . ."

Stella smirked at that. "A bit too old fashioned. I was thinking a billboard."

I kicked her suggestion around. The more I thought about it, the more I liked it. "One in the downtown core, near where the attacks have happened?"

"Yes, but maybe two billboards. One for Main Street and one for King Street."

Main and King were the two main one-way streets that ran through the core, so by putting one on each, it doubled our chances of the lich spotting it. I had no idea what a billboard cost to rent but suspected it wasn't cheap. While it might be expensive to rent the billboards, if it prevented another Russian immigrant from coming to a horrible end, it was worth the price.

Blue returned and said that the headpiece was secure. By the gleam in her eye, I pitied anyone who tried to touch it. Stella brought Blue up to speed on the billboard idea and Blue nodded in approval.

I wanted to get started on contacting billboard companies immediately, but Stella pointed out that it was Sunday. She said she and Blue would contact them first thing in the morning. She also pointed out that that allowed us to vote on the expenditure with Liv and Bree that night at dinner and gave her time to create an image for the billboard.

The delay wasn't ideal but there wasn't much that we could do about it. I just hope that our delay wouldn't cost someone their life in the meantime.

I helped Stella and Blue with the crime map, but as it had been less than forty-eight hours since the lich vanished to its new location, the crime incidents on the map were sparse and didn't provide enough information for us to narrow down a location.

The rest of the afternoon, we kicked around ideas for finding the lich and planning how to do a full grid search of the city. Stella came up with the idea of starting the search at the warehouse where we found the lich and working out in a widening pattern from there. Her reasoning was that teleport spells were usually limited in distance, so there was a chance the lich may not have teleported far from the warehouse. It felt a bit thin to me but neither I nor Blue had a better suggestion, so we went with it. We would begin our new plan tomorrow.

Chapter 22

Monday, October 17

The next morning, it seemed our luck was improving. Stella and Blue had managed to contact a billboard company and one of the two billboards was up.

I blinked at that news. It was only just gone 11:00 a.m. Assuming the billboard company kept regular business hours and opened at nine, they'd managed to get a billboard up in under two hours. "How?"

Stella smiled. "The sign on King Street is digital. We dropped off a check and a USB drive with the image earlier this morning and the company uploaded it right away." Her smile disappeared and she added, "We aren't so lucky with the Main Street one. They will print the sign today, but it won't go up until Wednesday morning."

I pondered that and still thought it wasn't bad. "This all seems really quick; how did you make it happen this fast?"

"I pointed out that we were working with the police and EIRT and that these billboards would save lives. The owner was very cooperative after that. We also cut a check for thirty thousand, which helped with the owner's motivation."

I flinched at the number, but if these billboards stopped the lich from killing more people in its search, it was money well spent. "We have the billboards for a month?"

Stella's expression changed to one of concern and she shook her head. "No, just until the end of the month. We have first rights to the billboards for November but have to let the owner know by the twenty-fifth. If we want the billboards for November, it is another eighteen thousand."

I kicked around the chances of us needing the billboards for November and figured we probably wouldn't need them. The bigger concern was losing Bree's services this upcoming Saturday when she left for her pack duties. Another thought hit me. "What does the billboard image look like?"

Stella pulled out her phone and fiddled with it for a moment and then turned towards me. The picture on her phone was of me in my armor holding the headpiece. Behind me in the shot was Stella in her full Hyde persona, Bree in her standing Werepanther form, and Liv and Blue. The ad was captioned, "We have your headpiece," and had a phone number under it I didn't recognize.

"The phone number is to a live answering service. I provided them with a list of questions to use to screen callers. I also mentioned that if a caller threatens to devour their souls or something similar to put them through to us," said Stella with a grin.

The answering service was a good idea, as it saved us from being inundated with calls from the general public. As always, it looked like Stella and Blue had everything covered. I thanked them for their hard work and retired to the office upstairs to make some calls quick calls before we began our search for the headpiece.

My calls with Agent Chambers and Detective Little were brief, as neither of them had anything new to report about the lich. Agent Chambers mentioned that the two vampires taken into custody couldn't remember anything about their time with the lich. The last thing either remembered was being at home on the Friday before all of this started; the last week and a half was a complete blank for them.

I wondered if they were faking the memory loss to try and get out of the murder charges and mentioned that to Agent Chambers. He said he'd considered the same thing, but they had a telepath scan their thoughts and confirmed that they had no memories of the events with the lich. Agent Chambers added that the Crown wasn't happy because it complicated their case against the vampires, and they were concerned that they might not be able to press charges.

I freaked a bit at the idea of the two vampires walking free, but Agent Chambers said that both were being detained due to public safety concerns. I had mixed feelings about that. Generally, I disagreed with detention for that reason alone, as this was something only Enhanced Individuals were subjected to. The law basically allowed the government to detain any Enhanced Individual for an indefinite period of time if they were deemed a threat to the public. I felt the law was discriminatory towards Enhanced Individuals and that it should be changed. This time, though, it worked in my favor, which was why I had mixed feelings.

With the calls out of the way, I went to my room to put on my armor and get Walter's magic-detecting device.

Once I was suited up and ready, I joined Stella and Blue in the kitchen. Blue already had her communication glasses on, and Stella had the list of search squares laid out in front of her ready to go. I followed Blue to the living room, and she opened a shadow portal to the first search area on our list.

I stepped out of the shadows on the roof of the warehouse where the sniper team had been set up during our attempted ambush. I glanced over to the lich's hideout and saw there was yellow police tape blocking the entrance to the property and all around the building itself. There was also a police cruiser parked with an officer in it at the front entrance to the property. I assumed the officer was stationed there in case the lich returned, and I approved of that decision.

I was a bit confused about why Stella picked this as our first search area and got on the comms and asked why I was here.

"Teleporting spells are usually limited by range. The lich may have just teleported to another warehouse nearby," said Blue.

I was pretty sure that the police and EIRT had done a search of the area after our assault on the warehouse, so this was probably a waste of time. On the other hand, it would only take a minute to check, so it really wasn't worth arguing about it. *"Roger that."*

I called on my Air power, lifted myself into the air, and flew to the center of our search area. I turned on the magic-detecting device and did a slow circle. The needle stayed dead still the entire time. I opened a channel and said, *"Area clear, what is the next address?"*

Blue gave me the address and I entered it into the GPS on the helmet's visor and flew towards it. The plan was to search eight one-kilometer squares around this location and then keep expanding the search out from there. As I was flying from one adjacent square to the next, it was quicker for me to fly than to have Blue shadow travel me each time.

As I flew towards the next search area, I took a moment to appreciate the day. It was a cool sunny day and much nicer weather than we usually got at this time of year. The cooler temperature kept me from overheating in my suit. I could see the thick line of trees along the mountain brow off in the distance with all their pretty fall-colored leaves on them and enjoyed the sight.

The next area was a mix of older residential homes and some warehouses and light industry. I turned on Walter's magic detector and did a slow circle. Once again, the needle didn't budge. I was starting to get the feeling this could be a long day as I called in for the next address.

The next eight areas in the vicinity of the warehouse were a bust. The needle didn't so much as twitch during that time. My luck improved at the tenth, though, as the needle shot over about three-quarters of the way to the right. I rotated back and forth slightly in the air until I got the strongest reading from Walter's magic-detecting device. The movement of the needle relieved the growing fear I had that the device hadn't been working and needed new batteries or something.

I set off in the direction the device was pointing to, which was towards a bunch of modest World War II-era houses. The neighborhood, with its mature trees lining the street and quaint-looking houses, didn't seem to be where I would have imagined a lich would have set up shop, but anything was possible.

I flew over a small yellow-painted house that was well kept and as I passed it the needle dropped instantly back to the left. I banked around in the air and the moment I was pointed at the yellow house, the needle shot back to the right again. I spotted a house number on the mailbox and used my GPS to get the street name and opened a channel on the comms. *"I have a reading on the device."* I gave Blue the address and waited for her to check it out from the shadows.

While I waited, I took a low pass over the house to see if I could sense the lich's presence. I got a slight tingle across my body as I hit the closest point of my flyover but no overwhelming feeling of death or despair. I assumed the tingling sensation must have been from whatever wards were protecting the house. I cursed at that, as I probably alerted whoever resided there to my presence. I hoped they were friendly.

Blue's voice grabbed my attention. *"The house is occupied by a middle-aged lady. By the herbs and various spell components on the shelves, I suspect the woman is a witch. Shall we assault the house?"*

I rolled my eyes at the last part of Blue's statement. Blue didn't have a high tolerance for witches due to a past experience she and Stella had with a witch that practiced black magic. The majority of witches were peaceful and beneficial to mankind. *"Did you find anything to indicate that she was practicing black magic?"*

"No. There was nothing out of the ordinary to indicate that she was causing harm to anyone."

"Then we have no reason to disturb the witch. Our focus is on the lich. Make a note of the address for our files and give me the next search address."

"Roger that."

I swore I heard the disappointment in Blue's tone on the comms with that last transmission. Only Blue would be down about not being able to attack a magic user in their home. I shuddered at the thought of trying it, as there could be years' worth of spells, wards, and traps defending that place, which would make any type of assault a dicey proposition at best. Not taking down a magic user in their home was like Bounty Hunting 101. You only did it if you didn't have any other choice.

Blue gave me the address of the next search area and I punched it into the GPS and flew towards it.

***

I had Blue shadow travel me home once it started to get dark and a light rain began. The afternoon had been a bust, other than we'd managed to eliminate seventy-two of the search squares on our grid. I was pleased that we'd managed to get that many done, but it still left us with just over 300 more to search. At that rate, we still had three or four more days until we covered every search square.

By the time I got changed out of my armor and joined the team downstairs, Blue was back with the food. There was a buffet of Thai food laid out on the counter and Blue and Stella were already building plates for themselves. Stella handed me one as I got in line behind her, and Bree just growled under her breath at me jumping the line. "Hey, you know the rule," I said.

The house rule for any buffet-type dinner was Bree went last so the rest of us would actually get food.

Bree nodded but frowned. "Less talkie-talkie," and she pointed insistently at the food, trying to get me to build my plate quicker.

I was tempted to make a smart-ass reply but wisely focused on building my plate instead. Delaying a Were from her food was never a smart idea. In my rush, I almost made the tragic mistake of putting some of Blue's special vegetable dish on my plate. The sheer amount of angry red flecks in the dish gave me a good idea of just how spicy it was. I liked spicy food, but Blue's tolerance for spice was next level. I was willing to bet that a single mouthful of that would have me sweating and crying profusely and draining a gallon of milk to stop the burn while praying for death.

I joined Blue, Stella, Liv, and Alteea at the table while Bree happily loaded her two plates. Oddly enough, Liv barely acknowledged me and just slowly sipped her pint glass of blood like she was in her own little world. I was tempted to ask what was up, but my stomach rumbled, and the food just smelled too good to ignore.

As I ate my dinner, I noticed that Stella also seemed to be in a down mood. It dawned on me that she was probably upset that her theory about the lich teleporting somewhere close by and using that as our search starting point hadn't panned out. I swallowed a mouthful of pan-fried noodles and said, "Stella, cheer up. It was a good theory and better than any ideas the rest of us had. You win some and you lose some; that is the nature of bounty hunting."

Stella nodded and gave me a half-smile. "You're right. I just thought that I really had something there. I realize, though, that my theory was flawed."

"In what way?"

"The distance you can teleport is proportional to the spellcaster's power. That limits how far they can teleport. The one thing I failed to take into account was how powerful the lich is."

It took me a second to understand what Stella was getting at, but I figured it out. The lich was an exceptionally powerful magic user, which meant he could cast a teleport spell that would send him a much further distance than most magic users. I mean, he raised a zombie T rex. for Odin's sake, so he probably had damn near enough power to teleport anywhere in the world.

I was about to reassure Stella that her idea still had been a good one when Liv suddenly sat bolt upright and went dead still.

After a few long seconds, she said, "The lich is calling out to vampires. I can feel his voice whispering in my mind."

Stella was quicker than me to react and said, "Can you tell from where?"

Liv shook her head but got to her feet and slowly started turning in a circle. She stopped for a moment and then moved back and forth slightly. She held up her arms about a foot and half apart and said, "Somewhere in this direction. I can't narrow it down more than that."

She started to lower her arms and Stella said, "Stop. Keep your arms up."

Liv shrugged and raised her arms back up to where they had been pointing. Stella dashed from the table and started frantically opening drawers in the kitchen until she pulled out a roll of masking tape, a ball of twine, and a pair of scissors. She moved over to Liv and ripped off a small piece of masking tape and stuck it to the floor directly between Liv's feet. Stella then unwound a large length of twine and snipped it off.

I frowned in confusion as she picked up a saltshaker from the table and tied the end of the twine around it. She moved to the end of Liv's right hand and lowered the saltshaker from the tip of Liv's middle finger. Stella stopped lowering it barely an inch from the floor. Blue must have been on the same wavelength as Stella, as she took the roll of tape and tore off a small piece. Stella nodded in approval as Blue stuck the piece of tape directly on the floor below the saltshaker. The moment the tape was in place, Stella repeated the process from Liv's left hand and Blue put another piece of tape down on the floor.

"Okay, you can lower your arms and sit down," said Stella.

As Liv moved away, Stella taped a length of twine to the floor between the piece of tape that had been between Liv's feet and the one under her middle finger on her right hand. Stella ran another piece of twine to represent Liv's left arm and then stood up and nodded in satisfaction.

It finally dawned on me what Stella had been doing. She was going to use the strings on the floor as another starting point to find the lich. She could take the angle on the floor and superimpose that on a map to give us a search area to look for the lich. I started to get excited but reality kicked in. While the angle was fairly narrow, we lived on the far southeast corner of Hamilton, and once that cone was put over a map and extended to the far northwest corner of Hamilton's city limits, it would end up being a fairly large search area. On the other hand, it would probably eliminate two-thirds of the city, which would cut our search time down considerably.

Stella got up and headed for the stairway with Blue right behind her. I assumed they were going to get started on working out our new search area.

The moment Stella left, Bree asked, "Are we going out on patrol after dinner?"

As I pondered her question, the rain outside picked up and helped me reach a decision. I shook my head. "The lich is trying to recruit another vampire or two. I doubt he will be out tonight. The rain is coming down out there and my power is running next to empty thanks to all the flying around I did today."

Bree seemed disappointed at my answer, but Liv perked up at that. At first, I was excited that she wanted to spend some time together. She'd been a bit standoffish recently and I was wondering what was up with her. My excitement vanished as she turned to Bree and talked about getting caught up on some series on Netflix. I was a bit disappointed at her choosing Bree but then realized that Bree would be leaving Saturday so it made sense that Liv wanted to spend as much as time she could with her before she then. It hit me that I'd probably get a lot more Liv time after Saturday and that cheered me up.

After dinner, Liv, Bree, and Alteea retired to the living room to binge-watch TV and I joined Blue and Stella up in the office to plan out our new search area.

Chapter 23

Monday, October 17

I'd been asleep for less than an hour when my phone buzzed insistently from my side table. I groaned as I woke up and saw that it was just coming up on midnight. I picked up the phone and saw Detective Little's name.

"*Hurricane, we have another victim. Grigori Sidorov, 43, owner of the Gas and Go in Westdale. The MO matches earlier lich attacks.*"

"*We'll be there shortly,*" I said and ended the call.

I quickly got dressed and into my armor.

I opened my door and jumped as Liv suddenly appeared in front of me. I mentally cursed vampire speed and their ability to move so silently.

"I've already woken up Blue and she is waiting for us in the living room," said Liv, who then disappeared down the stairs.

I was about to add vampire hearing to my list of annoyances, but in this case, it had been useful. Liv waking up Blue had saved us a couple of minutes.

As I headed down the stairs, Bree's earlier words about patrolling haunted me. I let a little rain and my low power levels stop us from going out on patrol and wondered if Grigori Sidorov would still be alive if we'd been out there. The low power level excuse was just laziness on my part; I could have easily had Blue shadow travel me to the lab after dinner. Thirty minutes between the Tesla coils and I would have been up to full strength.

I pushed those thoughts to the side, as I couldn't change the past. I entered the living room and Blue said, "The portal is open. The Gas and Go is across the street from where the portal is. It is also raining heavily."

I called on my Air powers, so they were ready and stepped into the shadows. I came out to a cold rainy night and immediately thickened the air above me to keep the water off us. Liv and Alteea popped out of the shadows behind me. Liv nodded in approval at my makeshift umbrella. Alteea had her glamor up so I couldn't see her reaction to my air shield keeping the rain off of us, but I suspected she disapproved as she loved playing in the rain. She did, however, stay perched on Liv's shoulder rather than flying off ahead. I assumed that was because she realized that if she got wet, she'd leave a trail of water behind her, which might give her presence away.

Across the street was the gas station and it was a hive of activity with police cruisers, EIRT SUVs, and uniformed police officers all around it. I recognized the area, as it was in the west end of Westdale. The location helped ease my guilt about not patrolling earlier. This attack was farther west than any of the previous ones. Bree and I wouldn't have gone out this far on our patrol and likely would have missed it even if we had been out.

Traffic was light and didn't delay us in crossing the street much. Halfway across the road, the familiar shroud of death and despair hit me, which confirmed for me that the lich had been here.

An officer I didn't recognize became alert as we approached the yellow police tape that had been erected. I reached slowly for my wallet as we got closer and pulled out my hero ID. I stepped onto the sidewalk and said, "Zack Stevens and Olivia Dick. We are here as representatives of the English Vampire Court. Can you please let Detective Little or Agent Chambers know we are here?"

The young officer nodded and lifted his radio handset from his vest. He turned and said something into it. I heard the response that ordered him to let us through and the officer nodded. He faced us again, lifted the yellow tape, and said, "Detective Little is inside."

We ducked under the barrier and headed for the store. I gritted my teeth, as the feeling of death and despair increased with every step. The feeling became so overwhelming that for a brief second I lost control of my air shield. Liv glared at me as I hastily thickened the air above us again.

The fluorescent sign above the gas station had seen better days. One of the bulbs was out, leaving the lower part of the sign dark. The red lettering of the Gas and Go had faded to a dark pink color after years in the sun. There was also a small crack in the upper right side of the sign's glass.

Detective Little met us at the front entrance to the small store and handed us plastic boots and gloves. "Sorry to have gotten you out of bed on such a miserable night."

I shrugged and we followed him inside once we put on the protective gear. The interior was older and worn-looking and probably hadn't been changed for the last twenty years or so. I spotted the auras of Mac the mage and Agent Chambers deeper inside the store, and both were behind the counter examining the body. There was a single deep neck wound on the body that looked like a vampire had fed. One wound rather than two made me hopeful that the lich had only managed to recruit one new vampire.

Detective Little's partner was on the near side of the counter talking with Bobby Knight.

The seven of us inside made the place feel very cramped.

I ignored them and the body for a moment and looked around. The inside of the store was tiny and had just two aisles separated by some mid-height metal shelving. To my right was a small row of glass display fridges stocked with sodas, juice, and energy drinks. In front of me was a bank machine with a self-serve coffee station beside it. The rest of the displays held chocolate bars, chips, and snacks. There was a video camera above the counter, and I hoped that meant there was also one on the gas bar itself.

"Any witnesses?" I asked Detective Little.

He shook his head. "The body was discovered by a uniform. He stopped to grab a coffee and found the body and called it in. We rewound the video surveillance; the camera covering the gas bar goes fuzzy just before 10:30 p.m. A minute later, the one covering the cash gets scrambled as we assume the lich and his companion enter the store and the camera covering the gas bar clears up. The camera over the cash stays fuzzy until just before eleven, after which time the gas bar camera malfunctions again. Once the gas bar camera clears up again, nothing happens, and no one comes by until twenty minutes later when the officer pulls up. The good news is the one on the gas bar gave us a picture of the car and plate number."

"What is the make and model?" I asked.

"A silver 2016 Sentra."

I was disappointed with the car model. That car was so generic that it would blend in anywhere. I was willing to bet there were hundreds in Hamilton that matched that description. It would have been nice if they'd stolen a bright yellow Corvette or something similarly eye catching.

"We ran the plate, and it belongs to a senior who lives in a large apartment complex in West Hamilton. We sent some units by to check on her. They radioed in just before you got here to say that the lady is fine but can't find her car key and has no memory of giving the keys to anyone. The last time she remembers having the keys to the car was just before 10:00 p.m. when she came back from the pharmacy after picking up a prescription."

I considered that for a moment. "The vampire or the lich probably mind rolled her and took the keys and the car. The lady is lucky to be alive."

Detective Little nodded. "That is the part I don't understand. The lich hasn't shown any mercy before, so why now?"

I thought about it for a moment and Liv said, "The lich may not have been there. He might have sent the vampire out to get transportation. The vampire waits at the lot of the apartment building for someone to drive in or come out. The vampire approaches the lady, mind rolls her, and instructs her to give him the keys, and then go to her apartment and forget it ever happened. If the vampire had killed her and taken the keys, once the body was discovered and the car was missing, you'd be searching for the car. This way, no one knows the car is stolen and no one is looking for it."

I pondered Liv's theory and it made sense. I was also impressed at how insightful it was. Olivia came across as flighty and distractible at times, but when she put her mind to it, she usually had good ideas.

Her theory fit, as it was much better to be driving around in a car that hadn't been reported stolen. If that was the case, then I suspected the car would turn up abandoned somewhere in the near future. The vampire would just do the same thing the next time they needed a car.

Detective Little said, "That also would explain why the car was stolen before ten but didn't show up here until 10:30 p.m. West Hamilton to here at this time of night is about a ten-minute drive, but if the vampire had to go somewhere first to pick up the lich, that would account for the missing twenty minutes."

Mac and Agent Chambers came out from behind the counter and approached us. Agent Chambers said, "The coroner and the forensic team are en route, so if you want to examine the body, I'd suggest you do it now."

I steeled myself and headed for the area behind the counter to get a closer look at the body. Grigori seemed to be just a normal mid-aged man. He had short brown hair with a growing bald spot at the crown of his head and touches of grey creeping in. He was tied to the chair, so it was hard to guess his exact height, but he was probably around five foot eight or nine. A slight gut overhung the belt of his pants, which wasn't uncommon to see for someone in their forties, especially in a sedentary job like manning a cash counter.

His mouth was open in the familiar silent scream of agony that matched the other victims. He had cuts and bruises on his face from where the vampire or the lich had worked him over but not as many as some of the victims had. I wondered if the open location had something to do with that. Most of the cash area had windows around it and was visible from the street. The lich and vampire may not have wanted to linger here.

The left side of his neck was torn open from the vampire feeding on him. That wound would have been fatal if the lich hadn't killed him first. I figured the autopsy would show the five distinct bruises on his chest around the area his heart was and the heart itself would be shriveled. The damage to the heart would be listed as the cause of death.

I spotted a pair of eyeglasses on the floor beside the chair. The left lens was badly cracked and the frame on that side was bent too. The right lens had a blood smear on it. I idly wondered if the vampire or lich had hit the glasses and knocked them off or if they'd just fallen off during the scuffle. I realized that in the end, it didn't matter.

It was odd that at most traumatic scenes I'd seen in my career, it usually wasn't the images of the victims that stayed with me the most. It was details like the glasses on the floor. There'd been a bad car accident earlier in my career where a whole family had been killed, and to this day the discarded plush pink bunny lying near the wreck on the road still haunted me.

I took a deep breath and caught the scent of blood, which reminded me why we were here. "Liv, you getting any odd scents?"

Olivia closed her eyes and inhaled deeply. "Blood is the strongest one, but the musty scent of the lich is there too . . ." She frowned and inhaled again and added, "There is a trace of women's perfume that is here too. I'm pretty sure it's Angel; my mom used to wear it."

"Can you go to the other side of the counter and make like Toucan Sam again?"

Liv gave me a confused look and I added, "Follow your nose," which didn't clear things up for her. "See if the perfume scent is stronger there."

She shrugged, blurred around the counter, and inhaled. "It is weaker here."

Our actions were getting strange looks from the peanut gallery, so I said, "Liv's sensitive nose picked up traces of perfume on this side of the counter. I doubt the lich is wearing it or that Grigori was, so our vampire might be female."

I watched as Bobby and Detective Little each added that to their notes. Little's partner just rolled his eyes dismissively at my statement and went back to sucking up to Agent Chambers.

The door opened and three members of the police forensics services team walked in wearing protective gear. That meant my time was up. I took one last quick glance around the victim and then exited from behind the counter to get out of their way.

Bobby, Mac, Agent Chambers, and the two detectives moved to the far side of the store to get out of the way, too, and I joined them. Liv hovered near the counter and watched the forensic people with interest.

I was starting to feel a bit claustrophobic in the small store and realized that I didn't need to be here. I said goodbye to everyone and reminded Liv to call Blue for a lift tomorrow when she was done here. Liv just waved me off and continued to pester the forensic people with questions as they worked.

I kicked around the idea of calling Blue for a lift home and decided to let her sleep. I discarded my plastic boots and gloves in the box just inside the door and stepped outside. I used my powers to lift myself into the air and headed for home.

As I flew home, I went over the day. The speed at which the lich operated suggested a sense of urgency on his part. He'd recruited a vampire and completed an attack all in the same night. When he recruited the first two vampires, he waited until the following night before going out with them. I wondered if us flushing him from the warehouse was the reason or if it was something else. If he was picking up the pace of his attacks, then we needed to find him sooner than later, or the body count was going to get uglier.

Chapter 24

Tuesday, October 18

It was still raining when I awoke the next day. I sighed, as it was just rain and no thunder and lightning. A good juicy lightning storm would have made things much more enjoyable. Today the plan was to start our new search pattern and the rain would just make the day longer.

I joined Stella and Blue at the table for a late breakfast. They'd had a busy morning, as they had refined and prioritized our search grids for the day. The far end of the search cone overlapped with some of the areas we'd searched yesterday, so Stella had eliminated those from the list. She put the search areas on the mountain as secondary targets since the lich so far hadn't strayed even close to that area. The mountain was in the narrowest part of the search cone, so putting it second only saved less than twenty search squares, but that was better than nothing. The revised list left us with just over sixty squares to cover.

Stella suggested that I start from the edge of the mountain brow and work north towards the harbor. It seemed as good a place as any, so I agreed.

Thanks to my late night at the gas station crime scene, it was gone eleven by the time I arrived at the first search area. The rainy skies made it hard to get motivated and cast a grey pall over the city. I missed the nicer weather I had yesterday during my search.

The houses near the brow were larger, part of a more affluent neighborhood, and as a consequence, it took longer to search those areas. A number of the houses had powerful wards that tripped the magic detector. Either that or the houses contained magic items or the homeowners were magic users.

In the fourth search square on our list, in a particularly nice neighborhood, the magic detector went haywire. The needle jerked hard to the right but stayed there even as I turned in a circle. It took us a bit to understand what was going on but eventually we figured it out when I flew to the edges of the search area. It turned out there were four different houses in the area that tripped the detector. Three of them contained magic items and the fourth house's wards were leaking magic. It took almost an hour to sort through that mess.

Farther away from the brow, the houses turned into more modest dwellings and three-story apartments, which sped up the search time, as the detector didn't react.

After three hours of fruitless searching, I started to worry that this was another theory that wasn't going to pan out. The lich might not have been at his new hideout when he summoned the vampire last night.

Shortly after that thought, I arrived at one of the search squares that was on the far western edge of our grid and the detector's needle jumped hard to the right as I turned in the air. I found the direction where the reading was the strongest and my heart rate picked up as a saw a cemetery in the distance. A lich hiding out in a cemetery seemed almost too on point, though, and I forced myself to tamper down my excitement. The cemetery was a good size and probably one of the larger ones in Hamilton. I guessed its area would take about six city blocks.

As I flew toward the cemetery, the needle remained steady to the right. I approached a large mausoleum that was tucked away at the southeastern back corner of the lot. Just as I was about to fly over it, I was hit by a familiar feeling of despair. Oddly enough, rather than it building negative emotions in me, it did the opposite. I almost cheered when I realized we'd found the lich.

I confirmed this by flying over and past the mausoleum. The shroud got stronger the closer I got to it, and the moment I passed by, the needle dropped back to the left.

I opened a channel on the comms. "*Found him. West Church Memorial Gardens. He is in a mausoleum on the southeast corner of the lot.*"

"*Roger that. Hold on,*" said Blue.

I flew far enough away that I was out of the shroud of death and despair but still close enough that I had eyes on the entrance to the mausoleum, and I hovered there to wait for Blue.

"*I cannot view the interior via the shadows, just like the warehouse, which means you are likely correct. The lich seems to be here. How do you wish to proceed?*"

I eyed the imposing structure. It wasn't that big, but the stone masonry it was built out of and the heavy-looking door would make it a tough nut to crack. If it had been located in the center of the cemetery, I'd have been sorely tempted to let Blue use her anti-tank missile on it. The problem was there were backyards of neighboring houses less than twenty-five feet away, and that took that option off the table. I'd also promised Agent Chambers to work and share information with him, and us cowboy-ing the lich with an anti-tank missile on our own really didn't fit that agreement. Doing it solo would also deprive us of all the extra resources EIRT could bring.

It struck me, too, that Agent Chambers had more than lived up to his end of the bargain, which was impressive considering our first meeting. I owed it to him to include him on this takedown.

I turned my attention back to the mausoleum. I was willing to bet that the entire structure was warded to the nines. Odin only knew what nasty surprises those wards might hold.

As I rapidly thought about options while Blue waited for my reply, it dawned on me that I didn't need to decide what to do right now. Assuming the vampire was in there with the lich, they weren't going out for at least four and half hours, which was when the sun went down. "Blue, can you open a portal nearby for me? I want to come home and discuss our options."

"Hold on."

Less than a minute later, Blue said, "There is a large apartment across the street. On the roof is a commercial air conditioning unit. I've opened a portal in the shadows there."

"Roger that. Be there shortly."

I banked in the air and headed for the building. As I flew towards it, my mind was already going over options and tactics. We'd found the lich, now we just needed to take him down.

***

Twenty minutes later, Agent Chambers, Bobby Knight, Stella, and I were gathered around our kitchen table discussing how to handle the lich's new hiding spot. Mac the mage and Blue were out at the cemetery. Mac was using his ward-detecting goggles to see if the mausoleum had wards around it or not.

Agent Chambers had already gotten in touch with Hamilton police to start blocking off traffic on the street the cemetery was on and evacuating the houses that backed on to it. The ETA on the evacuation was a minimum of three hours, which left us almost no time before nightfall. The rest of Agent Chambers' makeshift GRC13 team were loading up the SUVs and would proceed to the cemetery once they were done.

"I requisitioned a new toy to help deal with the lich that arrived this morning," said Agent Chambers with a smile.

"A tactical nuke?" I was only half-joking about that, as a part of me would have liked nothing more than to nuke the lich into oblivion.

"Sorry, no. I did get a flamethrower, though."

I blinked at that. I was a bit surprised that they were willing to use a flamethrower in a densely populated place like Hamilton. I thought about it some more and realized that with his Fire elemental powers that he would be able to contain whatever blaze was started. "You sure that is for the lich and not just so you have a nice way of recharging your powers?"

Chambers grinned sheepishly. "Well, it was mostly for the lich, but having a quick power boost may have influenced my decision."

"I suspect that flamethrower will come in handy in the next few hours. Thanks to the evacuation, we'll probably have to hit the lich at sunset, which means we are going to be dealing with a lot of zombies."

"The timing isn't ideal, but those homes are too close for us to risk an assault without clearing them out first," said Agent Chambers.

"At least you'll have your vampire's services," said Bobby, trying to make the best of a bad situation.

I was happy to have Olivia in the upcoming fight, but nightfall still worked in the lich's favor. He had another vampire on his side, which took away our vampire advantage. But he also had a cemetery's worth of zombies to bring to the fight as well. I was about to point that out when Mac and Blue stepped out of the living room and joined us in the kitchen.

Mac got right to the point, "The mausoleum is heavily warded. The goggles put a green glow around wards and the intensity of the glow signifies the strength of the wards. These ones glowed so bright, it was almost like looking at the sun."

I mentally cursed at that. I'd been hoping, as this had been the lich's fallback site, that it wouldn't have wards, or if it did, they'd be weak.

Doug looked at Mac and said, "Any chance you have a spell or device tucked away to disable those wards?"

Mac shook his head. "No. I'd strongly recommend not tripping or activating them."

Stella said, "Could we use one of the two remaining dispelling grenades to disable the wards?"

"That wouldn't work. The dispelling grenades only work against active magic; wards are by their nature passive magic. They only become active once someone touches them or crosses them," said Mac.

I grinned and said, "We could have Murdock trip the wards and then use a dispelling grenade to deal with them once the magic goes active. At least he'd be useful for once in his life."

Doug frowned, as he didn't get my humor, but Bobby and Mac both smothered their grins at my suggestion.

"You're terrible," said Stella, shaking her head at me.

To alleviate Doug's confusion, I took a moment to explain who Murdock was.

Doug nodded. "Remind me not to get on your bad side." He then paused and added, "Looks like we either wait until he comes out or we need to lure him out."

Bobby frowned at that. "What is to stop the lich from just teleporting out of there once he sees us?"

I was taken back by that as Bobby had a point. During our first encounter with the lich in Westdale, he stayed just long enough to distract us and then fled while we dealt with zombie T. rex. During the second encounter at the warehouse, he teleported out and hadn't even attempted to fight us. I'd assumed that due to him being so powerful, he'd stay and fight, but I realized that hadn't been the case. The lich was focused and disciplined. There was no upside for him to fight us; his goal was to recover the headpiece. I smiled at that last thought, as that was the key. "We make him stay and fight."

"How?" asked Bobby.

"We have what he wants—the headpiece."

Stella gasped. "No, we can't bring the headpiece to the cemetery. That is playing right into his hands."

I shook my head. "We don't need to bring it. We just need to let him know we have it. The moment we do that, he'll come after us like a shark that smells blood in the water."

I got nods around the table at that.

Bobby said, "Assuming we can get him to stay and fight, how do we take him down?"

And that was the million-dollar question. The biggest issue was the energy shield the lich cast around himself. The dispelling grenades could bring that down for a few seconds until he recast it which gave us our window, but how could we take him down in that small amount of time?

Stella got a thoughtful look on her face and said, "During our first encounter with the lich, you said that the ruby was the key to his power. If that is the case, then that should be our focus."

Necromancers used objects to transfer their life force to cheat death. I assumed the lich had transferred its life force to the ruby, as it had been the only part of the Staff of Darkness that had stayed with the lich. Assuming this was the case, then we just needed to figure out how to snatch it from one of the most powerful magic users on the planet and destroy it. I smiled as an idea came to mind. I turned to Doug and said, "How good is your sniper team?"

Doug rubbed his chin. "The agent is one of the best shooters in the country, but hitting a ruby that is about the size of a quarter from a couple of blocks away within a window of a few seconds while the lich's energy shield is down would be a hell of a shot."

My excitement waned at his answer. While Mac and Blue had been scoping out the mausoleum, we briefly discussed where to set up for the fight. The sniper team was to set up on the roof of a three-story apartment across the street from the cemetery. This was farther back than we wanted but it kept them out of the cemetery and, therefore, out of the line of potential zombies. The raised height also meant that if we stayed on the ground, none of us would cross the sniper team's line of fire if they got a clear shot at the lich. The rest of us were going to encamp along the roadway that ran through the cemetery. The roadway had low walls along it that we could use to hide behind and would act as a natural barrier to the zombies. The road's closest area to the mausoleum was about fifty feet, which was a good range for my lightning and Doug's fireballs.

Stella looked at me and said, "What about Lyudmila?"

Lyudmila was a vampire from the English Vampire Court that was part of Sarah's security team. She had been one of the vampires that joined us in our final fight against the Master last month. She was a sniper who used a rifle that was big enough to be called a cannon. Images of what that gun did to armored Acolytes still haunted my dreams.

After the battle with the Master, Stella had been intrigued about Lyudmila and asked Sarah about her history. Lyudmila had been a decorated World War II sniper that served with Soviet forces. She'd been turned just after the war and had been a member of the English Vampire Court ever since. This made her a combat sniper with over seventy-five years of experience. If anyone on the planet could make that shot, it was her. I nodded at Stella and then turned my attention to Doug and said, "Can I have a word with you in the living room?"

Doug shrugged but got to his feet.

Once we were out of earshot in the living room, I explained who Lyudmila was and what she could do. I mentioned that Lyudmila also had a camouflage cloak that made her damn near invisible.

When I was done, Doug stayed quiet for a moment, pondering what I'd said. "I assume we are having this conversation in private due to Lyudmila using what sounds like what would be a highly illegal anti-tank rifle on Canadian soil?"

I cocked a sly grin and said, "If no one sees her, was she really on Canadian soil?"

"So, if she makes the shot and takes out the lich, we'll just claim that it was our GRC13 sniper team that made the shot?" I nodded and he went quiet again.

I could tell by his expression that he was struggling with this, but then his shoulders straightened, and he said, "I normally wouldn't even think about doing something like this, but the lich is too dangerous a threat. Make the call."

I nodded and we joined everyone back in the kitchen. I turned to Stella and said, "Call Sarah and arrange for us to have use of Lyudmila's services. If there is a fee for that, agree to it. The bounty on the lich will easily cover it."

Stella got up and disappeared into the living room to make the call. Doug brought Mac and Bobby up to speed on what was going on and neither of them had an issue with Lyudmila being added to our team.

Stella returned and I was relieved to see a smile on her face. "She's available and will be ready to go once the sun goes down here."

With that settled, we continued planning tonight's operation.

Chapter 25

Tuesday, October 18

We'd been set up in the cemetery since just after sunset. The rain had tapered down to a barely noticeable light drizzle. Lyudmila and the GRC13 sniper team were both in position on the roof of the apartment across the street.

Doug was beside me on my left. I shook my head at his outfit. He was wrapped in a heavy grey wool blanket for warmth and wore a pair of sneakers that had seen better days. Under the blanket, he was wearing his fireproof orange underwear. The idea was that at the start of the fight, he'd drop the blanket and go full Fire elemental. The shoes would go out in a flaming blaze of glory.

We both stood behind the low wall at the side of the road that ran inside the cemetery. Blue was about ten feet to my right. Mac was about the same distance away from Doug on his left. Beyond Blue and Mac, there were two groups of five EIRT agents in full tactical gear loaded for bear. Extra ammo was stacked at their feet and tucked against the low wall, and additional ammo was also against the wall on the far side of the roadway. The agent in the center of the left flank had the flamethrower strapped to his back. An agent beside Blue on the right had a grenade launcher loaded with one of the two remaining magic-dispelling grenades. Stella and Liv were on the far-right edge of the formation and Bree and the EIRT werewolf were on the left. Alteea flew fifty feet or so overhead and acted as our eyes in the sky.

Hamilton SWAT had both of their teams positioned outside the main gates of the cemetery in case anything tried to break out.

It was a formidable force that was assembled to take on the lich, yet part of me wondered if it would be enough. I certainly wouldn't have said no to adding a couple of modern battle tanks, some artillery pieces, and maybe a fully loaded attack helicopter or two to our forces. That was just a fantasy on my part, as there was no way that type of military equipment would be authorized for use in the city.

Other than some faint traffic and city-related noises in the distance, the place was unnervingly quiet. You could actually hear the light wind blowing through the wet leaves of the few trees nearby. Nobody said a word as we waited. Everyone's attention was focused on the foreboding mausoleum sitting off in the distance.

The EIRT agents tightly clutched their weapons. Mac intently studied his spell book, as if trying to memorize an extra spell or two that might make the difference. I checked the time on my visor for, like, the fifth time in a minute. The shroud of death and despair all around us certainly didn't help ease the tension.

The plan was to wait for the lich to come out and if he hadn't appeared by 7:30 p.m., we would try and lure him out. It was times like this that I missed my hero days. As a hero, most of the time I was reacting to threats, so there wasn't any of this sitting around, dreading when the action was going to start. The waiting was the hard part.

The lich had already cost me Charlie. I knew this fight was going to be ugly and worried who else the lich might take down before it was over. I made a silent prayer to Odin that if someone had to die to take down the lich for it to be me and not any of my teammates. I'd grown very attached to all of them and wasn't sure I could deal with losing any of them.

Two minutes before the deadline, I opened a channel and did a final comms check. Over the next twenty seconds, all the different teams and people checked in until all were accounted for.

My eyes lingered on the fifty or so graves that lay between us and the mausoleum. Each one could be a zombie, but we had a plan in place for how to deal with them quickly. The graves in front of me, though, reminded me of the thousand or so graves that were behind me. The idea of taking on a nightmare creature of legend while having my back to hundreds of brain-thirsty zombies didn't have me jumping for joy. At least thanks to the police, the nearby houses had been evacuated and the high walls around the cemetery should keep the fight contained to the cemetery itself.

As the clock on my visor ticked to 7:30 p.m., I opened the channel again and simply said, *"Prepare to engage."*

I took a deep breath as I picked up the bullhorn that had been resting on the low wall in front of me and flicked it on. I cringed as the feedback noise briefly cut through the night air like a scream. I raised it to the front of my helmet and simply said, "Night Lord, we have your headpiece."

I turned off the bullhorn and put it down on the wall again. Doug dropped his blanket and lit up the night as he went full flame. I could swear I heard him moan in pleasure as he did. Freezing your ass off as a Fire elemental couldn't be fun. Finally being able to warm up must have been a relief for him. The EIRT agents all raised and readied their weapons. I spotted Liv draw her sword and give it a couple of swings. Both Bree and the EIRT werewolf let out challenging growls into the night.

The hinges to the mausoleum's door creaked ominously as it swung inwards, revealing nothing but darkness beyond. The dark, cloaked figure of the lich emerged from its depths. Its casual pace was unnerving, as though it didn't care or fear whatever we had out here.

The raspy voice of the lich filled the air. "Give me the headpiece and I promise you and your companions will receive a quick death."

I was about to make a smart-ass reply to his offer when a soft *thoomp* echoed to my right. One of the EIRT agents fired the magic-dispelling grenade towards the lich. I immediately began building up a large strike of electricity, hoping to hit the lich when his shield went down due to the grenade.

A blur of a black and red aura with blonde hair snatched the grenade out of the air and disappeared deeper into the cemetery. Not for the first time in my life, I cursed vampire speed. Out of the corner of my eye, I caught Liv jump the low wall and take off in pursuit of the lich's vampire minion.

A soft pop in the distance meant the grenade had detonated. The fight had barely started, and we'd wasted one of our two precious dispelling grenades.

The lich began waving his staff about and mumbling a spell incantation. I released the blast of lightning at him, hoping to distract him from his spell casting. A massive fireball and a green beam of energy also hit the shield as Doug and Mac commenced their attacks.

I swore under my breath when the pink energy bubble appeared as the lightning, fireball, and green energy beam slammed home. Two rounds from the sniper team and Lyudmila hit the shield as well. The GRC13 sniper's bullet was barely noticeable against the small explosion Lyudmila's round made against the shield.

Before the fight, when we explained what we wanted Lyudmila to do, she stated that she'd use High Explosive (HE) rounds. By using them, even in the unlikely event that she missed the ruby, if she was close enough it would likely take it out anyway. Her statement, at the time, filled me with confidence. Now that the lich's shield was up, it didn't matter how accurate she was.

I kept pouring lightning into the pink shield, hoping that I could overpower it or weaken it; Doug, too, continued launching fireballs at it, and Mac blasted another spell at the lich.

I groaned as I felt the ground under my feet begin to rumble and figured that wasn't a good sign. My premonition proved correct. Seconds later, zombies began bursting from the ground in front of us.

A soft *whoosh* caught my attention, and I watched the EIRT agent with the flamethrower launch a thick stream of fire at the zombies on the left side. Doug turned and launched a series of fireballs to the right to hit the zombies there. The volume of the fight intensified as the rest of the agents opened up with shotgun blasts and automatic weapons. Stella, Bree, and the EIRT werewolf turned around to start dealing with the zombies behind us.

To my right, a zombie burst from the ground just in front of the low wall. This was unexpected as all the grave markers were at least ten feet back from the wall. Either it had tunneled ten feet towards us or there had been an unmarked grave there.

Blue lit her sword and moved to intercept the zombie. It blocked the EIRT agent with the grenade launcher who was in the middle of reloading our last dispelling grenade. I watched in horror as he fumbled the grenade and it slipped from his hand. The agent desperately lunged after it, but the precious grenade bounced off the low wall and disappeared deeper into the cemetery grounds.

Blue didn't hesitate and leaped up onto the wall. She cut the zombie in half and then sprang off the wall after the wayward grenade. Thankfully, between the fire from the flamethrower and Doug, as well as the massive expenditure of rounds from the EIRT agents, most of the zombies were down for the moment.

The huge chorus of low groans behind me had my sphincter tightening more than ever. The EIRT agents turned around and sprinted to the other side of the roadway to help Stella and the two Weres hold off the zombie horde behind us.

The lull in the gunfire while they did this allowed me to catch snippets of the lich's chanting. He was casting another spell. I dropped the lightning attack that didn't seem to be doing anything and hastily erected a thick air shield to cover Doug and me.

I poured more into the air shield as the lich's chant came to a crescendo and he pointed his staff directly at us. A black beam of energy erupted from the end of the staff and shot towards us. It went through my shield as if it wasn't even there and hit both of us.

Doug screamed beside me and the fire around his body disappeared. My own screams echoed his as it felt like a giant ice-cold hand was trying to rip the very core of my essence from existence. The pain was mercifully brief but was followed by the worst wave of nausea and dizziness that I'd ever experienced, and I dropped to my knees. I caught the edge of the low wall with my hands to brace myself and then closed my eyes in a desperate attempt to steady myself. My stomach churned violently, and it was only through a supreme act of will that I managed not to puke.

That effort barely lasted five seconds. As soon as I heard Doug vomiting beside me, I hastily popped open my visor and proceeded to lose all of my dinner over the side of the road.

Chapter 26

Tuesday, October 18

A voice in my head screamed at me to get up and fight. Puking as I leaned on my hands and knees wasn't ideal, as a few bricks and mortar weren't going to be enough to save me from whatever follow-up attack the lich had planned.

Between the dizziness and the nonstop vomiting, I couldn't get back on my feet and start fighting again.

I dry-heaved for the fourth time in as many seconds and a part of me began to pray for death. The lich, the battle, and everything around me ceased to exist as I just focused on sucking in air between heaves.

Ten seconds later, I'd finally stopped upchucking and took a deep, steadying breath.

Blue's voice on the comms echoed in my helmet. *"I have the grenade; get ready to take the shot."*

Like an avalanche, her words slammed home the reality of our situation. I still had a fight to finish, and that grenade might be our only shot at taking down the lich. I opened my eyes and was grateful the world was only a bit wobbly and not spinning around like it had been before. I closed my visor and struggled to get to my feet.

Doug was still down beside me but seemed to be alive. Mac was off to his left about ten feet away and had a bright beam of white energy extending from his fingertips. By the way he was trembling and sweating, that spell was taxing him to his limit. I followed the white beam with my eyes, and about fifteen feet out it crashed against the black beam of energy that was coming from the lich. With each passing second, the white beam was being pushed farther and farther back.

"Get ready," said Blue over the comms.

She was close enough that I could hear her voice as well, which created an odd stereo effect. I turned and spotted her beside the EIRT agent with the grenade launcher. He closed the breach and aimed it towards the lich.

My gaze flicked over to Mac as he gasped in pain and the white beam from his hand was now only five feet out in front of him, the black energy surging forward.

This is going to be close.

I turned towards the lich. I raised my hands and tried calling on my lightning, but something felt off. I didn't have time to figure out what was wrong as Blue's voice called out, "Fire in the hole!"

The soft *thoomp* went off as the grenade launcher fired. I dug deep and called on every ounce of power I could muster. The moment that grenade went off, I planned to hit the lich with enough electricity to fry an elephant.

Out of the corner of my eye, I watched Mac dive for the roadway as the black energy surged again. I silently cheered as it flashed over his head and missed.

A raspy cry came from the lich as the grenade went off and he staggered on his feet.

This was our one window and we had to make it count.

Eat this, fucker! I thought as I gleefully released the blast of lightning from my hands.

My glee turned to complete confusion when I felt a soothing coldness on my fingertips, and I watched in disbelief as a thick six-foot-long shard of ice shot from me and across the battered cemetery grounds like a missile.

I blinked as the ice spear slammed into the lower waist area of the lich and pinned him to the side of the mausoleum like a butterfly in a science display.

What the f—? My thoughts were cut off as Lyudmila's round slammed home, dead center in the lich's chest.

The lich screamed as the sickly red glow of the ruby under his dark robe disappeared. I briefly saw the stone wall of the mausoleum through a six-inch hole in his chest. I then had to look away as a radiant glow erupted from the area around the lich. The automatic tinting on my visor kicked in and lowered the brightness enough that I could look towards it.

Hundreds if not thousands of bright white specters swirled around the lich and then began shooting skywards. I could make out individuals in the mass smiling and cheering as they shot towards the heavens. One of the phantoms sped out towards me.

My eyes instantly welled up as Charlie's ghostly form stopped just in front of me. Charlie lifted her ethereal catcher's mask, and she gave one of her trademark smiles and an approving nod. Charlie then gave me a small wave and launched towards the sky. Tears streamed down my face as I watched her go. I knew that was the final time I'd see Charlie and prayed she was going to a better place.

A sharp raspy "No!" cut the air and I turned my attention back to the lich. The ground beneath his feet blackened and shimmered. The small black circle rapidly grew to fifteen feet in width, and something began to rise from the ground.

My knees shook as the air was filled with something so primal and powerful it made me question life itself.

A huge glowing aura of the purest grey color I'd ever seen surrounded the figure that emerged from the ground. A massive black scythe appeared and rose like a dark tower in the night. The scythe was clutched in a boney hand that extended from the blackest robes imaginable. The robed figure stood over ten feet tall and its aura extended out another ten feet. That aura absolutely dwarfed any that I'd ever seen. Elizabeth of the English Vampire Court had one of the most powerful auras I'd encountered. Until now.

In disbelief, I knew I was looking at a reaper or possibly Death itself.

A skeletal hand shot out and gripped the lich by his neck and effortlessly yanked him from the wall. The specter of Death shifted the lich and forced him to look at the ground.

The lich screamed and the moans and cries of the Damned erupted from the hole in the ground.

And then, in a blink of an eye, the lich and specter of Death vanished into the Earth and the black circular hole disappeared behind them.

A second after that, there was a huge bang as an explosive round slammed into the very top of the mausoleum. A cloud of stone fragments rained down in front of the tomb.

Two things happened instantly after that. First, it hit me that Lyudmila had just tried to kill Death or its minion. Second, I felt warmth around my inner legs and realized that I'd pissed myself as the implications of that hit home. Whatever that creature had been, it was so far out of our league that the idea of ticking it off was just too much for me to even bear thinking about. If Lyudmila had been a second quicker, things would have gotten ugly fast.

Thankfully, Liv blurred up and lightened the mood by dropping a severed blonde vampire head at my feet and said, "What did I miss? Is it over?"

Words failed me and I just nodded.

The silence in the air made me realize that not only was the lich defeated but the zombies were done too. I glanced around in astonishment as there were no zombie corpses on the ground. The graves, too, were now back to grass-covered undisturbed plots, as pristine as they were when the fight started. I wondered if Death or its minion had put the zombies back to their rest. A small part of me also cursed at that; without bodies, we would be out the bounties on each of the zombies. That, though, was the very least of my concerns.

The agents by the opposite wall were securing their weapons and standing down.

Blue wandered up, took a quick look at the blonde vampire head on the ground, and said to Olivia, "That was a nice clean cut; your swordsmanship is improving."

I shook my head and laughed. Only on my team would someone look at a decapitated head and comment on the skill of the kill. Most normal people would be throwing up or running away screaming. For us, it was just another day at the office.

With the fight over, I had other concerns. The first was getting rid of a vampire sniper that was crazy enough to take a shot at Death itself. "Blue, thank Lyudmila for her service and take her back to the English Court. You might as well take Liv, Bree, and Alteea home, too."

Blue nodded and walked away with Liv to go find Bree.

Doug groaned and softly said, "I can't access my powers . . ."

I looked over and saw him sitting and shivering against the wall about four feet from his puke pile with the grey blanket around him. I wandered over and sat down beside him, on the opposite side of where he'd tossed his cookies. Mac was getting slowly to his feet and dusting off his robes.

Doug's statement had me thinking about my own powers. I lifted my visor and then raised my right hand and focused on calling my Electrical powers. A tiny blue spark danced in my hand for a moment and then disappeared. I tried again and put a little more into it and barely managed to get a small one-inch-high bit of electricity going. I pushed harder and it grew a few inches higher and then winked out of existence. I was about to try again but realized that I now felt totally drained. I freaked out a bit myself as by the amount of power I had poured into that last attempt, I should have lit up the sky with a massive lightning blast.

I tried calling my Air powers and felt absolutely nothing. I hoped that my powers were just drained and that was why nothing happened, but another part of me knew it was more than that. There was something drastically wrong with me. I'd hoped that pain, vomiting, and dizziness were the only side effects the black energy beam the lich hit us with created, but deep in my heart, I knew it had done something much worse.

Mac stood in front of us and looked towards the mausoleum and frowned. He pulled me from my thoughts when he said, "Why is there a chunk of ice sticking out the side of that wall?"

"Um, that was me."

"Impossible, you're an Air elemental," said Doug.

I shrugged. "I think whatever the lich hit us with messed with our powers. I've always had just the barest amount of Ice elemental ability. Other than not feeling the cold as badly as most people do, that was the extent of them. If I tried to make a snowball it would drain me completely."

Doug gave me a half-smile and said, "And I thought I didn't like you because of your personality."

It took me a second, but I chuckled as I got his humor. Being a Fire elemental meant that he'd not be comfortable around his opposite element of water/ice.

"It drained me to produce that little spark show. I can't even seem to access anything wind-related at all."

Mac rubbed his chin. "Try making some ice."

I was going to argue that I didn't know how, but seeing as I somehow launched a six-foot-long ice spear, I decided to humor him. I held up my hand and focused on making some ice. I gasped as ice crystals began rapidly forming along the armor covering my hand. They kept growing until my entire hand was covered in a half-inch of ice. I quickly stopped, as I could feel the Ice power in me wanting to get out. I somehow knew I had plenty more of that power in reserve.

"Fascinating," said Mac. "In mage school, we had a lecture about elementals. There is a theory that elementals are children of mages that were incredibly proficient in one element. The concept is that a mage uses so much, say, fire-based magic, that it gets into his blood, and he passes that on, and creates children that are Fire elementals. The Mage Council had no record of any elemental being able to control two elements equally. There have been a number of cases like yours where an elemental was able to control one element and had a touch of another but nothing more than that. It was speculated that an elemental's main element suppresses the minor one. You might have just proved that."

"Huh?" I said.

"Doug can't access his powers, and you can't access your Air and can only barely access your Electrical powers. I think whatever spell the lich hit you with did that. Once he removed your Air powers, nothing was holding back your Ice. Those Ice powers are why you can't access your full Electrical abilities, as they are suppressing it."

Doug went white at that. "Surely this has to be temporary, right?"

Mac shrugged. "No idea. Whatever dark magic the lich used isn't anything I'm familiar with. I didn't even know it was possible to strip an elemental of its powers. So, you might wake up tomorrow and be back to normal or . . ."

The implications that this change could be permanent hit me like a punch to the gut, and I desperately wanted another answer.

I was about to pester Mac with another question when Bobby yelled over. "Mac, we want to search the mausoleum; can you check it for wards?"

Mac looked down at us and said, "Duty calls. We'll talk later."

He wandered off, leaving us to our thoughts.

Mac's words lingered with me, and I wondered out of Doug and me, who was worse off. Doug had no powers, but at least if his Fire powers came back, nothing was stopping them from regaining full strength again. In my case, if my Air power came back, I might not be able to access it due to my Ice powers being stronger. The idea of not being able to fly again shook me and I almost started to panic. I forced myself to stay calm. As Mac said, we might wake up tomorrow and be back to normal. I prayed he was right.

Chapter 27

Tuesday, October 18

It was almost 10:00 p.m. by the time Stella and I joined everyone back at the house around the kitchen table. I was still shocked and stunned about the loss of my powers. Not wanting to dwell on that now, I focused on the more mundane issues. We had bounty claim numbers for the lich and the vampire, but as I'd feared earlier, no claims for zombies, as we had no pictures of zombie corpses to prove our claims. The extra bounties for the zombies would have been nice, but I suspected that we were looking at a minimum seven-figure payout for the lich. A small part of me even thought that an eight-figure payout might be possible.

The reason for the unknown amount was that no one had ever taken down a lich since the UN Bounty program was founded. The claim would be assessed and we'd find out what the payment would be in the next couple of weeks.

We'd wrapped up everything at the cemetery by 9:00 p.m., but once we were done there, I had Blue shadow travel the three of us over to Charlie's house. Charlie's grandmother smiled and nodded approvingly when I told her the lich had been destroyed. Charlie's mom, Diane, barely even reacted at the news, though, and just wore the same look of despair and loss that she'd had when we arrived. I knew how she felt. The destruction of the lich didn't bring Charlie back.

I told them about the spirits that had been released when the ruby was smashed and about Charlie appearing before me before leaving for the heavens. Diane did react to that, and tears streamed down her cheeks, but she was also smiling. I'd hoped that knowing Charlie was in a better place would bring her some comfort. We said our goodbyes and left them to their grief. As we were leaving, I felt in some ways even more drained than I had been after the battle.

The moment we got home, I made a beeline for the bathroom and grabbed a shower and washed out my armor. No one had commented about my little bladder leakage, and I hoped that no one had noticed. I took that as another small victory for the night.

I was hungry but my throat was sore and raw, and my stomach was still a bit sensitive, so I opted for some chicken soup and a glass of water. Blue and Stella each had a cup of tea. Liv and Alteea were sharing a pint mug of blood. Bree had already eaten when she got home but that didn't stop her from enjoying a box of donuts. I smiled to myself as Bree protectively pulled the box closer to her, and Alteea eyed them with a hopeful look.

The team was in good spirits as we discussed and celebrated our victory. Liv filled us in about her quote *epic* fight with the blonde vampire while she also avoided and battled the zombie hordes. Her excitement and enthusiasm lifted my mood a bit, but I was still dwelling on my powers being gone.

Once Liv was finished with her story, Bree turned to me and said, "So you're an Ice elemental now?"

I shrugged as I honestly didn't know what I was now. I hoped that I'd wake up tomorrow and whatever this was would be gone and I'd be back to normal.

"Make some ice," said Bree.

A part of me wasn't interested in doing this, as it just reinforced my fears, but another part of me realized that this was a chance to try a different elemental power. I held out my hand and smiled in wonder as a one-inch ball of ice appeared there. Bree and Liv clapped, and I dropped my new ice ball into my water glass. The hardest part of the whole thing was making just a small amount of ice, as I could feel it wanting to surge out of me. It was scary. I felt like I was twelve again and just coming into my powers but lacking control of them.

It had taken me years to learn how to use my Air powers and that was under my mother's training and guidance. I realized that if this change was permanent than I'd have to learn to use them safely. Ariel at GRC13 was a powerful Ice elemental, and I wondered if she'd be willing to train me. I pushed that thought aside for the moment. I was still praying that this was just temporary.

Liv perked up and said, "If we go out into the backyard, can you make it snow or make a skating rink?"

I shook my head. "I don't know. I might be able to, but I don't want to risk it." I explained that I had no idea how to fully control this new element and how dangerous that was.

When I finished, Liv got a concerned look on her face and asked, "Are you doing okay about losing your powers? Do you want to talk about it?"

The rest of the table mirrored Liv's worried look. I was touched by their concern but also felt a bit awkward being the center of attention. "No, I'm good. There is a good chance that with a full night's sleep I will wake up tomorrow and be back to normal."

"You sure?" probed Liv.

I nodded and put on a hopefully reassuring smile and said, "I'm beat and just want to get some sleep. Why don't you and Bree finish watching that Netflix series you were excited about?"

Liv gave me a long hard stare and then slowly nodded. She got up and she, Bree, and Alteea disappeared into the living room.

I followed Stella and Blue upstairs, as they too were turning in for the night. As I walked behind them, I prayed that my new condition was temporary.

***

The next morning, I got up and the first thing I did was try to access my Electrical powers. A small spark danced in my hands but that was about it. I sighed as nothing from last night had changed.

After a quick breakfast with Blue and Stella, I retired to my room and called Doug Chambers to see how he was doing. The call was short. Nothing had changed for him either, and he couldn't access his Fire abilities. I tried to put a positive spin on it by saying that it had been less than twenty-four hours and hopefully tomorrow would be different. The call ended shortly after that.

My next call was to Mac the mage. After the battle last night, he promised to bring up Doug's and my situation with some of the academics at that Mage Archives to see if they had any way of reversing what the lich had done or if anything like this had happened before.

"*I haven't heard anything yet. It will probably take them a few days to find something,*" said Mac just after we'd exchanged greetings. I didn't say anything to that, and he added, "*I have been giving your situation some thought, though. As you know, while mages are able to access all the elements, we are usually stronger in one of the four primary elements. There have been mages that have changed which element is their primary element."*

I perked up a bit at this, as this was something I hadn't been aware of. *"How does that relate to my situation?"*

"I was getting to that. It's how they do it that is relevant. A mage who wants to change their primary element does it by casting spell after spell using only the element they want to master and never casting any spells from their original element."

I pondered that for a moment and said, *"Sort of like building muscles. If you keep exercising one certain group of muscles, you'll make them stronger."*

"Exactly. So, as you can still access a bit of your Electrical powers, you need to keep exercising that and avoid using your Ice powers. You were also born an Air elemental, so I'm hoping that as your body heals from this spell that it will naturally start getting stronger towards the element you've always had an affinity towards."

I was excited about Mac's theory, but his tone didn't seem overly optimistic. *"Mac, that is great but why do I feel that you aren't telling me something?"*

There was a long pause on the line and then Mac said, *"I didn't want to say anything until I got more information from the experts at the Archive, but I worry this spell might be permanent. This type of spell would be classed as a curse spell. For most curse-type spells, if you kill the caster, the curse is broken."*

I followed his line of reasoning. The lich was destroyed and yet the spell still remained. If this had been a normal curse spell, it should have been lifted once the lich was killed. *"So, give me the odds on this being permanent."*

"Zack, I can't say anything for sure, but if I had to guess, I'd say there's an eighty percent chance that it is permanent."

That number was higher than I liked, but at least I still had a chance that this would go away on its own. We chatted for a bit longer and Mac promised he'd call me as soon as he had anything from the mages at the Archive and then we ended the call.

Mac had given me lots to think about. Assuming this change was permanent, I had a decision to make. I could embrace my newfound Ice powers and work with Ariel to learn to control them, or I had to purposely not use them and keep trying to make my Electrical ones stronger in the hopes that they'd overcome the Ice power and become dominant again. The issue with the second option was I had no guarantee that they'd ever become the dominant power again.

I could hear Stella and Blue working in the office beside my room and that pulled my thoughts in another direction. Whether I embraced my Ice powers or tried to bring back my Air powers, I was off the team until either of those things happened. In my current state, I was a liability to the team while we were in the field. I needed to discuss that with them.

As I walked into the office, Stella looked up from the computer and smiled. "The bounties for the vampire and lich are now filed. I also called the billboard company and told them we didn't need the signs anymore. We won't get any money back on the digital sign, but they are giving us some money back on the other one."

"Good work," I said. "With this case over, we need to talk about the future . . ." I went over where I stood with my powers, or lack of powers, and everything Mac had said. I then talked about my options to either embrace the Ice powers or try to work my Air powers back up. ". . . in either case, I will be a liability in the field and need to excuse myself from the team while I get this resolved," I explained.

Stella gave me a look of sympathy and understanding, whereas Blue seemed disappointed. I was going to ask Blue about her reaction, but Stella said, "Maybe we put the entire team on hiatus for a bit. Come Saturday, we lose Bree's services for three months while she is on pack business. And—," Stella paused for a brief second. "—And Blue and I have a new project to keep us busy for the next while. Emma Turner called me a couple of days ago and wants Blue and I to help teach her to use her powers."

The name rang a bell, but I was having trouble placing it. "Emma Turner?"

"She was the girl who came into her powers at the Home Depot a few months ago."

That filled things in for me. Emma was a young Enhanced girl who had the power to project pain. The problem with her power was that she had no control of it and was hit by the same pain herself. Her body then would attempt to protect itself by using more of her power and bring her even more pain in a weird and nasty feedback loop. The girl, if she could control her power, would be an exceptionally strong

Super. The big question was whether she could overcome the pain to keep control of her power. "Why does Emma suddenly want to learn how to use her power? The last thing you told me was she was wearing power-blocking bracelets to keep her power at bay."

Stella nodded. "Those bracelets are the reason. It seems the kids at her school are making fun of her for wearing them and for being Enhanced."

This wasn't an uncommon problem for teens with powers. Most of the teens that had joined the Acolytes did so because they were tired of being called freaks or being shunned by their peers. "That sounds like a worthy project. As your Hyde form doesn't feel pain, and Blue can shadow travel you and Emma to somewhere remote, you two are uniquely suited to help her. That said, I think you have a long, hard road ahead of you with this. When do you start?"

Stella shrugged. "Emma still needs to get her parents' permission. When we talked yesterday, they had their reservations but seemed to be coming around. The other issue is I need to create a power-blocking platform; nothing huge but something big enough for Emma to stand on. Trying to put power-blocking bracelets back on Emma in my Hyde form is challenging. A platform would allow me to just push her back onto it if she loses control, which would be a much more practical solution. I sketched out some designs but haven't started making it yet. I was waiting until this case was over."

"The platform sounds like a good idea."

"Yeah, as long as I can make one. It might also be useful when we are back to bounty hunting; if we force an Enhanced to step on it, it will be easier for us to take them down," said Stella. She then added, "So getting back to the team. With Bree gone, Blue and I working with Emma, and you figuring out your power issues, taking a break from bounty hunting wouldn't be a bad idea. Financially, we were already in good shape and that is even before the bounty for the lich. Even if that bounty is on the low end of your estimates, it will easily keep us flush with cash during the break."

On the money side, Stella was right. I already had enough money in the bank to retire if I wanted to. The only reason I was still bounty hunting was because the rest of my team with their long lifespans needed more of a nest egg to retire on than I did, and I hadn't wanted them out there hunting without me. My foundation also had enough money in it to cover the member salaries for the next three years as well. "What about Liv?"

Stella got an odd look on her face for a second but then said, "I'm sure Olivia will find something to do during the break. She'll probably spend the next month trying to figure out what her new car will be."

The girl did like to shop, and Stella was right, as Liv still hadn't figured out what to buy to replace her six-wheeled SUV that the zombie T. rex destroyed. Another part of me figured that Liv and I could also spend some more time together once Bree left.

We chatted for a bit longer and Stella suggested that we have a small going away dinner for Bree on Friday. The conversation ended when Stella said that she and Blue needed to go out to get some supplies for the power-blocking platform.

I found myself at a loose end and decided to go for a walk. The day was cold and windy but thanks to my handy new Ice powers, feeling the cold was even less of an issue than it had been before. With the team on hiatus, I had three months to figure out what I was going to do about my powers. I still had a chance that I'd wake up in the next day or two and things would be back to normal, but I couldn't count on that.

The walk really didn't resolve anything and when I got home to the quiet house, I ended up spending the afternoon drinking in my room, trying to figure out what to do.

During dinner that night, Stella brought Bree, Olivia, and Alteea up to speed on what we'd discussed this afternoon. The food helped sober me up a bit, as I'd gone a bit heavier with the drinking than I intended to. I'd hoped to spend some time with Liv this evening, but that hope vanished when dinner ended, as she, Bree, and Alteea retired to the living room to hang out and watch TV. Stella and Blue left to go back to the lab to work on the platform, leaving me on my own.

I probably could have joined Liv and Bree in the living room, but I wasn't feeling it and figured I'd just bring them down. I was disappointed about not being able to spend time with Liv, but I knew she was just trying to pack as much time in with Bree as she could before Bree left. I retired to my room and went back to thinking and drinking. I passed out later that night.

***

I woke up the next day with a hangover. I called Doug and nothing had changed for him or me power-wise. I then had a large breakfast by myself, as Blue and Stella were already at the lab. I popped a couple of aspirin and went back to bed to try and sleep it off.

I felt better when I woke up but was a bit rough around the edges. Dinner with the team was a strangely quiet affair and there seemed to be an unspoken tension in the air. Pointed looks were being exchanged, but barely anyone said anything other than a bit of small talk. I wondered what was going on.

After dinner, I got my answer as Liv said, "Zack, we need to talk."

I mentally groaned at the words, as generally nothing good ever came from them. Liv suggested we go to my room, and I followed her up the stairs. She stopped just inside the threshold to my room, and I sat on my bed.

Liv closed the door and said, "With Bree leaving on pack business and to learn more about her kind, I have decided that I need to do the same. Stella has arranged a three-month apprenticeship for me with Sarah at the English Vampire Court. I'm leaving on Saturday when Bree does."

I blinked at that for two reasons. The first was Liv's unexpected departure, but the bigger surprise was her and Sarah spending three months together. The two of them got along like oil and water, and Liv tried to avoid Sarah whenever possible. On the other hand, Sarah was the champion of the English Court and over 500 years old. I had no doubt Liv would learn a lot from her. I was just surprised that Liv was able to swallow her pride and have Sarah boss her around for months. "But what about us?"

Liv shook her head. "To be blunt, there is no 'us.' Right from the start, I told you this was casual." The pain and hurt I felt must have shown on my face because Liv's expression softened and she added, "Zack, I do love you and I enjoyed our time together, but if you look deep in your heart, can you honestly say that I'm the one?"

I was about to immediately say yes but stopped at the last moment and thought about Liv's question. I also loved Bree, Stella, Blue, and Alteea, as I considered them family. Was my love for Liv that different from my love for my other teammates?

Liv walked over and sat down beside me. My silence must have spoken volumes as Liv said, "I thought so. You deserve more than me. I can't give you the one thing you've longed for . . ."

I wanted to argue that it didn't matter but Liv was right, I had always wanted kids and a family. The team functioned as my family, and I was good with that, but a big part of me still wanted kids of my own. I'd found visiting Rob and Annette since Ian was born had become bittersweet for me. I loved seeing how happy the three of them were, but another part of me was envious of that and wanted that for myself. "We could adopt."

Liv laughed softly at that. "Zack, I'm not mother material and you know that. It's not just you wanting kids. We already get odd looks from people when we go out on dates. Just think about how that will be in ten years. People will think we are a father and daughter, and that will only get worse with each year after that."

I knew that Liv wouldn't age, and we were already a decade apart in age and looks. She was right that things would get more awkward going forward. "I don't care about that."

Liv sighed. "I know but there are other issues like my severe allergies to the sun, the blood diet, and the whole undead thing. I know the timing of this sucks. You aren't in a good mental space right now due to your power issues, but I think this is for the best. Take this as an opportunity to not worry about bounty hunting, your powers, or being the Hamilton Hurricane, and just work on what is best for you. You have the money, get out there and enjoy the world and find someone who can give you what you want."

I tried to muster the words to change her mind but by her tone, I knew she'd made up her mind.

Liv leaned over and lightly kissed me on my forehead.

She walked to the door and opened it, but then turned to me and said, "If I can give you some advice?" I nodded and she added, "If you do meet someone, don't try so hard. You have a lot of great things to offer; just be yourself."

And with that, she softly closed the door and left me to my thoughts. I felt the tears starting to come and tried to hold them back, as I didn't want Liv to hear them. I fished out a bottle from the bedside table and took a long pull from it. The burn as it hit the back of my throat felt good, and I took another hit. I found my earbuds and called up a playlist on my phone and listened to sad songs. I thought about Liv, Charlie, and my powers, and let the music and the booze flow through me until I was drunk enough that sleep took me.

***

The next morning, I woke up with another hangover. I stumbled downstairs and found a note on the counter from Stella. She and Blue were at the lab and wanted to remind me that tonight was the going away dinner for both Bree and Olivia.

I thought about making some coffee but having the house to myself gave me another idea. I grabbed a bottle of vodka out of the cupboard and some orange juice out of the fridge and made myself a little pick-me-up.

A few minutes later, it had started to kick in and I felt better. With nothing better to do, I made myself a pitcher of OJ and vodka and retired to my office upstairs. I called Doug to confirm that nothing had changed for him either today. Afterwards, I poured myself a tall glass and fired up a videogame to lose myself in.

By the time the celebration dinner rolled around, I was pretty drunk. I caught the looks of disapproval from my teammates but ignored them. My team, my love life, and my powers were in shambles. Why shouldn't I be too? I took another drink and hoped for oblivion.

Epilogue

I groaned as I cracked my eyes open and saw it was just past noon. My head pounded like a drum, and I was confused about a few things: one, I was still fully dressed, and two, I had a power-blocking cuff on each wrist. Thankfully, they weren't chained together so I had full movement of my arms. I tried entering the code to open the cuffs, but it came back with an error. I tried the code again and got the same result.

I tried to recall how I got to bed or how I ended up wearing the cuffs. As I focused on trying to piece things together, some of last night came back to me and none of it was good. I remembered ranting at my team about how I wasn't the Hamilton Hurricane anymore and was now the Hamilton Snowflake. I was also pretty sure I said some shitty things about them leaving me in my hour of need. A few other dark bits and pieces came flashing back and I mentally cringed. I badly owed all of them an apology for my behavior.

I got out of bed and headed downstairs to find some answers about the cuffs or at least something to deal with this headache. In the kitchen, I proceeded directly to the cupboard with the booze and was disappointed to find we were out of vodka. I spied some rum and decided that would work. I got the bottle out and placed it on the counter. I turned to the fridge to find something to mix it with and jumped when I spotted Blue sitting at the table glaring at me.

"We need to talk."

I let out a half-hearted laugh and said, "You breaking up with me too?"

Blue got up and ignored my comment. "Put the bottle away. You have five minutes to make yourself a coffee and consume a couple aspirin and then we are leaving."

My anger rose and I was tempted to lash out. Who was Blue to tell me what to do? The dead serious look in her purple eyes quickly made me reassess my options. I took a deep breath and remembered my behavior from the night before. Blue didn't deserve my resentment and

I really didn't want to piss her off while I was wearing power-blocking cuffs.

I put the bottle away and plugged in the kettle. I dry swallowed a couple of aspirin and prayed they'd kick in soon.

Five minutes later, coffee in hand, I followed a silent Blue to the living room.

"Put the coffee down for a moment," said Blue.

I placed the coffee carefully on the side table and Blue moved closer. She took my left arm and punched in a code on the power-blocking cuff. The cuff clicked open, and Blue took it off my wrist.

"Um, how did these end up on my wrists?"

Blue took hold of my right arm and said, "I thought they were a sensible precaution due to your inebriated state last night."

I pondered that as Blue entered the code on the other cuff. It hit me that 'sensible precaution' was a massive understatement and how foolish I'd been drinking while I had powers that I could barely control. I was lucky that I hadn't encased myself in a tomb of ice or something equally fatal. It wasn't only me who was at risk; I could have easily harmed one of my teammates. That thought sobered me deeply.

The moment Blue removed the second cuff, I gasped as I felt my new power surge. Ice crystals began rapidly forming at my fingertips and I had to use all of my focus to reign it back in. The ice stopped forming and I breathed a sigh of relief. That little demonstration underscored how stupid I'd been with my drinking. "Thank you."

Those two words seemed lacking to express my gratitude for Blue putting them on me in the first place and for removing them now.

Blue just gave me a brief nod and then opened a shadow portal. She picked up my coffee then said, "Follow me through the portal very slowly."

Her words suddenly made me nervous and she disappeared into the shadows. I took a slow step forward and followed her through.

I gasped at the drop in front of me and Blue placed her hand firmly on my chest to stop me from going forward and over the edge. I was hit by exotic scents and sights in the dark night, and like Dorothy, I knew I wasn't in Kansas anymore. I was about to ask Blue where we were, but the question died on my lips as I spotted the two large stone pyramids sitting in the desert sands in front of us. I looked down the stone-stepped side of the pyramid we were on and spotted tour buses with Arabic writing on them. They were another big clue to our location.

Blue handed me my coffee. "Take a seat, but check for scorpions first," said Blue with a pointy-toothed grin.

Her smile had me hoping that she was joking about the last part, but just to be sure, I took a long glance at the stone I was about to sit on, and it seemed clear.

As I sat down beside her and looked off into the distance in awe at the sights before me, Blue said, "I come here when I need to reflect. This place reminds me of the capital of my home world, as it too had three large pyramids. They were a sight to behold as they gleamed in the twin suns. The pyramids here were once covered in polished white limestone. In my world, only one of the three pyramids had a limestone covering. The second one was covered in a polished crimson red stone, which I haven't found an equal to here on Earth. The last was adorned in polished deep black obsidian."

"Was there significance to the three colors?"

Blue nodded. "Yes. The colors were the God-King's three colors, which were used on his banners, flags, and emblems. Much like here, the pyramids on my home world were the final resting places of the God-Kings. When a God-King died, a vote was taken by every citizen of the Empire to determine which pyramid he'd be interned in. Most God-Kings went to the White pyramid, some went to the Red pyramid, and the greatest of them were honored by being entered into the Black pyramid."

From what I'd learned from Blue up until now, the God-Kings that ruled her world had absolute power. I kind of liked that the people got the final vote on his resting place, as it seemed like an incentive for the God-King to rule well.

"Seeing these pyramids, stripped of their limestone, and showing their age also helps remind me that the world I came from is dead to me and in the past. I brought you here because I hoped that you, too, might find the peace of mind I get when I gaze out on their magnificent size."

I had to admit it was peaceful up here. To my left and right were the lights of the city but in front of me were the pyramids and vast tracks of uninterrupted sand that made this place seem ancient and otherworldly. "Thank you. This is amazing."

Blue gave me a half-smile and said, "I also brought you here as I am concerned about your recent behavior and your mental state." I was about to apologize, but Blue held up her hand and continued, "My concern isn't about the absence of your Air powers or your lack of control of your new ones. Nor is it about your recent drinking. It was your statement about being a liability to the team."

I frowned at that and failed to see why that was Blue's biggest concern.

"You have had decades studying and fighting Enhanced Individuals. Add in your ability to see auras, which gives you an idea of someone's powers and capabilities, and that makes you a very dangerous opponent. Even if those two things were gone too, it is your heart that makes a worthy warrior. You are willing to sacrifice everything to do what is right and are not afraid to make hard decisions. I fear, though, that you have placed too much importance on your Hamilton Hurricane persona, and with your Air powers gone, you feel like a large part of you is dead."

Blue's words hit home. My Air powers being gone did make me feel like I was missing one of my senses. The lack of Air powers also made me feel like the Hamilton Hurricane part of me was truly dead.

I stayed quiet as I sensed Blue had more to say.

"I, too, have lost a part of me. You know about my assassin past, but what you do not know is why I became an assassin in the first place. I was Paired back on my home world. It is similar to your marriage but on another level. Paired are mated for life. At the Pairing ceremony, a spell is cast that binds the two as one. If one of the Pair dies, the other is destined to remain alone."

"What about you and Dmitri?"

Blue gave me a small grin. "Different world, different rules." I nodded and she continued, "The bond between Paired allows you to sense your mate no matter where they are. I knew the moment my mate had been killed. It felt like a part of me had died. Most Paired cannot take the anguish of losing their mate and end their own lives as a consequence. I was close on many occasions to doing just that, but I needed to know how he had died."

Blue got a sad and far-off look in her eyes and then said, "My mate was an officer in the God-King's army and had been stationed to the far eastern end of the Empire on a peacekeeping mission. I was at the capital and had a career as an arena fighter. We were like your MMA fighters of today, though probably closer to your ancient Roman gladiators.

"It took months, but finally, a report came back. The entire garrison had been wiped out. It seems a traitor opened the back gate of the fortress and allowed the rebels to enter freely. The sentries were killed before any could raise the alarm. The rebels then slaughtered all the soldiers in their beds."

Blue clenched her fists and slowly exhaled. "I was beyond furious when I learned of this. My mate had been a kind, fair, just, and honorable man. If he had been killed in battle, I could have accepted that, but this was plain murder. He'd deserved better. I used to tease him that he was too gentle to be a soldier and would be much more suited to being an artist or a poet. I think he probably would have been, but his family had a long line of decorated and famous officers he was expected to follow.

"The report had been delivered personally to me by the commander of the God-King's Hand. The Hand were the intelligence arm of the God-King's forces, but they were also assassins at the God-King's call. The commander made me an offer to join the Hand and hunt down all that were involved.

"I immediately accepted his offer. After training, I set about my task. I will not go into the details, but it took me close to twenty of your Earth years to complete my quest. I saved the traitor for last and by the end of my time with him, he pleaded for death. . ."

I shivered at the intensity of Blue's tone and didn't even want to imagine what Blue might have done to him.

Blue exhaled and said, "After that was done, I stayed with the Hand for a few years but eventually resigned and returned to the village of my birth to start a new life. My thirst for vengeance had saved me from killing myself but those were dark times that I regret. It had given me enough time to find myself again and find reasons to live.

"I see a lot of my younger lost self in you at this moment and do not want you to walk down the wrong path. The drinking and the self-pity need to end. You need to find the reason to go on. The Hamilton Hurricane isn't dead unless you truly give in. I will end with one question for you to consider. What would Charlie think about you giving up?"

Hurt and anger flared in me at that, but I forced it down. Charlie had given her life by entering into a fight she had no chance of winning because it was what she believed in and because it was the right thing to do. Blue was right, I owed Charlie more than just sitting around moping about my lack of Air powers. I needed to make a decision to either work towards getting them back or to embrace these new Ice powers.

I smiled, as Blue was also correct about the Hamilton Hurricane persona. That identity wasn't about me being able to make vivid blasts of lightning or powerful gusts of wind. It was about doing what was right and trying to make the world a safer and better place. I knew I could do that whether I got my powers back or not.

***

After we returned to the house, I remembered that I hadn't called Doug yet. The call started the same as our previous ones, as neither of us had our powers back, but it ended very differently.

"I think we should stop these calls," said Doug. *"I will call you if anything changes and please call me if anything changes on your end."*

"Sure. Are you doing okay?"

"Yeah, actually I'm doing better than okay. I have been on leave since the fight, and it has given me a lot of time to think. I've decided to resign from GRC13. I have been doing some consulting work over the last couple of years for a friend that owns a very successful private security firm. I talked to him early this week about my new situation and he made me a job offer. It pays more than double what I currently earn and has tons of benefits too. It is a training and marketing position. It is also a normal job, so Monday to Friday. No night shifts, weekends, or holidays."

"Wow. Sounds great."

"Yeah, it will also be a new challenge for me that I'm excited about." The line went quiet for a second, but I sensed Doug had more to add. *"It's funny, ever since I was a teen, all I wanted to do was join GRC13, but this week showed me that GRC13 isn't the most important thing in my life. My wife didn't say anything about me losing my powers, but I could tell it rattled her. I think the strain of worrying about me every time I go to work was starting to grind her down. I also realized that you and I were both lucky; that spell that hit us could have done much worse than just taking our powers. Knowing that*

if that spell had been different I wouldn't be around for my wife and kids made me realize that they are the most important things in my life. This new job will allow me to spend more time with them and that is probably the best part."

A small part of me worried that Doug was just trying to put on a brave face, but I clearly heard the joy and eagerness in his voice and knew that he really was looking forward to this new chapter in his life. I congratulated him on his decision and wished him the best. We talked for a few minutes more and then ended the call.

I loved that Doug had managed to take a negative and turn it into something very positive and drew some inspiration from that.

I came to a decision about what to do about my own future. Liv and Bree were gone for three months. I was going to use that time to work on getting my Air powers back. If they didn't return by then, I would embrace the Ice powers and learn to use them effectively. I also swore to myself I would avoid any alcohol until either I had my powers back or had learned to control my Ice ones.

The next few months would be a long road, but I knew I'd have Stella and Blue to help me, and that I didn't have to do this by myself.

The End

Author's Note

I'm having trouble believing that this is the seventh book of The Bounty Series. I'd like to thank you for supporting the series and making this book happen.

I struggled with the ending of this story, as I always strongly try to end on a happy note and I realize this one doesn't exactly scream Happily Ever After.

I also try to avoid cliffhangers, and you could probably argue that leaving the story here is a bit of a cliffhanger, but I'd like to point out that the lich was the main storyline, and it did get wrapped up, so hopefully you won't count this as one.

The next book will be more focused on Zack as he deals with all these issues, and I can't wait to share it with you.

If you want to keep up to date on what is happening with The Bounty Series, please visit my Facebook page (https://www.facebook.com/TheBountySeries). It is updated weekly. There is also a link there to my website (www.markusmatthews.com) and links to all the other social media I'm on (Goodreads, BookBub, Instagram, etc.). Lastly, if you have comments or suggestions for the series, please e-mail me at me@markusmatthews.com.

-Markus Matthews
April 15, 2022

www.ingramcontent.com/pod-product-compliance
Lightning Source LLC
LaVergne TN
LVHW091537060526
838200LV00036B/643